"MY POOR BABY," HE SOOTHED. "TELL DADDY WHAT'S HAPPENING TO YOU."

With a halting motion that made her arm quiver, Jessica pointed toward the hall door. But there was no one there.

Grant looked back at Jessica. She was still pointing. "What is it?" he pleaded. "Show Daddy."

Again her head barely moved, but now he understood. There was something he must see—something down the hall. Suddenly he knew—it was in the nursery. He stumbled forward, his knees sagging with every step. Pressing his hands against the doorjamb, he pushed himself into the pale pink room.

They were both there—Sarah in her crib and Emily on the floor beside it. Grant stared at them stupidly for a moment; then he turned away from the sight of all that blood and death.

Dell Books by
BARBARA PETTY
THRILL
BAD BLOOD
DON'T TELL DADDY

DON'T TELL DADDY

Barbara Petty

A DELL BOOK

Published by
Dell Publishing Co., Inc.
1 Dag Hammarskjold Plaza
New York, New York 10017

Copyright © 1982 by Barbara Petty

All rights reserved. No part of this book may be
reproduced or transmitted in any form or by any
means, electronic or mechanical, including photocopying,
recording or by any information storage and retrieval
system, without the written permission of the Publisher,
except where permitted by law.

Dell ® TM 681510, Dell Publishing Co., Inc.

ISBN: 0-440-12096-9

Printed in the United States of America
First printing—March 1982

*To Jane Rotrosen and Linda Grey
with gratitude and affection*

PROLOGUE

A cold rain fell, tapping out a dull rhythm on the glass walls of Grant's office, obscuring the Manhattan towers around it. Grant glanced up from the accounting sheet he was pretending to study and frowned. The sky had turned gray and glowering, matching his mood.

He leaned back in his chair, took off his horn-rimmed glasses, closed his eyes, and rubbed the indentations on the bridge of his nose. He felt old, much older than his thirty-eight years. He knew he looked it, too. In the last nine weeks he had watched the faint creases in his forehead grow into deeply etched furrows, the slight circles under his eyes sink into dark hollows.

People had commented on it—the office staff, his clients, and even his squash partners at the racquet club. Everyone had more or less made a joke of it: "Those two o'clock feedings getting to you, Grant, old boy? Heh, heh, that's what you get for waiting so long to have a second baby."

And when they laughed, he would fake a good-natured grin, taking their ribbing—anything to keep them from guessing the truth.

And what was the truth?

Grant opened his eyes and stared sightlessly out at the rain. The truth was that the last nine weeks had been the most miserable and most damning of his whole life.

Nine weeks—was that all it had been? Nine weeks since he and Emily had brought home Sarah, nine weeks since Emily had been herself. In such a short time Emily had begun slowly, almost imperceptibly, to slip into a personality so radically different from what she had been before—so different from the lovely woman he had married. He bowed his head forward, closing his eyes slowly, almost painfully.

Oh, for the first few days home from the hospital, Emily had seemed fine, even contented. She had been a doting mother to their newborn infant and to their eight-year-old daughter, Jessica, and a loving wife to him. Then something had happened. She changed— terribly.

Once rather vain and particular about her appearance, Emily became slovenly, rarely bothering to change out of her nightgown and bathrobe. She stopped having her hair done, letting it go tousled and uncombed and often unwashed. Then she started drinking. A little wine at first, but then Grant noticed the level in the Scotch bottle going down; then it was replaced by another, and still another. After that she didn't bother to hide it.

She was an odd drunk. She didn't even seem to enjoy it, for she closed her eyes and wrinkled her nose in distaste whenever she took a drink. In fact Grant was quite sure that she drank only to deaden the pain of whatever was eating her up inside. But nothing he did or said seemed to penetrate the dark hole she was retreating into, leaving the children and her husband far behind her.

Far worse than the sloppiness and the drinking was the paranoia. Her eyes became hard and watchful, and her mouth formed vile accusations: "Where have you been—having a little 'conference' with your secretary? Do you like to sleep with her? She's a bitch, you know," she would say snidely if he was late coming home from the office. If he tried to protest, she would pounce on that as confirmation of her suspicions, and if he tried to ignore her, she would wail tearfully, "Oh, you *hate* me. I know you hate me."

The fact is he did hate her. Not so much for what she had done to him, but for what she had done to Jessica. Poor Jessica had taken the brunt of her mother's madness. At first Emily had just attacked Jessica verbally, calling her hateful names and accusing her of lying or of spying on her. But then one day he had caught Emily slapping the child viciously, and when he pulled her off, she had refused to tell him what the child had done to incur her wrath. Jessica herself said that she had only gone to pick up Sarah, who was crying in her crib, and that Mommy had swooped down on her and had begun beating her.

After that, Grant had urged Emily to see her doctor. But she had refused. "There's nothing wrong with me," she insisted listlessly, fingering the soiled fabric of her dress. Then in a half-wistful, half-ironic tone of voice she had added, "Nothing that a doctor can help, anyway."

"What is *that* supposed to mean?" Grant asked.

"Nothing." She sighed, assuming the silently suffering expression of a martyr. "Nothing at all. Forget I said it."

Grant had walked away from her then, refusing to get sucked into another one of her verbal games, where now he always seemed to play the helpless victim to her frenzied ravings.

Day by day she was becoming worse, so much so that he didn't want to leave her alone with the baby, even though the baby was the one thing she seemed to care about. Oddly, despite her venomous attacks on Jessica and Grant, Emily was usually vaguely tender to Sarah. But when he had suggested getting a nurse for Sarah, Emily had said, "You do, and you'll never see me or Sarah again." He was quite sure that she meant it, so he let the subject drop.

The worst of it all was that he felt that somehow it was his fault, that he had failed Emily in some way—some way that he wasn't aware of or couldn't remember. And she seemed to go out of her way to reinforce that impression—when she wasn't making veiled accusations, she did it with pathetic wounded looks that froze his soul.

He had wracked his brain trying to remember if he might have said or done something to upset her after they brought the baby home. But all he could recall was that for those first few days he had perhaps not paid enough attention to her or Jessica because he had been so wrapped up in Sarah.

He tried several times to ask her what, if anything, he had done wrong. But she almost seemed to enjoy taunting him by withholding what was her dark and solitary secret.

This morning, after Jessica had left for school and Emily appeared to be in one of her calmer moods, he had asked her again. "Emily, please. What is it?" he had begged her. "What's bothering you? Is it something I've done?"

Pushing back her dirty hair, resting her forehead in her hand, she had looked at him with those doleful blue eyes of hers. Grant felt moved by the look of despair and confusion he thought he saw there. Her fingernails, he noticed, were torn and painful looking, so far from the careful appearance she had once projected. Touched, he longed to take those injured hands into his own.

"Why? Are you feeling guilty?" she lashed out suddenly.

"Yes, damn it! You make sure of that!" he had wanted to shout at her. But instead he gripped the table's edge with his own whitened fingers and had answered patiently, "I want to help you, Emily. I can't go on living with you when you are like this—you are destroying me—you are destroying this family. But I can't do anything if you won't tell me what's eating at you. If it's something I've done, I want to rectify it."

Her eyes gazed back at him, and in them for the barest moment was something he had not seen for weeks—hope. But then she quickly lowered her eyes. "You've done enough already," she said dully.

Grant winced. "You really know how to twist the knife, don't you?"

She responded to this by pouring herself a drink.

"For Christ's sake, Emily!" Grant snapped. "You're disgusting!" He pushed himself away from the breakfast table and got to his feet. The smell of Scotch was overpowering, making him want to retch, and it followed him even as he stormed from the kitchen.

He thought he could hear her puttering around in the kitchen as he was on his way out the door, but he didn't bother to say good-bye. At that moment he didn't care if he ever set eyes on her again.

Now he gazed at the silver-framed photograph sitting on his desk. It was a mother-daughter portrait of Emily and Jessica, taken two years ago. If only he could bring back the woman in that picture—so vibrant, so lovely. Where had she gone? And would she ever return?

His eyes were drawn to Jessica's half of the portrait. What a beautiful child she was. She was smiling in the photo, gazing straight into the camera with the clear sapphire eyes she had inherited from her mother. Emily's eyes had long since lost the depth and luster that had first enticed him, but she had passed those attractions on to her older daughter. Emily always used to accuse him of spoiling Jessica, but he had never been able to deny the child anything. And it hadn't hurt any—Jessica had never given him a moment's anguish.

Poor Sarah, her birth had brought nothing *but* anguish. *What kind of effect would that have on a child?* For perhaps the hundredth time, Grant regretted the fact that he had talked Emily into having another baby.

It had been selfish of him—perhaps even a misguided means of hanging on to his youth; he should never have forced the issue when Emily had initially said no. But he had accused *her* of being self-centered and unfeeling and had eventually worn her down. But as the months of the pregnancy had passed, Emily too had begun to eagerly prepare for the birth, or so he had thought.

Now he picked up the phone and listlessly punched out his home number. It was time for his usual call. He let the phone ring several times, hoping Jessica would pick it up so that he wouldn't have to hear Emily's slurred "H'llo." But there was no answer. He checked his watch again—three forty-five—*somebody* should be there. Jessica was usually home from school by this time.

He waited fifteen more minutes and tried again. Still no answer. A knot of tension began to form at the back of his neck. *Something was wrong.* Emily wouldn't have taken the baby out in this weather. An image sprang into his mind: Emily in a drunken stupor, unable to respond to the telephone, and helpless Sarah, squalling for her mother, who couldn't hear her cries.

He rubbed at his neck. All the fatigue had left him, drained away by the anxiety gnawing in the pit of his stomach. *What was happening to him? How had he turned into such an alarmist?*

He tried the number again, and still it went on ringing. Slamming down the phone, he strode to the closet and got out his trenchcoat and rain hat.

He opened the door to his secretary's office. "Faye, I'm leaving for the day," he said. "If anybody needs me, they can get me at home." He saw the curiosity in her eyes but didn't stop to wait for her response.

A severe woman in her late fifties, Faye had no idea of what was going on in Grant's life because she'd only worked for him for two weeks. Emily had finally chased his other secretary away.

Suzanne had been a remarkably efficient, attractive young woman in her early thirties who had worked for Grant for seven years. Emily had always seemed to like her—up until just a few weeks ago. Then she had begun a campaign of harassment on the telephone. Suzanne didn't bother to mention the unnerving calls to Grant until later, when Emily bared her claws for the full-blown attack. Then she accused Suzanne of being in love with Grant and of carrying on an affair with him behind her back. Suzanne's response was to hang up on her, but then Emily would call back, shrieking "Whore! Homewrecker! Lying slut!" As these calls increased in frequency it didn't take long before Suzanne broke down and tearfully told Grant about them. Furious, Grant ordered Emily to leave Suzanne alone; she seemed to take this as some sort of sign that she had been right all along and only stepped up her barrage of maniacal calls—until she'd hounded Suzanne into quitting.

Once Suzanne was gone, Emily stopped calling Grant at his office. It was as if her suspicions of Suzanne had given a focus to her paranoia. And with Suzanne gone she turned her attention to her children. She began a strange sort of love/hate obsession with her two daughters, usually choosing her favorite in Sarah, abusing, often striking Jessica.

Grant pushed through the revolving door of his building onto Madison Avenue, turned up his collar against the rain, and stepped off the curb, his eyes scanning the traffic for a cab. From where he stood at the corner of Forty-third Street, he could look down Madison to the crest of a hill at Forty-first Street; the rainswept avenue was dotted with numerous golden-yellow taxis—all of them occupied.

He turned to look toward the old Biltmore Hotel behind him on Forty-third Street and spotted a cab pulling up to the entrance to discharge its passenger. Like a sprinter exploding from the starting block, he splashed across the street and raced toward the cab, reaching it just as the rear door swung open.

Grant stepped back to give the startled passenger room to exit and then heaved himself into the back seat. "Park Avenue and Eighty-third," he barked to the driver through the cloudy Plexiglas partition.

Grant sank back against the seat, pulled off his glasses, and wiped them with his handkerchief. He left them off, letting the world go blurry as the cab alternately crawled then sped through a mass of swirling shapes and haloed lights. He wished he could turn his mind off the same way. He knew he was acting crazy, but he couldn't stop himself. He couldn't let himself stop. Only now and with great grief could he admit that he despised his wife. That he couldn't trust her. That he believed her to be mad.

When he got out of the cab, Patrick, the ruddy-faced Irish doorman, met him with an umbrella.

"Did you happen to see my wife go out this afternoon?" Grant asked tersely as the two men walked together to the entryway.

Patrick's eyes clouded up. "Oh, well now, let me see. I think I saw her a little while ago—or was that Mrs. Curtis?—well now, I really can't say. It's possible I saw her earlier today—but I just can't remember."

Grant frowned. If Emily *had* gone out with the baby, perhaps they got caught in the rain and decided to wait it out somewhere. "How about my daughter?" he asked.

Patrick brightened. "Oh, she's been home quite a while now—of that I'm positive. See, she always stops to have a little chat with me. Such a polite child she is—and so smart. Talks like a grown-up, she does."

Grant nodded. "Yes, we're very proud of Jessica."

Patrick's attention had been drawn to the curb, where another tenant was alighting from a cab. "Well, have a good evening, Mr. Cameron," he said and hurried away.

Upstairs, the foyer of their apartment was dark when Grant let himself in, so he switched on the light. "Hello?" he called out, taking off his hat and coat. "I'm home."

Black silence greeted him.

"Jessica, where are you?" he said, louder this time. "It's Daddy."

The sound of his own voice was all that broke the oppressive silence.

Then slowly he smiled to himself as he caught on: Jessica must be playing her favorite game with him.

"Okay, Jessica," he called. "I'm coming to find you." He walked into the living room, turning on lamps as he went, and looked in all of her usual hiding places: behind the couch or the pair of overstuffed chairs, then behind the draperies. She wasn't there.

"So you're really playing hard to get," he said. "Well, I'm not giving up yet." He made a cursory search of the dining room, kitchen, and his study before crying out, "Okay, okay. I give up—you win. You can come out now."

But there was no answering giggle, no sudden rustling of the curtains or furniture pushed aside to reveal his quarry.

Grant muttered under his breath. The child was carrying the game too far. "Please, Jessica," he sighed loudly. "Daddy's tired. I don't want to play the game anymore."

When there was still no response, Grant felt a sudden chill travel along his spine. The silence seemed to mock him, to defy his efforts to penetrate it. "Jessica!" he shouted suddenly. "Where are you?"

And then he heard a sound so faint that it could have come from outside, perhaps the rain dashed against a window by a flurry of wind. But it was closer than that—it was coming from somewhere in the apartment. He turned down the hall to the bedrooms. There it was again—a whimper. Yes, a child's whimper. *Jessica.*

He ran to her room—it was empty. Again came the soft bleating cry—there, *there* it was—from his and Emily's room next door. He burst into it, calling harshly, "Jessica!"

She was not in the room, but he could hear the sound closer now—yes, it was coming from their bathroom. The door was shut, and he twisted at the knob frantically. Locked.

"Jessica! Are you all right? It's Daddy!" He pounded on the door. "Please! Open up!"

The whimpers grew louder now and became long, gasping sobs. But the door remained locked.

"Jessica," he pleaded, trying to calm himself so he wouldn't frighten her. "It's all right now. Whatever's happened to you—it's all right. Daddy's here. I'll take care of you."

The sobbing ceased momentarily. Seconds passed, and then he could hear the lock being slowly turned. He had his hand out to grasp the knob, when the door silently swung open.

Jessica was still in her school uniform—but it was torn and spattered with dark splotches. Her blond hair was hanging over her face, and it wasn't until Grant brushed it away that he saw the look of dazed terror in Jessica's eyes.

"My God," he moaned, dropping to his knees and pulling her to him. Her slender body went slack against his own, and he held her there until the sobs became intermittent sighs.

"My poor baby," he soothed. "Tell Daddy what's happened to you." He pulled back from her and searched her small, tear-swollen face.

Jessica stared past him, her eyelids puffy and drooping, giving her a dull, drugged look. She made no attempt to speak.

Grant glanced down at her bedraggled clothes and realized for the first time that the rusty stains on her navy blue blazer were blood.

"Jessica!" He shook her gently. "Please tell Daddy—are you hurt?"

Her head moved the tiniest fraction of an inch from side to side, and Grant let out a sigh of relief. "Thank God for that," he said. "But now *please* tell Daddy what happened."

With a halting motion that made her arm quiver, Jessica lifted her right hand and pointed toward the hall door. Grant jerked his head around to look over his shoulder.

But there was no one there.

Grant looked back at Jessica. She was still pointing. "What is it?" he pleaded. "Show Daddy."

Again her head barely moved back and forth, but now he understood. There was something he must see—something down the hall. He lurched to his feet. Suddenly he knew—it was in the nursery.

He stumbled forward, his knees sagging with every step, down the long hall toward the door at the end. Pressing his hands against the doorjamb, he pushed himself into the pale pink room.

They were both there—Sarah in her crib and Emily on the floor beside it. Grant stared at them stupidly for a moment, and then he turned away from the sight of all that blood and death.

CHAPTER ONE

Karen stole another glance at her watch. Only five minutes had passed since the last time she checked it. She had promised herself to spend at least an hour at this party, and she still had over half an hour to go. She didn't think she was going to make it.

She took a sip of her whiskey sour and let her eyes sweep around the room over the rim of the glass. It was a big old-fashioned room, but so packed with people that the walls seemed to be closing in on her. Or was that only her imagination?

She had never been in one of these Fifth Avenue grande dame apartment houses before and had spent the first fifteen minutes of the party skirting chattering knots of people so that she could admire the intricately carved *boiserie* of the mantelpiece, the breathtaking expanse of mullioned windows overlooking the treetops of Central Park, the rich workmanship of the parquetry underneath her feet along with a scattering of jewel-toned Oriental rugs, and the handful of oil paintings adorning the walls. An artist herself, she had given each painting a close look. They were mostly still lifes and landscapes and were all by obscure artists, but she knew they were really quite good.

The furniture in the apartment was substantial but dull—pea green velvet chairs and sofas and some sturdy little mahogany tables—except for a genuine Tiffany lamp, a magnificent rosewood sideboard, and a grand piano that would have filled Karen's entire living room. Here, it barely took up one corner of the room. Seated at the piano was a handsome young black man in a dinner jacket. He was singing Cole Porter songs and trying his best to sound like Bobby Short.

Much as she would have liked to ignore the other guests at the party, Karen knew she ought to make at least some small effort at being sociable. But these people looked so unapproachable. She felt uneasy, almost threatened by the confidence they projected. The men all had that high-powered executive demeanor, and the women had the glossy chic of Upper East Side matrons.

But even among all their designer outfits, Karen thought she looked acceptable. Her black challis dress was years old, but it had a timeless quality to it, and she knew that it draped her figure well. Although she had always fretted over what she considered her "average American girl" looks and the somewhat nondescript coloring of her brown hair and green eyes, she had secretly prided herself on her well-proportioned body. People often told her that she had the body of a dancer—which she found rather amusing because in truth she was quite clumsy.

There was a lot of money in this room, Karen realized. But nobody was flaunting it; they were all much too secure, too well bred for that. No, these were the kind of people for whom money was a given: they all had it, everybody knew it, and therefore there was no need to try to impress anyone.

And that's why you're so impressed, Karen heard herself thinking. *You might as well admit it. These people intimidate the socks off you. They've got everything you want—and what's more, they've had it all their lives.*

For perhaps the tenth time since she walked through the front door, Karen told herself, *You don't belong here.* Then a mocking voice seemed to answer back: *But Karen old girl, don't you wish you did?*

That was absurd, she tried to tell herself. She had a good life, a life she had carved out entirely on her own after picking up the pieces from her divorce. And most of all, she had her career—a growing reputation as a commercial artist. Why would she want to put herself in the place of any of these silly, superfluous women?

Her eyes fell on a woman perched on the arm of a chair, listening to a man seated with his back to Karen. She looked like one of those sleek, privileged creatures who haunt the pages of *Town & Country,* and Karen felt a stab of envy. Then the woman turned her head, and her eyes met Karen's. She smiled, but it was a wintry, arrogant smile, and Karen quickly looked away.

What insufferable snobs, she thought cheerlessly. Why should she waste her time on them? To hell with sticking out the hour. She looked around for a place to put down her drink.

Out of the corner of her eye she spotted Fran, the hostess, bearing down on her. *Oh no. Now she'd have to lie to Fran, tell her what a wonderful time she was having*—and probably have to stay around awhile longer.

Then she saw the tall, rather attractive man trailing behind Fran. Funny, she hadn't noticed him before. He wore horn-rimmed glasses, and his dark brown hair was flecked with gray. Karen guessed that he was about forty. His features, sharp and angular, were softened by the polite smile he was wearing.

"Karen, darling," Fran called out to her. "I've got someone here I want you to meet." She drew up to Karen and gave her a conspirator's smile, then turned back to the man. "This is the woman I was telling you about," she said. "This is Karen."

The man smiled and extended his hand. "Hello, I'm Grant. Grant Cameron."

Karen shook his hand. "Karen Bellinger," she said. She felt oddly warmed by his smile and returned it with one of her own. She lingered just a moment gazing into his dark eyes, intrigued by the intelligence and quiet strength she saw there. Then she pulled her eyes away.

He was interested in her, that was apparent—but not enough to cross the room and introduce himself to her. Instead, he had relied on Fran's nearly incurable penchant for matchmaking. Why was he so cautious? Karen wondered.

Fran was talking, saying something obviously designed to put them at ease with each other, but Karen found it hard to keep her mind on the conversation. Her eyes kept drifting back to his face, roaming over it, noting the appealing way the flesh at the corners of his mouth dimpled up as he laughed, the clean, squared-off angle of his jaw, the almost harsh, bony jut of his nose, and the way he had of touching his glasses to make sure they were sitting properly on that aristocratic nose. It was a handsome face—yet not really good-looking, Karen decided. Its separate parts were not esthetically perfect, but they came together in a pleasing congruity. It was a face she would love to sketch.

"Oh, darlings, I've got to see to my other guests," Fran said suddenly, tossing her flaming red hair. "So I'm going to leave you two to get to know each other." She squeezed Karen's hand and darted away, her purple silk caftan floating about her ankles and her gold bracelets jangling on her wrists.

Karen looked at Grant, and they both broke into unabashed grins. "I've never seen her quite like this," Karen said wryly. "What is she doing—her Perle Mesta imitation?"

Grant chuckled. "I take it you've never been to one of Fran's parties before," he said. "Otherwise you would have known what to expect."

"No. We really don't know one another very well. Actually, I just met her a few months ago," Karen responded. "We took a course together at NYU."

"Yes, she mentioned that," Grant said. "Some sort of women's workshop, wasn't it?"

"Yes, that's right—career planning. I went because I wanted to see if they could tell me anything I didn't know already."

"And did they?"

"Not really." Karen smiled. "But I got a lot out of it anyway—I met Fran there."

"That must have been when Fran was thinking of getting a job," he said. "She goes through phases like that periodically."

"You sound as if you've known her for a long time," Karen commented.

"Ages," he said. Then he laughed.

Karen nodded. She was pleased to hear the affection in his voice when he spoke of Fran. It made her feel as if they had a common bond. "Fran went out of her way to befriend me," she said. "I think she saw me as some sort of waif that she was taking under her wing."

His eyes flickered with amusement. "You hardly look like a waif to me."

Karen smiled with genuine pleasure at the implied

compliment. "I'm not. But don't tell Fran—she'll be so disappointed."

He grinned. "It's our secret."

Karen liked the sound of that. But more than the words, there was a special quality to the tone of his voice in everything that he said—as if he were speaking to the heart of her, piercing through all the cocktail party repartee, and addressing a hidden part of her. . . .

"Can I freshen that up for you?" he asked, extending his hand toward her drink.

"What?" Karen said, suddenly realizing that she had been daydreaming. Then she looked down at her glass. "Oh, no thanks, I'm not really much of a drinker. But I would like some plain club soda—or Perrier, if you don't mind."

"Not at all." Grant took the empty glass from her hand and left her. The bar was on the opposite side of the room, and Karen watched him as he made his way through the clustered groups.

He moved gracefully, but with a coiled reserve in his step, like an athlete who knows his own strength so well he has no need to flaunt it. But there was energy there, energy and power—sexual power, she suddenly acknowledged. And for the first time in what seemed like an eternity, Karen felt the beginnings of sexual longing. She had been without a man's body for far too long.

God bless Fran, Karen thought with renewed appreciation for her friend. *This time she's come up with a winner.* Of course, Karen had no idea what the rest of Fran's attempted matches were like since she had never given in before to Fran's persistent efforts at fixing her up with eligible men. But she had suspected when Fran invited her to this party that there might be an ulterior motive.

And there he was—all gorgeous six feet plus of him.

She definitely should have had more faith in Fran's taste in men—after all, Fran's husband, Jerry, was attractive. That is, if you went in for the captain-of-the-football-team-at-forty look. She didn't particularly.

But Grant—even his name had a mature, worldly sound to it—was quite clearly an urban sophisticate.

She was glad she had stayed. Grant was interesting; he could be special; she could feel her attraction already. And if she wasn't mistaken, that feeling was reciprocated. Even from across the room, his eyes were sending out discreet but very clear messages that made Karen feel like a very desirable woman.

Suddenly, Fran was at her side. "Well? What do you think of him?" she asked, her eyes following Karen's.

"I don't know," Karen said guardedly, turning to face her friend. "Why are you so eager for us to get together?"

Fran's eyes met Karen's. She had dropped her role as hostess-of-the-hour. "Because," she said, "I would give anything to see Grant happy again."

"Oh?" Karen glanced at him as he stood talking to the bartender. He did not look particularly unhappy. "What's the matter with him?"

Fran sighed. "He's a widower. His wife died three years ago—" Her voice broke off as she saw Grant walking toward them. "Oh, I'd better not tell you anymore now, darling." She turned on her heel and disappeared into a group bunched around the piano.

Grant came up to Karen and put a glass in her hand. "Perrier," he said. "I'm having the same." Behind his glasses his brown eyes were studying her. He glanced toward the group at the piano and then back to her. "Did Fran tell you that I asked to meet you?" he said suddenly.

Karen shook her head. "No—no, she didn't."

Grant smiled to himself. "Actually, she told me

about you a few weeks ago. She said she'd met somebody I'd like, but I told her I wasn't interested. But then tonight I walked in here and right away I asked her who the beautiful woman in the corner was. You should have seen the look on her face when she said, 'That's the one I've been telling you about.' "

Karen laughed self-consciously. She managed to mumble something about being flattered.

"Oh, but I wasn't trying to flatter you," Grant said. "If you knew me better, you'd know that I don't go in for that sort of thing. I was simply telling you the truth."

Karen looked at him closely. There was something so straightforward about him that she was suddenly convinced he was sincere. "Then you're very different from most men I meet," she said.

"I suppose I am," Grant said, an almost hidden tinge of irony in his voice. He stared into his drink for a silent moment and then raised his eyes to hers. "Fran said that you're an artist." His tone was again light and conversational.

Karen nodded. "Well, of sorts. I'm a commercial artist."

"That sounds fascinating."

"Does it really?" Karen smiled ruefully. "Well, it's not. Mostly it's uncertain—you never know where your next job is going to come from. Usually, it's feast or famine."

"I take it you work free-lance," Grant said. "That must mean you have a lot of self-discipline."

Karen sighed. "Yes, well, motivation has a lot to do with it, too. There's nothing like a stack of unpaid bills staring you in the face to really get you motivated."

Grant gave her a quick grin. "I know exactly what you mean."

Karen wasn't sure that he did. From the cut of his

expensive—if somewhat conservative—suit and his air of self-assurance, she was certain he was a stranger to any kind of deprivation or insecurity. "What do you do?" she asked.

"I'm an accountant. Actually, Jerry—you know, Fran's husband—and I are partners in an accounting firm."

"Oh, so *you're* Jerry's partner!" Karen exclaimed.

He cocked an eyebrow at her. "Why? Has Fran mentioned me to you?"

Karen smiled at him sheepishly. "Well, yes. But I always thought—" She bit at her lip, letting the sentence go unfinished.

He finished it for her. "You thought that an accountant couldn't possibly be the sort of man you'd be interested in meeting. Isn't that right?"

Karen nodded dumbly, hoping he wasn't offended.

He leaned toward her and lowered his voice. "Well, I have a confession to make, too."

"What's that?"

"When Fran told me she had a friend who was an artist—well, I expected you to be a bit of a Bohemian. You know, paint-smeared clothes, living in a loft somewhere in Soho. Rather a ridiculous stereotype, wouldn't you say?"

Karen laughed. "Not really. I know quite a few artists who are just like that."

"Well, I'm glad you're not," he said, his eyes giving an extra level of meaning to his words.

Karen stared back at him, unable to tear her own eyes away. She felt as if she were intoxicated by him—by the sound of his voice, his searching gaze, the very nearness of him. The party continued to surge around them, but the noise, the smoke, the festive smell of flowers and alcohol faded into the background, and she was aware only of him.

* * *

The next morning Karen was lying in bed rerunning the previous evening through her mind and fantasizing about what it would have been like if Grant had come home with her, when the phone rang.

"Hi," a cheery voice said. "It's Fran. I hope I didn't wake you up—but I couldn't wait any longer to call you."

"That's funny," Karen said, snapping herself out of her reverie. "I was just thinking about calling *you*."

"I know. You wanted to tell me what a *fabulous* time you had at our party, that it's been *ages* since you met such *fascinating* people—"

"Something like that," Karen said dryly.

"Yes, well, I know most of the people there weren't your type. But they don't matter. There was only one person I wanted you to meet—"

"And you managed to pull that off rather successfully, didn't you?" Karen said, unable to resist a little good-natured banter with her friend before getting down to brass tacks.

Fran ignored this. "Well?" she said. "Are you going to tell me what you thought of him?"

Karen laughed. "You just can't wait till I tell you whether or not I liked him, can you?"

Facetiously, Fran said, "Are you always this evasive so early in the morning?"

"Okay, I liked him, Fran," Karen said. Then she let her voice get serious. "I liked him a lot."

"Mmm, I thought so," Fran said with just a trace of smugness.

"Well, what's not to like?" Karen came back. "He's handsome, charming, intelligent, and obviously well off. So the question is . . . what's wrong with him, Fran?"

It took Fran just a few seconds too long to respond. "There's nothing 'wrong' with him, Karen," she said, sounding a trifle defensive.

"Then why do you have to do his matchmaking for him?"

This time there was a longer hesitation. Fran seemed to be making up her mind about something. "I suppose you ought to know," she said at last.

Uh oh, here it comes, Karen thought, realizing that she had been more or less expecting it. *The fatal flaw. I should have known he was too good to be true.* "Well, don't keep me in suspense," she said, not bothering to soften her sarcastic words by the tone of her voice.

"I'm sure he'd want you to know," Fran went on as if she hadn't even heard Karen. "Although he'd probably find it difficult to tell you himself—"

"Fran, *please*," Karen interrupted. "What *are* you babbling about?"

"I'm sorry, Karen, but it's even a little hard for me. It's been three years, but I still can't forget her—"

"You mean his wife?" Karen asked brusquely. "Is that who you're talking about?"

"Yes, his wife—Emily. You see, she was my best friend. I suppose I'll never get over the feeling that I failed her."

Karen was struck by the overwhelming sadness in Fran's voice. In their short friendship, she had never experienced this side of Fran before. To her, Fran had always appeared to be the larger-than-life, self-assured woman who never let anything get her down. Then she realized how brief their contact had been. She really knew very little about Fran. And Fran knew almost nothing about her. Now she realized that Fran had unhappy secrets.

Gently, Karen said, "What happened to her?"

"She killed herself," Fran said, her voice strangely dispassionate. "And she killed her nine-week-old baby. It was a tragic, horrible incident."

Karen was genuinely shocked. "Oh, my God—how awful."

"They said it was an acute postpartum depression. I just couldn't believe it—I saw her in the hospital right after the baby was born and she was fine. But Grant said she changed after she came home. I tried to talk to her, but she would barely speak to me on the phone, and she refused to let me into the apartment. I suppose she was trying to hide the fact that she'd started drinking."

Karen thought about Grant and marveled that he seemed so cool and collected. The man must have tremendous inner reserves of control and resilience to have come back so staunchly from such a nightmare. "Tell me about Grant," she said. "How did it affect him?"

Fran sighed. "Very badly. If it hadn't been for Jessica, I think he would have gone out of his mind with shock and grief. But for her sake, he held himself together."

"Who's Jessica?"

"The older daughter. She's eleven now—a really lovely child. And surprisingly unaffected by the whole tragedy. I guess Grant deserves the credit for that."

A daughter, an eleven-year-old daughter. Karen couldn't help feeling a sense of misgiving. Of course, it wasn't surprising that a man of his age should have a child. But why was she worrying about that now? My God, she hadn't even gone out with Grant yet.

"Karen, he likes you," Fran said. "I can't tell you how happy that makes me. You're the first woman he's shown any interest in since Emily."

"Why do you suppose that is?" Karen asked. "Why me?"

"I'm not sure," Fran said uncertainly. "I've tried introducing him to a few other women, but he couldn't have cared less. When I talked about you to him, he only seemed mildly curious, but he noticed you right away at the party and asked me who you were—which I thought was rather ironic. Anyway, I could actually see a change in him. There was something in his eyes and the way he looked at you. . . ." Fran let the last words trail off, as if there were something else she couldn't bring herself to say.

"Do I detect a note of hesitation in your voice?" Karen asked. "Is there something you're not telling me?"

"Well . . . I don't know if Grant saw the same thing I did," Fran said reluctantly.

"What?" Karen said, wondering how much more Fran was keeping back.

Sounding vaguely apologetic, Fran said, "I forgot all about it as soon as I got to know you—but, well, the first time I saw you at the workshop I couldn't help thinking that from certain angles, you reminded me a little bit of Emily."

Karen let this sink in for a moment. Finally, she said, "That seems somewhat inauspicious—to say the least."

"Oh, but you're really not at all like her," Fran tried to reassure her. "Even physically. Your coloring is quite different—she had blond hair and blue eyes—and you have a much better figure than she did. And your personalities are totally unalike. She was quiet—too quiet probably—and she had absolutely no desire to do anything with her life, other than being a wife and mother."

Somewhat mollified, Karen said, "Then you think that my resemblance to her is incidental? As far as Grant is concerned, I mean?"

"Oh, of course, he may have noticed it, but I don't think that would be the reason for his interest in you. He's not the kind of man who would want to relive the past."

God, I should hope not, Karen thought. Anyway, what did it matter if she resembled his dead wife? It was a well-known fact that people were often attracted to the same physical type—it was simply human nature. So there was no point in her getting apprehensive about it. Besides, Fran hadn't even told her whether or not he intended to pursue this relationship.

"Well, is he going to make the next move—or what?" Karen asked.

"I gave him your phone number—I figured you wouldn't mind."

"I hope he at least asked for it. You didn't force it on him, did you, Fran?"

"Darling, of course not. He was here this morning—he and Jerry go jogging in the park every morning, although how they managed to do it *this* morning I'll never understand—anyway, he came in and practically *grilled* me about you. He wanted to know absolutely everything about you."

"So what did you tell him?"

"Well, he wanted to know more about your work. So I dug up one of your magazine illustrations. I think he was rather impressed."

"And? Was that all?"

"I told him about your divorce. Nothing much. That's up to you to tell him if you want to. I simply said that you'd been divorced for several years and that you weren't seeing anybody in particular."

"Fran, why did he have to come to you to find all this out? He could have asked me himself last night."

"Caution, my dear. The man is the soul of caution. Always has been, Jerry says. And he's known Grant since time immemorial."

"How long is that?"

"Can you believe since prep school? They met at Choate. Then they went to Yale, which is where I met them. And then they went into business together as soon as they'd finished graduate school. Honestly, I think Jerry would divorce *me* before he'd break off his friendship with Grant."

"What about his family—where are they?"

"He was an only child. His parents are both dead— lovely people but a trifle too reserved, if you know what I mean. They lived in Connecticut—Norwalk— and had this wonderful old place right on the water and a gorgeous sailboat. But Grant sold them both after his parents died. Emily didn't like the water."

"Does he live in the city?"

"Just a few blocks from us—on Park and Eighty-third. It's the same place he lived with Emily. I know he thought about moving but decided against it—he wanted to disrupt Jessica's life as little as possible. So they stayed in the apartment—but he had it completely redone, of course."

Karen heard all this with a troubled mind. Grant had a lot going for him, it was true, but he had drawbacks, too—serious drawbacks: a dead wife, a daughter who must bear the scars of the most appalling incident of her youth. "Fran, I've got to be honest with you," she said suddenly. "I don't know if I'm up to dealing with a man who has such a horrendous past. You know, I've been hurt myself—not anything like he has—but still, I don't need anyone with a lot of problems. Maybe we just ought to forget the whole thing...."

"Do what you want, Karen," Fran argued, "but I guarantee you that Grant is a lot less neurotic than all of those lecherous art directors you're always telling me about."

"That I can believe," Karen said half-heartedly.

"Then what are you afraid of, Karen?"

"I wish I knew," Karen said slowly. "I really am attracted to him—more than anyone in a long, long time, I must admit. But—trite as it sounds—maybe that's what I'm afraid of: my own feelings."

Fran was silent for several seconds. Then she said, "All I'm asking you to do is go out with him once. Just once—is that too much?"

"No." Karen sighed, wondering why she was fighting it. In her heart, she knew that she was dying to go out with Grant Cameron. Men like him came along so rarely.

She remembered the way he looked at her with those penetrating brown eyes, and the memory was enough to flood her with feelings that surprised her with the intensity of their raw sexuality. But she knew it was more than sex that attracted her to Grant. There had been an instinctive rapport between them, a recognition of a secret spark that drew them together, shutting out the rest of the world. Her protests were a sham; the truth was she didn't care about what had happened to him in the past—all she cared about was the future.

CHAPTER TWO

At thirty-four, Karen Bellinger was convinced that she was condemned to live out the rest of her days alone. True, she might let herself have a casual fling now and again, but the great love, the all-consuming passion—well, she just didn't see that happening to her ever again.

Her last romance—ended nearly a year ago—had been with a sweet, serious boy six years her junior. She had never considered it more than a pleasant interlude, and neither, it seemed, had he. But when it was over, she had missed him more than she thought she would. She let three months go by before she got up the courage to give him a call. When a woman answered, she pretended to be a wrong number and hung up the phone in embarrassment.

Men had always been a mystery and a source of frustration to Karen. Her father, a salesman for a pharmaceutical company, had been away from home a great deal, and he had seemed to her little more than a stranger. Even now, if she and her father were left alone in the room together, on the rare occasions when she went home to New Jersey, they had difficulty keeping a conversation going.

All through the years when she was growing up, Karen was sure that her father had been disappointed that she, his firstborn, had not been a boy. And try as she might, she was not capable of transforming herself into a tomboy—although she doubted that even that would have satisfied him. Nothing she did was enough for him.

She could never remember receiving a word of praise from him. For years she had brought home report cards filled with superior grades, showed them to her duly appreciative mother, and then timidly tapped her father on the arm as he sat in his favorite chair reading the evening paper.

"Dad," she would say because he did not like to be called "Daddy." "Here's my report card. It's pretty good. Do you want to look at it?"

"Not now," he'd grumble. "I'm busy. Later."

But Karen knew that "later" would never come.

She felt singled out by his apathy—although he was as remote and unaffectionate with her younger sister, Janet, and Karen could not recall ever seeing him kiss her mother or even put his arm around her. But his coolness to *her* seemed unique; it was an utter indifference to her—whatever she might do or say, he simply didn't *care*.

In the years since she had left home, Karen had occasionally talked to her mother about her father. Her mother always insisted that Karen's memories of her childhood were distorted: "Your father loved you, Karen," she'd say. "He just didn't know how to show it—and you never let him."

Karen didn't argue with her mother about it, for she thought that her mother must have her own reasons for seeing things the way she did. In any case, Karen knew that her perceptions of her childhood were all that really mattered. If that's the way she saw things, then that's the way things were.

But there was one time when she was a child when her father had paid her attention, and she was aware of how profoundly influenced by it she had been: although she had always shown some artistic ability, it wasn't until she was ten years old that it was recognized by a first-place award in her school's annual art fair for a pen-and-ink drawing of their house. To Karen's great surprise, her father actually had the picture framed and hung it in a place of honor in the living room—where it was still hanging.

From that day on, Karen nurtured secret dreams of becoming an artist, hoping to garner further plaudits from her father. And although he never responded the same way again, she had the feeling he approved of her artistic efforts.

Of course, Karen only realized all this years later. At the time, all she knew was that her father seemed to like her drawing, so she kept it up.

Because she had only a sister and very few boys of her age lived in their neighborhood, as a child she had no close or extended contact with boys. She never had a boyfriend during all the years she was growing up—never knew a boy whom she could simply call a friend. Even though Janet was three years younger, she was always surrounded by boys from the time she was twelve. Karen pretended not to care, but she secretly envied Janet and wondered what there was about herself that made boys shy away from her so. Janet once told Karen that she seemed to stiffen up whenever boys were around, but Karen countered by saying she wasn't about to stoop to acting like Janet did in front of boys—all googly-eyed and simpering.

Then she went away to college in upstate New York, and there she found herself singled out—quite literally picked out of a crowd of freshmen women—

by one of the big wheels on campus, Randy Bellinger.

Randy, along with a group of other upperclassmen, had posted himself outside the hall where an orientation meeting was being held for the newly arrived freshmen women. When the girls exited, these men-of-the-world submitted them to their keen-eyed scrutiny, searching for likely prospects to date.

When Randy spied Karen, he immediately fell in step beside her and introduced himself. Karen, deeply embarrassed by such attention from an upperclassman on practically her first day at college, could barely look him in the eye. But she already knew who he was, for he had been pointed out to her as one of the best-looking and most sought-after men on campus. With his sandy blond hair, deep-set gray-blue eyes, and lingering tan, he looked like a California beach boy—which was exactly what everyone was trying to look like in those days. It seemed quite incredible to Karen that anybody like that should be interested in her. But she didn't want to discourage him by seeming unfriendly so she managed to stammer out her own name in response to his introduction.

"Karen Sinclair," he repeated. "That's a pretty name—but then it should be to go with such a pretty girl."

At that, Karen blushed and turned her face away. She knew she was behaving like a silly goose, but she couldn't help it—she had no experience flirting with boys, and here she was attracting the attention of a terrific-looking upperclassman. Then she quickly realized that even if she couldn't carry on any clever, coquettish repartee, she could at least talk to him, couldn't she? So she looked back at him and gave him what she hoped was an encouraging smile. "I think I've heard of you," she managed to say. "Aren't you a jock of some sort?"

He grinned. "Jock-of-all-trades, that's me. Football, baseball, skiing—you name it, I do it."

When he smiled, Karen noticed that there was a tiny gap between his two front teeth—which she found utterly adorable. "Well, what's your favorite?" she asked, suddenly finding it easier to talk to him.

"Skiing," he said without hesitation. "It's my passion."

"Oh," Karen said, wishing she was a bit more knowledgeable about sports. "I wouldn't know anything about that. I've never been on a pair of skis in my life."

"Then you'll have to learn," he said simply. "I'll teach you."

Karen looked at him with surprise, but he didn't seem to notice, as he had gone on describing to her the raptures of skiing.

He then proceeded to ask her to have coffee with him in the student union, and by the time they finished drinking their coffee, he had asked her out for that night.

For their first date, they went to a movie, stopped for pizza, and then spent an intoxicating fifteen minutes necking in the shadows outside her dorm. Before he said good night, he arranged for a date for the following evening.

After only a few dates, he had quite systematically managed to take over her life: he saw to it that they ate all their meals together, walked to and from classes hand in hand, and studied together in his carrel in the library. And by the end of her freshman year, he had persuaded her to sleep with him.

Karen held out as long as she could on that final step. It was still the middle sixties then and girls were supposed to stay virgins until they were married—or at least engaged. It was only when Randy started talking about their future together—which she interpreted to mean marriage—that she finally submitted to him.

But sex turned out to be not quite what she had expected. It was pleasant enough and certainly exciting—especially since it was accomplished on a blanket in the woods where they might have been discovered at any moment—but it was not the overwhelming experience she had read about in D. H. Lawrence and all those other authors she had read in her English Lit class. But she never let on to Randy that she was disappointed by their sexual encounters, afraid that he might think less of her because "nice" girls were not really supposed to be all that interested in sex.

Randy blocked out their life together as if it were a game plan: he graduated two years ahead of her and moved down to New York City, where he got his master's in business at Columbia; in her junior year, he gave her a small ("tasteful" he called it) diamond on Homecoming Weekend; during her junior and senior years, he called her practically every night, saw her nearly every weekend, and supervised her curriculum, making sure that she took plenty of home ec courses in addition to her art major and minor in education; they were married two weeks after her graduation in an elaborate, expensive wedding that Randy insisted they have rather than the smaller, simpler wedding she had wanted.

They moved into New York after their marriage and rented a small apartment in a luxury building on the fashionable East Side. Randy had a good job on Wall Street as an investment analyst, and she worked occasionally as a substitute art teacher.

"Don't worry, you won't have to work long," he had informed her. "I'm going to keep you too busy having babies."

Karen laughed when she heard this. "Don't I have anything to say about it?" she asked good-humoredly.

She thought that Randy was being just a mite too old-fashioned, but as always she knew she would defer to his wishes.

And then she got pregnant, and Randy acted as if he were the first man who had ever fathered a child.

His excitement communicated itself to her, and she began to share it—in spite of a lingering desire to do something more with her artistic talent. But she knew Randy would disapprove of her wanting to be anything other than a wife and a mother, so she tried to pretend to herself that it didn't matter.

Then one bright spring afternoon when she was out for a walk in the park, she began to get violent cramps in her abdomen. Frightened, she found a cab and went directly to her doctor's office. He confirmed what she feared most: she was miscarrying. But he assured her that there was no reason why she couldn't get pregnant again.

Randy took the news stoically. "When you're ready, we'll try again," he told her. Karen was hopeful, sure that next time everything would be all right. Ten months later she was pregnant once more. Again, she miscarried. And again the doctor told her that she was perfectly healthy and capable of having children.

But Randy didn't seem to be so sure. Something changed in him after the second miscarriage. He began coming home late from work, and night after night he fell asleep in front of the television set. Karen began to suspect that he was avoiding having sex with her. She wondered whether that was because he was afraid of getting her pregnant—or because he was sleeping with someone else.

When Karen finally confronted him, he admitted that he was having an affair with a young woman who worked in the research department of his firm. It meant nothing, he insisted. He promised to break it off. Three weeks later he asked for a divorce. His girl friend was pregnant—or so he said. Karen didn't believe him.

She wormed the woman's name out of him and—full of self-righteous indignation—called her up. "Are you going to have Randy's baby?" she demanded. The woman reluctantly admitted that for a time she had thought she was—but it had turned out to be a false alarm. Karen didn't understand. Why had Randy lied to her?

Confused and hurt, she had asked him for an explanation. He couldn't give her one. They quarreled bitterly, and he walked out. The next thing she knew she was being served with divorce papers—the grounds were incompatibility. She was too stunned to contest it.

The suddenness, the capriciousness of Randy's behavior left her bewildered and tormented. There seemed to be no rhyme or reason for what he had done, and it was months before she could even begin to try to explain it to herself.

During the entire time that she had been with him, Karen had always considered herself to be the luckiest of women to have been singled out by Randy first to be his girl friend and then his wife. She often wondered why he had settled on her when he could have had any girl he wanted. She wondered, but she never actually questioned her good fortune.

Later—after the divorce—she realized that Randy perhaps had chosen her because he was looking for someone who would fit—or who he could mold to fit—his image of the ideal wife. When Randy met her, she was very young and inexperienced, eager to please, and even grateful for his attention. She was the perfect, pliable candidate for him to shape into the perfect, pliable wife.

But when the dust of the divorce had settled, she also realized that in order to become what *Randy* had wanted she had found it necessary to submerge many of her own needs and desires. Especially as far as her art was concerned. Randy had never thought of her talent as anything but a superfluous skill that she could turn to some advantage by teaching after they were married while she was waiting to get pregnant.

Karen never complained, never protested; she let herself be swept along by Randy because he seemed so sure that he knew what was right for her. And it was so much easier to have everything mapped out for her instead of having to think for herself—or fight with him about what she wanted to do with her life. So in many ways she was a fraud because she was not the docile little creature Randy had thought he had married. Toward the end she had slipped and let more of the strong, independent side of her nature show through, and she wondered if that was why Randy had left her: he simply could not live with a woman who would not kowtow to him.

But however much she tried to analyze what went wrong, her gut feeling told her that if she hadn't had those two miscarriages, if she'd been able to have a baby, she wouldn't have lost Randy. He divorced her because she was inadequate—she couldn't give him the children he desperately needed to confirm his virility and to fulfill his own particular version of the American dream.

The divorce caused a temporary rift with her parents, particularly her father. Randy was the all-American boy, everything her father had ever wanted in a son; the fact that Karen had been able to catch a man like Randy even seemed to raise his opinion of her. But after the divorce he was cooler to her than ever—as if she had deliberately meant to deprive him of the companionship of his son-in-law. Karen felt sure that he considered the divorce to be entirely *her* fault, that there was something wrong with her because she couldn't hang on to her man.

She had a small breakdown right after the divorce, and it forced her to get out of teaching. Floundering around, alone in the city, and wondering how she was going to survive, she saw an ad in the classified section of the *New York Times*. It was for an assistant to a commercial artist. Expecting rejection, she nevertheless forced herself to answer the ad.

When the artist asked her to come for an interview, she threw together a few of her illustrations from college for a makeshift portfolio and nervously went to his midtown studio. The artist was named Angelo Di-Bona, and he turned out to be a very energetic man with riveting brown, nearly black, eyes. They hit it off at once. He pored over her illustrations, demanding to know why she had let such talent go to waste. In response, she blurted out the whole wretched story of her divorce.

Angelo clucked sympathetically and hired her on the spot. "But you will not stay with me too long," he said. "I will train you, introduce you to people, but then you must go out on your own. You are too good to remain an assistant"—he winked at her—"even if it is to someone as brilliant as I."

Karen had thought that his words were meant merely to boost her wounded ego—which they did, tremendously—but she did not take him seriously.

She spent two years with Angelo. Two safe, very secure years while she learned to do things that she never dreamed she was capable of. She worked with Angelo on illustrations for some of the most prestigious magazines in the country, for best-selling books, and for million-dollar ad campaigns.

She met scores of new people—not dull, staid people like Randy, but people who were the movers and shakers in the world of advertising, publishing, art. And although she could never quite picture herself as truly one of them, she began to realize that her talent made her special to them, that it was something they would both recognize and pursue—and generously reward.

This realization eventually led her to the conclusion that it was time for her to strike out on her own, to leave Angelo's fatherly protection. When she reluctantly told him, he said simply, "I was wondering how long it would take you. I've been expecting this for months now. Of course, you must do this—and remember, you are too good to fail."

She had cried when she left him, lugging the beautiful black leather portfolio he had given her as a parting gift. She had called him often with many questions in her first few months as a free-lancer: Should she take a particular assignment? How much should she charge for it? What should she do about someone who hadn't paid her when he said he would?

But in time she learned to handle most of these questions herself, and she called on Angelo less and less as she became increasingly successful. They remained friends, however, and it had upset her greatly when he had a stroke and was forced to retire. He lived in Arizona now, and they exchanged Christmas cards with lengthy notes—although it pained her to see that his were written in an uncharacteristically feeble scrawl. She owed him a great deal, and in her heart she knew he was more like a father to her than her own father had ever been.

But Angelo had taught her well, and she soon discovered that she had developed quite a following. Art directors had begun to seek her out, and she found herself being given almost more work than she could handle. It kept her busy day and night, spending long hours at the drawing board set up in a corner of the living room of her apartment on the West Side, where she had moved after the divorce, and—aside from the fact that she of course needed the money—being continually busy was just fine with her because it left her with almost no social life to speak of. And she didn't want one, her work was everything to her.

It had only been within the last few years that she had begun to realize that perhaps all men weren't like Randy, and she had started dating again. But she had kept all her relationships as superficial as possible, vowing that she would never let herself be hurt again the way Randy had hurt her.

But lately, she had been forced to admit to herself that she was not quite the rational, dispassionate woman she had convinced herself she was. There were still powerful emotions hidden away somewhere deep inside her, smoldering, threatening to break out and engulf her.

One of those repressed urges had to do with children. A frightening incident happened when she had visited her sister Janet right after she'd had her first baby. When she picked up the child, a little girl named Melissa, Karen was struck by the family resemblance, not just to her sister, but to *her*—the baby could have been *hers*. Tears welled up in Karen's eyes, and she began to tremble. She wanted to take Melissa and squeeze her against her breast—and never let her go.

"Take her, please," she gasped to Janet, who was staring curiously at her. "She's so tiny, and I'm afraid I'm going to hurt her."

"Don't talk like that," Janet snapped as she scooped Melissa out of Karen's arms. "You're fine now, and I know you could never hurt a fly—let alone your own niece."

Janet was alluding to an incident in Karen's past, one that she would rather forget. But it was not the past that had upset Karen; rather, it was the sudden, intense desire she had experienced while holding Melissa to have a child of her own. Where that feeling had come from, she didn't know, for even in the days when she was married to Randy and was actively *trying* to become a mother she had not wanted to have a baby nearly so much as in that single moment of holding her niece in her arms. The feeling was so strong it was an ache—almost like a physical pain—but she still could not bring herself to mention it to Janet—even if her younger sister was her closest confidante. No, the feeling was too powerful, too confusing—too disruptive of the life she had etched out for herself.

But that moment had been a revelation to her. From then on she became increasingly aware of children around her, where she had formerly ignored them or thought of them only as nuisances. The couple in the next apartment had a three-year-old boy, and she offered to baby-sit for him if the mother ever needed to run out for a few minutes. Even though the child interfered with her work, she never really minded, and it was a sad day for her when the family eventually moved away.

Although she knew that there were women who were emancipated enough to have a child on their own without bothering with marriage, she could never do that. No, before she could even dream of having a child, she would have to find a husband.

And that was the biggest stumbling block. Aside from her own fears about marriage, where could she find a man—a man good enough to be not only a husband but also a father?

Meeting men was not the problem; her work brought her into contact with plenty of them. But the most attractive ones were usually married, and the eligible ones were often newly divorced—and dead-set against any serious involvement with a woman. Occasionally, she went out with these men, but it only took her a few dates to realize that they were lost causes—they were too steeped in their own bitterness, much as she had been after her divorce from Randy.

So, as time went by, she had begun to think that her dream of marriage and children would always be just a fantasy, a might-have-been. But she still had her work and the satisfactions it brought her—and this was no small comfort.

But now she had met Grant Cameron—and suddenly realized that she was far from finished with love.

CHAPTER THREE

Two days after the party, Grant called Karen. The conversation was short and to the point: would she like to have dinner with him the following evening?

Karen's reply was also short and shamelessly eager: Yes, she'd love to.

For that first date, he took her to Tavern-on-the-Green, a lovely, gardenlike restaurant set in the middle of Central Park. They sat in a floral-carpeted, glass-walled conservatory that was lit by ten antique Baccarat and Waterford crystal chandeliers and watched over by two large, whimsical, plaster-of-Paris reindeer. But Karen was hardly aware of either the surroundings or the cuisine, as she sat across the table from Grant.

Here she was able to observe something about him that she had not been aware of at their first meeting. There was an air of sadness to him, a kind of wistful melancholy that crept into his eyes at unguarded moments. It only made him all the more attractive to her. His eyes were like magnets to her own; she returned her gaze to them again and again, reveling in the frank desire she saw there.

As the dinner progressed their conversation turned from impersonal subjects to more personal ones. When Grant began asking Karen questions about her background, she found herself talking easily and eventually telling him things she had usually found too painful to reveal to a man—in particular about her divorce.

"You see," she explained after she'd given him most of the details, "Randy just up and left me—and I never understood why."

"But surely he must have given you some kind of reason," Grant suggested gently.

"None."

"Then what were the grounds for the divorce?"

"Incompatibility."

"Well, what kind of evidence did his lawyer offer?"

"I don't know, I didn't go to court—I couldn't face Randy."

Grant looked at her thoughtfully. "Do you ever have any contact with him now?"

"He sent me a Christmas card once," Karen said with a wry laugh. "I think it was just to let me know that he had remarried."

Grant shook his head. "Pardon my saying this—but he sounds like a real bastard."

"It's been eight years," Karen said with a shrug. "It doesn't bother me quite so much anymore."

A shadow suddenly passed across Grant's face, and his umber-colored eyes became pensive. "I wonder," he said, more to himself than to Karen, "does time really change things all that much?"

Several long moments passed, and then Karen said softly, "Were you thinking about your wife?"

"Yes." Grant sighed. "I suppose Fran told you."

Karen nodded.

"Good. I'm glad you know—and I'm equally glad that I don't have to be the one to tell you."

"I think Fran feels very protective toward you," Karen said. "I guess she wanted to make sure that I didn't ask you any insensitive questions."

"Good old Fran. She and Jerry are a couple of bricks—I don't know what I would have done without them." He sounded distracted, and his eyes swept around the room. "Would you like some dessert? Shall I call the waiter?"

"Oh, no. No dessert."

"Coffee? An after-dinner drink?"

"Just coffee," Karen said. Then she added casually, as if the idea had just occurred to her, "I have some wonderful old brandy at home. Maybe we could have that after-dinner drink at my place?"

"I like the sound of that," Grant said. He seemed at ease once more as he summoned the waiter over to the table.

After dinner Karen suggested that they walk to her apartment as it was a warm night for early spring, so they headed out of the park onto Central Park West. As they strolled along, Grant wordlessly took Karen's hand and put it in the crook of his arm. Through the fabric of his suit jacket, Karen could feel the sinewy strength of his muscles, and she suddenly longed to have those arms around her, holding her, pressing her close.

As if he had heard her thoughts, he abruptly stopped and drew her to him and kissed her. It started out as a tender kiss, but as she responded to him it grew more passionate, demanding, and arousing than either of them had expected. Finally, they both pulled away and gazed at each other longingly in the dim light.

"Remind me to thank Fran for being such a busybody," Grant said.

Karen laughed. "Are you sure you want to do that?"

"You're right," Grant said, taking her hand and starting to walk once more. "It would only encourage her—and we certainly can't have that."

Karen's apartment was in a renovated brownstone on Seventy-sixth Street, just off Central Park West. As they climbed the two flights of stairs, her own anticipation began to mount.

Once inside, Karen quickly took off her coat and headed for the kitchen. "Make yourself at home," she said. "I'll get the brandy."

But he followed her into the kitchen and came up behind her, wrapping his arms around her. "Forget the brandy," he said, his face buried in the nape of her neck. "All I want is you."

Karen let his words sink in, buzzing around in her mind, before she turned slowly, letting his kisses circle her neck, up her throat, seeking her lips. Then his mouth found hers, and she clung to him, their bodies pressing against each other, until she felt herself swept away by a wave of emotion, a passion more powerful than anything she had felt in a long time.

Ages seemed to pass before she could pull her lips away from his, gasping for air, trembling with excitement. "Please," she said weakly, "can we sit down? My knees are shaking."

But Grant didn't let her go. Instead he held her tighter. "Karen," he said, his voice barely a whisper. "I want to make love to you."

Karen lifted her head and looked deep into his eyes. The sadness was there again—along with something new: a reflection of the same aching need she felt in her own body. She knew they had both been hurt—each in a way too painful to dwell on. But they saw in each other an empathy, a compassion not easily found. Without saying a word, she took him by the hand and led him into her bedroom.

He was a wonderful lover. There was an urgency, a

kind of hunger to his lovemaking that drove Karen to an even higher pitch of arousal. Over and over again, he brought her to the heights of ecstasy. But then, as he reached his own climax, a low, strangled cry came out of his mouth—as if he were in intense pain. The sound of it tore at Karen's heart.

Afterward, they lay in each other's arms, silent for several long minutes. When Grant finally spoke, there was still a trembling, breathless quality to his voice. "It's been so long," he sighed. "I'd nearly forgotten how good it could be."

Karen looked at him intently. Without his glasses the fine, crinkly lines around his eyes gave him a look of vulnerability. "It's been a long time for me, too," she said tenderly, wanting to let him know that she understood what loneliness was.

Grant gazed at her thoughtfully and then rolled over and stared up at the ceiling. "I haven't been to bed with anybody since my wife died," he said. "I've been celibate—a veritable monk—for more than three years." He turned to look at Karen. "In these days of sexual liberation that sounds pretty strange, doesn't it?"

"Not at all," she replied. "Why? Do you think it does?"

"I don't know," he said, turning his face toward the ceiling again. "I guess for a long time after Emily died I was bitter. At one point I even promised myself there'd never be another woman in my life."

"I think I understand," Karen said gently.

Grant was quiet for a moment before he suddenly sat up, hunching himself over his knees. "I wish *I* did."

Karen sat up alongside of him. "What do you mean?"

His face was turned away from her. "I wonder whether I *should* get involved with another woman—

you, you seem so fragile, vulnerable—because maybe there's something in me. Maybe I'm a jinx. Maybe there's some fatal quirk in my nature that destroys the people around me. Maybe *I* drove Emily to do what she did."

"But that's absurd," Karen protested.

"Is it? Believe me, I've thought a lot about it."

"Fran said that it was postpartum depression—"

"It was. That and booze. But *I* lived with Emily. *I* should have known what she was planning to do."

"She probably didn't want you to know."

"I wish I could believe that."

Karen put her arm across his shoulders. His muscles were knotted with tension. "I think you're being too hard on yourself," she said.

Grant shook his head as if rousing himself from a stupor. "I don't know why I said all that," he said, twisting around to look at Karen. "I've never told anybody about those feelings before. It just came spilling out of me. I hope I haven't put you off."

"No," Karen reassured him. "You haven't. In fact, I'm glad you told me."

But Grant seemed to find it necessary to explain himself. "You know, I've done my best to cover up those feelings—mostly for Jessica's sake. She needed me, so I had to be strong."

"Of course," Karen said compassionately. "It must have been difficult for a child to understand."

"She was only eight when it happened. She—well, I don't know if Fran has told you any of the details—"

"She hasn't."

"Then you don't know that Jessica was the one who actually found the bodies. She came home from school and . . . there they were, the two of them, in the nursery. She was so frightened she went and locked herself in the bathroom and didn't come out until I got home from work a while later."

"How awful!" Karen gasped.

Grant nodded. "She was in a state of shock for quite some time. The doctor wanted to put her in the hospital, but she was terrified of being separated from me. She went into screaming fits if I even left her room for a minute."

"That must have been hard on you."

"It was, but worrying about Jessica helped keep my mind off . . . the other thing."

"Are you sure you want to talk about this?" Karen asked gently.

Grant heaved a great sigh. "Let me get this off my chest now. Then we won't ever have to talk about it again."

"All right. If you say so."

"But I don't want to inflict anything on you that you don't want to hear," Grant said hesitantly.

"No, it's not that," Karen said. "It's you. I can see that the subject upsets you."

"It does. That's why I never talk about it. I never wanted to discuss it with anyone—until now. Do you understand?"

Karen nodded. "Of course."

"Good. I just want to let you know a little of what I've been through—like you telling me about your divorce. Maybe it'll help you understand me. At least, I hope so."

"Then go ahead. But first tell me a little about your wife."

"Emily?" Grant frowned. "There's really not much to tell. I met her on a ski trip to Mount Stowe. She was working for a public relations firm then, but she quit her job after we got married. Our backgrounds were very similar: upper-middle-class Wasps—she went to Vassar and I went to Yale—and we were both only children. Somehow, our marriage seemed preordained.

"We were married for two years before Jessica was born. We'd originally intended to have another child right away because we had both known how lonely it could be growing up as an only child, and we didn't want that for Jessica. But there had been some complications with Jessica's birth, and Emily's doctor warned her not to try to have another baby too soon.

"So we waited until the doctor said it would be all right, but then Emily couldn't get pregnant again. It was very upsetting to her, so I told her we would forget about it—for a while, at least.

"And then, when I got into my middle thirties I had what I suppose the pop psychologists would call a 'life crisis,' and I began to realize that I was getting older and I suddenly, desperately wanted to have another child.

"So I talked Emily into trying again, and although it took a while, she eventually became pregnant with Sarah.

"I *thought* that Emily wanted this second baby as much as I did. And she seemed to—right up until the time Sarah was born, and even during those first few days in the hospital. But then when they came home—it was almost as if I had brought home the wrong wife from the hospital.

"Emily had always been a little high-strung, but suddenly she was wildly temperamental. I didn't dare look at her the wrong way or she would burst into tears. And she became so possessive of Sarah that she wouldn't let anyone else go near her. Then the drinking started.

"I couldn't believe it at first because Emily had never been one to have more than a glass of wine with dinner. But here she was, tossing the stuff down as if there were no tomorrow.

"I tried to get help for her, but she refused to go.

Every day she seemed to get worse, and I was at my wits' end when . . . it finally happened."

"You don't have to tell me any more," Karen interrupted him.

"No, wait," Grant said, needing to finish what he had started. "Just let me tell you about that day and then I'll shut up."

Reluctantly, Karen had to admit to herself that she felt a rather morbid curiosity about the circumstances of Grant's wife's suicide. But she didn't dare let him see this. "All right," she said grudgingly. "Go on."

"I went to the office as usual that day," Grant went on. "I shouldn't have. We'd had a particularly bitter argument that morning. She must have sensed my desperation, the hate I felt for her in my eyes. I should have known that Emily was near the breaking point. But so was I—and frankly, I could hardly stand to be around her anymore.

"Then in the afternoon I couldn't get any answer on the telephone, and I started to worry because Jessica should have been home from school by then, and she at least could have answered the phone. So I left the office a little early and went home.

"I didn't know if Emily and the baby were upstairs, but the doorman had told me that Jessica was definitely home from school. But she wasn't there when I got upstairs, and I couldn't find her. Finally, I heard a whimpering noise and found her locked in the bathroom off Emily's and my bedroom.

"She couldn't talk, but I could see that something terrible had happened to her. But when I tried to get her to tell me, all she could do was point down the hall."

Grant took a deep breath. "So I walked down to the nursery . . . they were there. Sarah—slashed to death in her crib. Emily—lying on the floor near her in a pool of blood. The butcher's knife was still sticking out of Emily's chest."

Grant rubbed a hand across his forehead as if to erase the awful image printed there. "Sometimes when I close my eyes I can still see them, and they're so real I could reach out and touch them." He paused a moment and then added dismally, "But the worst thing was the way it smelled, like a slaughterhouse. I could actually *smell* their blood—it was overpowering. In my mind I kept smelling it for months afterward."

He fell silent, and Karen let out the breath she'd been holding. "I-I had no idea it was so gruesome," she said. "I'm sorry if I've made you relive it."

"No." He reached for her hand. "I had to tell you. It's about time I let it out, anyway. I never told anyone what it was like before—except the police, of course."

"The police?"

"Yes, I had to notify them. There'd been a murder."

"But it was apparent what had happened. They didn't question you too rigorously, did they?"

Grant shrugged. "They made it as easy as they could. The most upsetting part of it was that they had to talk to Jessica since she was actually the first one on the scene. But they were surprisingly gentle with her."

Karen let her arm slip off his shoulders, and she started to get off the bed. "I think I could use some of that brandy now. How about you?" she asked quietly.

"Definitely."

Karen went into the kitchen and brought back the brandy bottle and two glasses. They propped up the pillows at the head of the bed and settled themselves against them, sipping the brandy and talking little.

Suddenly, Karen's gaze fell on the clock radio on

her nightstand. It was nearly eleven thirty. "It's getting late," she said. "How soon do you have to go?"

"That's up to you," Grant said. "I don't really have to go home at all."

"But what about your daughter?" Karen asked. "Won't she be expecting you?"

"She's spending the night at a girl friend's."

Karen smiled wryly. "You really plan ahead, don't you."

"I wasn't being presumptuous," he said quickly, a grin playing across his lips. "I didn't want her to be left alone for too long, and I thought it best that she just stay overnight with a friend."

"Does she know you had a date tonight?"

Two tiny furrows appeared in the space between Grant's eyebrows. "No. I told her I had a late business meeting. I hope she believed me—I hated lying to her."

Karen frowned. "Then why did you do it?" she asked, careful to keep any trace of the hurt she felt out of her voice.

Grant touched his hand to hers. "Don't get the wrong idea," he said. "I'm not ashamed of you, but I have my reasons for not telling her." He paused, obviously searching for words. "It's just that—well, Jessica is very possessive of me, and I don't know how she would react to my seeing someone. It might be threatening to her."

Karen heard the earnest concern in his voice. "You must be a wonderful father," she said.

"I do my best," Grant said solemnly. "I have to protect Jessica. She's so young and she's already been through so much."

"Is she very dependent on you?" Karen asked.

"Yes and no. Most of the time she hardly seems touched by what happened, but every once in a while she has nightmares about her mother. And she hates it if I have to go away on a business trip for more than a day or two."

"Does she ever talk to you about her mother?"

"Never. It's almost as if Emily and Sarah never existed. Perhaps it's better that way."

"I wonder," Karen mused. "Sometimes children get strange ideas that they're responsible for things if you don't explain it to them. You know, they think that they're the cause of their parents' divorce—things like that."

Grant frowned. "Yes, I know. I talked to a psychologist about it. But I'm sure Jessica knows that she didn't do anything to make her mother do what she did. And I really think she's handled the whole thing rather well."

"You're obviously right," Karen said. "Since you care for her a great deal, that must make up for a lot of things."

Grant stroked Karen's forearm with the back of his hand. "You know, I think Jessica would like you," he said. "I'll have to get the two of you together someday."

"I'll look forward to that," Karen said. "If she's anything like you, she must be a very special child."

Then Grant kissed her and his arms encircled her before he pulled her back down onto the bed.

CHAPTER FOUR

Love had happened to her again. Karen couldn't quite believe it, but every time she saw Grant she knew that a minor miracle had indeed occurred.

After that first night, Grant began calling Karen regularly and seeing her as often as he could. As they got to know each other better, their relationship became all that Karen could ask for—in every way but one: Grant never again brought up the subject of introducing her to his daughter.

Karen couldn't help but wonder why. She knew how important Jessica was to Grant, and it hurt Karen to think that he was shutting her out of that vital and demanding part of his life. Yet she was so afraid of spoiling what they had that she couldn't bring herself to ask him about it.

Weeks went by and then months, and their love deepened and grew. Eventually, Grant began talking about marriage; it was only then that Karen dared venture a question about Jessica and what she might think about his remarrying.

Grant admitted that he didn't know. He hadn't talked to her about it.

"Well, don't you think you'd better?" Karen asked. "What will you do if she's totally opposed to the idea?"

"I don't think she will be," Grant said. "She already knows that I've been seeing someone—and that it's serious. She's got to expect that I might want to get married again."

"But you haven't actually discussed it with her?"

"No. I thought that the two of you should meet first—and then I could tell her what our plans are. That way you won't just be an abstraction to her, but flesh and blood, someone she can relate to."

"And what if she doesn't like me?"

Grant smiled lovingly at Karen. "That's impossible. I know she will."

A week later Grant invited Karen to dinner at Uzie's, a chic Italian restaurant, for the following Friday evening. Jessica would be there. She had said she was looking forward to meeting Karen.

After the maître d' showed Grant and Jessica to their table, Jessica began to pepper him with questions about Karen.

"Daddy, what does she look like? Is she pretty?"

"Jessica," Grant said tolerantly, "I thought you told me you weren't going to do this. You said that you wanted to wait and form your own opinions about Karen, didn't you?"

Jessica smiled sheepishly. "I know I said that, Daddy. But I'm curious—I want to know. Can't you tell me just a little bit about her?"

Grant laughed and reached over and pinched Jessica on the cheek. "Just when I think you're growing up too fast, you do something that proves to me you're still a child," he said. "Thank God."

"Oh, *Daddy*," Jessica said, glancing around to see if

anyone had observed this little interchange. "I wish you wouldn't do things like that to me in public."

"Sorry," Grant said with mock solemnity. "In the future I'll try to be more well-mannered."

Jessica was still uncertain. "You won't do anything like that in front of Karen, will you?"

Grant shook his head. "I promise I'll be on my best behavior."

Jessica shot a quick glance toward the door and then back to Grant. "Are you serious about her, Daddy?" she asked.

"What do you mean by 'serious,' kitten?"

"Are you going to marry her?" Jessica asked, her blue eyes looking searchingly into his.

Grant studied her small, suddenly so vulnerable face. "Maybe," he said slowly. "How would you feel about that?"

Jessica lowered her eyes. "I don't know. I haven't even met her yet."

Grant reached discreetly under the table and patted Jessica's knee. "Sweetheart, you have nothing to worry about," he said. "Yes, I care for Karen, but that doesn't make any difference in the way I feel about you. You'll always be my number-one girl."

Jessica blinked at him. "Even if you get married?"

Grant gave her a reassuring smile. "Absolutely. Nobody could ever take your place, kitten. Don't you know that?"

Jessica responded with a quick, disarming smile. "I guess I needed to hear you say it, Daddy."

Grant gazed at her thoughtfully. Sometimes it amazed him to see how resilient she was, how little she seemed to be scarred by what her mother had done. But then there were other moments, times when she revealed how tenaciously dependent on him she was—a condition he was sure had not been there before the tragedy that had altered the course of their lives forever. Whenever he had a glimpse—as he had just now—of that dependency, it frightened him—for what would become of *her* if anything happened to *him*? For that reason alone, he might have considered remarrying—in addition to the fact that Jessica was entering a very tumultuous time in her life and could certainly use some female guidance. He had once thought that if he remarried these might be his overwhelming motivations, but then he had met Karen and had realized that he too had needs that had gone unfulfilled and that if he married her it would not be for the sake of his daughter alone.

"Daddy!" Jessica suddenly whispered sharply out of the side of her mouth. "Is that Karen?"

Grant followed her eyes in the direction of the restaurant's front door. It was indeed Karen who had just entered, and he felt himself involuntarily tense as he realized the importance of the meeting that was about to take place.

Jessica gave him a swift glance. "She's very pretty," she said, approval registering in her voice.

Grant smiled somewhat proprietorially as he watched Karen, led by the maître d', make her way toward them. He was aware that most of the other men in the room were watching her too—he had often noticed that Karen had that effect on men. She had a certain forbidding sexuality about her, an aura that both invited and denied interest. It made him feel good to know that she was his, that other men might lust after her to no avail. It was a new feeling for him; Emily had not been the kind of woman to make men's blood pound, not even his and not even in the beginning of their relationship. But satisfying his libido had not been the most important thing to him then either. Funny, now that he was older it had become more significant—and that was something he had only become aware of since meeting Karen.

She smiled as she approached the table, a smile that was at once warm but also revealed the extent of her nervousness. Grant wished he could say or do something that would lessen the look of apprehension in Karen's lovely green eyes, but at that moment he was not the calmest of men himself. He scrambled to his feet as the maître d' pulled out a chair for Karen. He leaned forward and gave her a quick peck on the cheek, wondering why he felt exactly as he had on the first day of the dancing classes that his parents had forced him to go to thirty years ago.

As he sat down he shot a glance at Jessica out of the corner of his eye. She was wearing a polite, demure smile and looking expectantly from him to Karen and back again while she waited for them to settle themselves and for him to make the formal introductions. Yet behind that pleasant exterior Grant could detect a shrewd gleam in his young daughter's eye: she was keenly sizing up both Karen and the extent of his feelings for her. In fact, Grant realized suddenly, Jessica had probably already assessed his intentions toward Karen and knew them even better than he did.

Karen too perceived the gleam in Jessica's eye and acknowledged that she was being cunningly appraised, much as if she were a specimen under a microscope. She had expected it, of course, but even so it was disconcerting to face that kind of minute observation.

She knew that she was off to a bad start as it was, having arrived late at the restaurant. Just as she'd been leaving her apartment she'd gotten a business call from an art director she could not afford to offend by cutting short. By the time she'd gotten off the phone she had begun to perspire nervously, causing her to worry about staining the jade green silk dress she was wearing. This necessitated taking the dress off, dousing herself with antiperspirant and dusting powder, and then slipping the dress back on and rushing out of the apartment. Amazingly enough, she had found a cab immediately, but they had gotten caught in the heavy rush-hour traffic, and as they inched their way across town, she became so jittery that she thought she might be better off getting out and walking—just to ease the tension. By the time they arrived at the restaurant on Third Avenue and Eighty-second Street, she was in such a dither that she stood outside on the sidewalk for several moments, forcing herself to take deep breaths, before she could walk in.

Now, sitting across the table from Jessica and being under such close scrutiny, Karen knew it would be impossible to conceal her nervousness. So she smiled and decided to look Jessica right in the eye. The child looked nothing like Grant, for she had luminous blue eyes and a flowing mane of tawny-gold hair. She was wearing a white middy dress, and Karen could see that her body was still that of a little girl's. But her face was that of a young woman. A young woman straight out of a painting by Botticelli—ethereal, exquisite, remote. She was a beautiful child. It was no wonder that Grant was so devoted to this charming daughter. Karen just stared helplessly at her while Grant made the introductions.

"How do you do?" Jessica said very formally, extending her hand to Karen. "I'm so pleased to meet you."

"Hello, Jessica." Karen shook her hand. It was surprisingly strong, but icy cold. "Your father has told me so much about you."

"Really?" Jessica responded, arching one delicate eyebrow a fraction of an inch.

"Why don't we order some drinks?" Grant interjected, signaling to the waiter who was hovering about the table.

"Oh, can I have a cocktail, Daddy?" Jessica said teasingly.

Grant ignored her. "She'll have a ginger ale," he said to the waiter. "What would you like?" he asked Karen.

"Oh, just a glass of wine," she said. "Red, I think."

Grant ordered a carafe of the house red wine. "It's really quite good," he said to Karen. "I hope you like it."

"I'm sure I'll like it, too," Jessica said loudly, diverting her father's attention away from Karen. "Can I have some with my meal?"

Grant looked askance at his daughter. "Of course not."

Jessica turned her blue eyes on Karen. "Don't you think I should be allowed to have just a little teensy taste of wine?" she said appealingly. "I think I'm old enough to be able to try it."

Karen glanced at Grant and saw that he was watching her, no doubt eager to see how she handled this situation. "Well, I—" she began uncertainly, then realized that the worst thing she could do as far as making a good impression on Grant's child was to appear wishy-washy. There was no reason for her to be uneasy with this child. "No, Jessica," she said, making sure all lack of confidence had vanished from her voice. "I don't think you should be allowed to taste the wine. Although you may think you're mature enough to handle it—and you very well may be—your father doesn't want you to, and in addition it would be against the law, and I'm sure the restaurant wouldn't permit it."

Grant gave her an approving smile. "Very good, Karen. I couldn't have said it better myself." Then he looked pointedly at Jessica. "I consider the subject of the wine to be closed now, do you understand me, Jessica?"

"Yes, Daddy," Jessica said quickly. "I promise I won't bring it up again."

"Good," Grant said. "Now I hope you will be able to behave yourself throughout the rest of the meal—otherwise Karen won't have a very favorable impression of you."

As the child meekly nodded her head, Karen realized that Grant's words were a trifle ironic. Perhaps Grant *was* concerned that she like his daughter, but far more crucial she was sure was Jessica's reaction to *her*. Should she fail to receive Jessica's stamp of approval, she was quite positive that it would mean the end of her relationship with Grant.

The waiter brought Jessica's ginger ale and the carafe of red wine and filled two glasses for her and Grant.

"How do you like it?" Grant asked as Karen sipped her wine.

"It's very good," she responded, taking another taste. "Nice and dry." She started to set her glass down, but inadvertently placed it on the tip of her knife. The glass wobbled and wine splashed over the rim, spreading a bright scarlet stain on the pristine white of the tablecloth. "Oh, how stupid of me!" Karen exclaimed as she grabbed for the glass to steady it.

"Don't worry about it," Grant said mildly. "There's no harm done."

Karen gave him an appreciative look, then glanced at Jessica, more than a bit embarrassed at her clumsiness. Expecting to see some kind of reproachful expression on the child's face, she was surprised to find Jessica staring fixedly at the stain on the tablecloth. Puzzled, Karen looked closer at the ruddy stain and wondered what the child could find so fascinating about it. Then with a sudden shock she realized how much the wine looked like blood against the whiteness of the tablecloth—and for Jessica the sight of blood must surely conjure up horrifying images of her mother and sister! Karen glanced again at Jessica, feeling a prickle of sympathy for her, and saw that she was still sitting, gazing blankly at the wine stain.

Grant did not seem to be aware of his daughter's abstraction. He was busily trying to regale Karen with descriptions of the delights on the restaurant's menu. Karen tried to pay attention to him, but she could not help glancing at Jessica every few seconds.

Then, the child shook herself and became conscious of her surroundings once again. Her clear blue eyes suddenly met Karen's, and for a fleeting second there was a look of apprehension in them—as if Jessica were afraid that Karen had seen her in an unguarded moment of weakness. Then the look was gone, and Jessica's eyes were calm once more. She turned them to gaze at her father.

The remainder of the meal was uneventful and even pleasant as Jessica seemed to make a special effort to be affable and charming. Karen wondered briefly if she was doing her best to wipe out any earlier, unfavorable impression Karen might have had when she caught Jessica staring at the wine stain.

Curious, Karen began to watch Jessica even more closely, intent on catching a sign that the child might be unstable. But Jessica disappointed her; she certainly seemed well-adjusted as she took a lively part in the dinner conversation. With her father especially she carried on an easy, bantering give-and-take. Karen envied the two of them; she had never had that kind of relationship with her father. As a child she had been lucky to get her father to even condescend to speak to her—let alone joke and play with her.

When the meal was over, Grant suggested that Karen come back with them to their apartment. As an inducement he added that Jessica had baked a cake in her honor.

"Really?" Karen said, turning to look at Jessica. "How very sweet of you."

An appealing rush of color tinged Jessica's cheeks. "I hope you like chocolate cake," she murmured.

Karen nodded eagerly. "It's my favorite."

Grant beamed at the two of them. "Well, then, ladies," he said, moving back his chair, "shall we push off?"

It was a short walk to their apartment on Park Avenue, and since she had never been there before, Karen was curious to see how Grant lived.

The building was old and solid and unremarkable among block after block of similar-looking brick and limestone luxury apartment houses. Karen did notice that the architect had added the flourish of a row of Moorish arches over the canopied entryway. The black-uniformed doorman gave both Grant and Jessica cheery greetings as he ushered them inside and gave Karen a discreetly inquisitive look.

Their apartment was on the eighth floor. Grant unlocked the door, turned on a light, and let Karen go in first. "Jessica," he said, "why don't you show Karen around while I get the coffeemaker started?"

"Would you like to see the apartment?" Jessica asked Karen.

"Yes, I'd like that very much."

Karen followed as Jessica led her into a room so large that her entire apartment could have nearly fit inside. Looking around, Karen said, "Oh, this is very nice."

The room was done in subtle shades of beige and blue and had a definite feminine touch. Beige-and-blue crewelwork covered a sofa and loveseat set at right angles to each other around a circle of buff-tinted marble serving as a coffee table. On the table were a number of ornate porcelain boxes and a blue glass vase containing a single cream-colored rose. Its musty, fragile fragrance lay faintly on the air. The carpeting and draperies were of a subdued blue that matched the shade in the crewelwork. On one wall was a fireplace edged with Delft tiles, and over the mantel hung a seascape in an antique gilded frame.

Directly off the living room was a small wood-paneled study lined with bookshelves. "This must be your father's retreat," Karen observed.

Jessica looked at her blankly. "No," she said. "This is where he comes to get away from it all."

Karen smiled at the child's back as she turned to lead her across the living room and through an archway to the dining room. Jessica flicked a switch and an ornate crystal chandelier began to shimmer with the light of dozens of glittering prisms. The chandelier was reflected on the gleaming walnut surfaces of the dining room table and chairs and china cabinet.

"What a lovely room," Karen said, her esthetic sense pleased by the room's elegance.

Jessica nodded, turned out the light, and led Karen out of the dining room to a long hallway, where she in quick succession pointed out Grant's bedroom and her own. Karen would have liked to have had more than the fleeting glimpse she had of Grant's bedroom, but Jessica hurried her on to show off her own bedroom.

Jessica's bedroom was the kind that Karen had dreamed of having when she was a young girl. It was a fairyland of pink ruffles; they adorned the canopied four-poster bed, the bedspread, a skirted dressing table, and the cafe curtains at the windows. "What a pretty room," Karen cooed. "It's so feminine."

Jessica walked over to one corner where a large

modern stereo with numerous dials and switches stood. "Isn't this neat?" she said proudly. "Daddy gave it to me last Christmas—only he doesn't like the kind of music I play so whenever he's around I use my headphones."

"What kind of music do you like, Jessica?" Karen asked.

In response, Jessica reeled off the names of about half a dozen groups that Karen had never heard of.

"I'm afraid I'm rather ignorant when it comes to today's music," Karen said apologetically.

"That's okay," Jessica said. "Most grownups are."

Karen threw a final, admiring glance around Jessica's room and then walked into the hallway. She spotted another door down at the far end. "Oh, what's that?" she asked Jessica. "Another room?"

"It's just a spare room," Jessica answered a little too quickly. "There's really nothing in it to see. Let's go back to the living room. Daddy's probably got the coffee ready by now."

Puzzled by the brusque way Jessica had ended the tour, Karen nevertheless dutifully followed her back to the living room.

Once there, she walked over to look at the painting hanging above the mantel. The seascape was done in the style of Winslow Homer and showed a tiny skiff with two fishermen riding over the top of a towering blue black wave that nearly blotted out a bleak expanse of gray sky.

"Do you like it?" Jessica asked, coming to stand beside Karen. "Since you're an artist, you probably like more modern things."

Karen glanced sideways at Jessica. The child's startling blue eyes were fixed on her. "Usually I do," Karen said. "But I happen to like this very much. Do you know who painted it?"

Grant had joined them. "Nobody special," he said.

"My father just picked it up because he liked it—he always loved the sea."

"Me too," Jessica chimed in. "Someday Daddy's going to buy a boat and teach me how to sail."

"I didn't know you were a sailor," Karen said in a slightly admonishing tone to Grant.

"I used to be," he said, draping his arm casually over Jessica's shoulder. "In my younger days I sailed with a group of friends—mostly around the Sound, but one summer we took my dad's boat down to Bermuda."

"That sounds like fun," Karen said, going to sit on the loveseat. "You'll have to tell me about it sometime."

Grant sat down on the couch, facing Karen. "Everything's set up for you in the kitchen, Jessica," he said. "All you have to do is cut your cake and serve it."

"Okay, Daddy," Jessica said, walking off toward the kitchen.

As Karen watched her cross the living room, she was struck by the similarity in the way father and daughter walked. Although Jessica's features bore little resemblance to Grant, in motion she was like a miniature female version of him: she had the same grace, the same long, fluid stride, the same suggestion of strength and energy in the spring of the step. They were both like efficient machines—no wasted movements, no part not contributing to the forward progress. Because Karen had always thought of herself as rather uncoordinated and clumsy, she had a jealous admiration for such unselfconscious physical grace.

Grant turned to Karen when Jessica was out of the room. "I think she likes you," he said, reaching for Karen's hand and squeezing it.

"How can you tell?"

"I know my daughter," Grant said simply.

Again Karen felt a twinge of envy as she thought of her own father and the lack of communication between them. "Yes, I can see how close you two are," she said, a trace of wistfulness in her voice.

Grant tightened his grip on her hand. "Don't get to thinking that there's no room for you here, Karen," he said lovingly. "Because there is."

Karen's impulse was to fling herself into Grant's arms and smother him with kisses, but she contented herself with a tender look. Just then, over Grant's shoulder, she noticed Jessica standing in the kitchen doorway, staring at them. Her face was frozen into an odd, almost vacant expression. What *was* the matter with the child?

Grant, seeing Karen looking past him, turned his head. "Oh, there you are, kitten," he called out gaily. "Is everything ready?"

Karen thought Jessica flinched at the sound of his voice. "Oh, uh, yes, Daddy," she said brightly. "I'll bring the coffee and cake out in just a minute." Then she disappeared into the kitchen.

Karen longed to ask Grant if Jessica often experienced momentary lapses of concentration. But she quickly berated herself for being insensitive, for reading too much into the young girl's behavior. And there was no doubt that the girl had been delightful—so eager to please and to satisfy Grant's obvious pride in his only daughter.

Karen waved away her critical thoughts. After all, she too had been a bit on show this evening—and her behavior hadn't been all that exemplary. It was obvious that both she and Jessica had been quite uneasy about meeting each other for the first time. They would come to like each other. Now, the important thing was to pretend that she found his daughter to be as pleasant and engaging as he obviously thought she was. After all, he was a package deal—she couldn't have the one without the other.

CHAPTER FIVE

"Well, what did Jessica think of me?" Karen blurted out the moment she heard Grant's voice on the phone the following day, knowing that her whole future might be riding on his answer.

"Now, don't take this the wrong way," Grant said, sounding more than a little defensive. "She said she thought you were okay."

"Okay?" Karen repeated incredulously. "Just 'okay'?" Then she moaned. "Oh, God, Grant, that's damning with faint praise."

"Wait a minute, Karen," Grant said quickly. "I don't think you understand what that means—"

"Well, I certainly hope you're going to explain it to me," Karen cut in sarcastically.

"It means," Grant said, sounding as if he were patiently explaining the latest permutations in the tax laws, "that she's willing to accept you. That's quite a concession for her to make, you've got to understand. Up to now she's had me all to herself for the last three years—now she's being asked to share me with another woman. I think that her saying that you're okay is her way of telling me that it's all right, that she's willing to share me. But you can't expect her to be too thrilled about it."

"No," Karen said, feeling a little sheepish about her earlier sarcasm.

"We also discussed my getting married to you," Grant said ever so matter-of-factly.

Karen couldn't hide her quick intake of breath. "What—what did she say?"

"She said she thought it seemed like a pretty good idea."

"Really?"

"Really."

"Am I to interpret that as meaning that she's not too crazy about the idea, but if that's what you really want, she's willing to go along?"

"You see, you're learning already."

"Oh, God, Grant, do you think she'll ever really accept me as a stepmother? I've never been one before—I won't know what to do."

"Well, you were a teacher, weren't you? You know how to handle kids."

"That was different. Anyway, it was a long time ago," Karen said curtly, hoping to dissuade Grant from continuing with this line of conversation.

But something in her tone of voice must have alerted Grant. "You don't like to talk about your teaching, do you?" he remarked. "Is it because it reminds you of Randy—or is there some other reason?"

Karen let out an exasperated sigh. "I wasn't very good at it, that's why I don't like to talk about it," she snapped. "Now, can we get back to the subject at hand?"

Luckily, Grant seemed satisfied with her response. "Well, as far as I'm concerned," he said blandly, "I don't see what you're so worried about. I'm sure that you and Jessica will both do your best to get along.

And once you've gotten to know each other, you'll probably grow to like each other."

"Do you really think so?" Karen asked, fishing for more reassurance.

"Absolutely," Grant said without hesitation. "Now, what we have to do next is decide when we want to get married."

Karen liked the tone of certainty in his voice; it helped to dispel many of her own misgivings. "You sound as if you're in a rush," she teased. "You've got to give a girl time to think about such things."

"Well, you'd better get started. Look over the calendar and pick out a date."

"All right, I'll put my mind to it."

When Karen hung up the phone, she was smiling fondly to herself. It was all working out very well, she decided. Jessica would not be a problem, after all.

From then on things moved so fast it was like a dream for Karen. They decided on a date in August—it was already June—and that they wanted to keep the ceremony itself small and intimate, instead throwing a large, extravagant reception later for all their friends and family.

Karen tried vainly to keep up with her work and to take care of all the wedding details at the same time, but the wedding won out. There was so much more to do than she remembered from her wedding to Randy. But then, of course, her mother—and Randy—had done much of the work. Now, it was all up to her.

Up until the day of the wedding she only seemed to see Grant in passing, and most of the time they spent together was devoted to making out guest lists or discussing the arrangements for the reception. They were rarely alone anymore, for it seemed that Jessica was nearly always around.

Karen still couldn't quite feel at ease in the child's

presence. She had the feeling that Jessica was watching her, judging her, comparing her—to her mother probably. Yet on the surface Jessica was always friendly and cooperative, and Karen wondered if perhaps she was projecting onto the child her own insecurities about remarriage and becoming a stepmother.

Wait until Grant and I are actually married, Karen told herself repeatedly. *Things will be different then. We'll have time to get to know one another.*

At last the day of the wedding arrived. Karen was up at dawn, wandering around her apartment, packing some things into boxes, glad to have these last few hours alone. She had lived in the apartment since her divorce from Randy, and it felt strange to know that she would never live there again. It had always been her refuge from the world—what would she do without it?

At seven thirty her mother called. "Just to make sure you were up, dear," she said.

"Oh, I've been up for hours," Karen told her. "I didn't sleep very well last night."

"You're not having second thoughts, are you?"

"No. Do you think I should?"

"Why no," her mother said tentatively. "I like Grant very much. I think he'll make a wonderful husband for you. It's just . . ."

"Just what?"

"Well, do you think you can handle having an eleven-year-old stepdaughter?"

"What do you mean by that?" Karen asked suspiciously.

"Oh, dear, do I have to remind you about what happened—"

"That's all in the past, Mother. It was only a temporary breakdown—which wasn't surprising, considering the circumstances. But I'm fine now, and there aren't going to be any repeat performances," Karen said calmly, her voice strong and sure.

"Does Grant know about your nervous breakdown?"

"No. And I'd appreciate it if you didn't tell him."

"Well, of course, I won't say anything if you don't want me to. But don't you think you ought to say something to him yourself?"

"Look, let's not discuss this now," Karen said with a laugh. "I've still got a million things to do. Remember? I'm getting married in a few hours."

"All right, dear. Forget I said anything." Her mother's voice sounded a trifle hurt.

She didn't have time to reflect on what her mother had said, for as soon as she'd hung up the phone it rang again. This time it was Grant. "Have you looked outside yet?" he asked.

"No. I haven't had time."

"Well, I just got back from jogging in the park—and I think it's the most glorious day I've ever seen in my life," he said excitedly. "The sky is a bright blue with these puffy little white clouds floating across it, the air is clean, there are birds singing like crazy—" He paused to catch his breath.

"Grant, I've never heard you talk like this before," Karen broke in. "What's come over you?"

"I don't know." He laughed. "But I feel like a kid—as if there were absolutely nothing I couldn't do today."

More than ever Karen felt very glad that she was marrying him.

"Karen, I love you," Grant said, his voice low and earnest. "You've helped me remember that I can be happy, that I can feel alive. It's very hard for me to put things like this into words, but I wanted to tell you this before we got swept up by the activities of the day."

When Karen got off the phone, her eyes were brimming with tears of happiness.

At eleven o'clock her parents, sister, and brother-in-law arrived from New Jersey, and Karen finished dressing. She had chosen an ivory-colored linen suit with a matching hat. She looked sophisticated and smart, yet very much like a bride.

The ceremony and reception were held in a rented townhouse at Seventy-third and Madison. The ceremony was performed by a judge in the townhouse's elegant Victorian parlor; only Karen's family, Jessica, and Fran and Jerry were present.

It was a sharp contrast to the three-ring circus that Karen remembered from her first wedding. Randy had orchestrated that whole show: he insisted that there be no less than six bridesmaids and groomsmen apiece; he chose the color of the bridesmaids' dresses (sea green—"to match Karen's eyes," he said); without consulting Karen, he selected the music for the ceremony; and he virtually overruled her mother and chose the dinner menu from the caterer. The day of the wedding he had been in his glory, glad-handing all the guests, receiving their congratulations and gifts with a practiced and phony humility, enjoying every single second of being the center of attention. Karen had felt like a stranger at her own wedding, but—mostly for her mother's sake—she had put on a determined smile and pretended to be happy.

Today, she was sure she would not have to pretend. She was happy—gloriously happy.

Karen barely heard the familiar words as they recited their vows. She wondered what Grant was thinking, whether he was remembering the first time he had done this—as she was doing—and the way it turned out. Both of their first marriages had been tragic—Grant's doubly so. But Karen trusted in their love. Believed there was nothing they couldn't do—couldn't have—together.

Then it was over; they were pronounced husband and wife. Grant gave her a quick, tender kiss, and everyone crowded around them, kissing and hugging and congratulating them.

When it was Fran's turn to embrace Karen, she burst into tears.

"Whatever are you crying for?" Karen teased. "Of all the people here, you should be the happiest—you engineered all this."

"I know," Fran blubbered. "That's why I'm crying."

Karen gazed fondly at her friend's tear-streaked face. "Stop that right now," she said in mock brusqueness. "Or else I'll start crying, too."

With that they collapsed in each other's arms in a mixture of tears and girlish giggles.

Later came the reception, with more people—some of whom Karen had never seen before—and an unending flow of music, food, champagne.

Karen drank glass after glass of champagne and danced with happy abandon with each man at the party. She was feeling positively buoyant—as if she could go on dancing all night.

Then suddenly Grant was there, gathering her in his arms, holding her as she swayed in time to the music.

"Don't just stand there like a stiff," she laughingly chided him. "Dance with me."

"Karen, I don't want to put a damper on your good time," Grant said, his hands tightening around her waist. "But I think maybe you ought to sit down for a while."

Karen blinked at him. "Why?"

"Because, my beautiful new bride—" he grinned at her—"you have been drinking champagne nonstop since we got here, and I think it would make our guests rather uncomfortable if you passed out on them."

"Oh." Karen digested this for a moment. Maybe Grant was right. Perhaps she'd had just a teeny tiny bit too much champagne. "Maybe I will sit this one out," she managed to mumble.

Grant led her to a nearby group of chairs, and as she eased herself down onto one, her sister Janet sat down next to her. "Grant, why don't you leave Karen with me?" Janet said diplomatically. "I haven't had a chance to talk to her all day."

Grant looked dubiously at Karen for a moment before he said, "I'll be back in a little while. Then we'll dance."

Karen dismissed him with an airy wave of her hand. "Don't worry about me, I'm fine. Go ahead and have a good time."

"You sound like a wife already," Janet observed as they both watched Grant walk away.

"Why shouldn't I?" Karen retorted quickly. "After all, I've had years of on-the-job experience."

Janet sighed. "Don't think about Randy. Not today."

Karen lowered her eyes to the new diamond-and-gold wedding band on her left hand. "You're right, Jan," she said. "This time is going to be different, isn't it?"

"Of course it is," Janet said emphatically. "This time you're marrying a man, not a boy. Grant will be good for you, Karen. He'll give you what you want."

"Mmm, yes," Karen agreed. "He's what Mom and Dad would call 'a good provider.'"

"Yes, that's true, but what I meant is that he can give you what you *really* want."

"And what's that?" Karen asked, amused that her kid sister thought she knew her so well.

"A child."

Karen was caught off-guard. "How do you know that's what I want?"

Janet was smiling at her with sisterly indulgence. "I've seen your face when you look at Melissa," she said.

"It's true," Karen reluctantly admitted. "I do want to have a baby. I thought I was over that. I thought Randy had cured me of that for good—but lately . . ." Her voice trailed off.

"I assume you and Grant have discussed this."

Karen shook her head. "Only vaguely. I don't think he knows how really important it is to me."

"Then what are you going to do? Not say anything to him, and just go along and hope that you get pregnant?"

"No, I—" The rest of the sentence died on Karen's lips as her eyes fixed on two figures on the dance floor: Grant and Jessica were gliding rhythmically to the strains of "Thank Heaven for Little Girls." Jessica's face was upturned, and her eyes were shining incandescently. Then Grant said something, and she giggled at what was obviously a private joke.

Karen stared at them. They were totally absorbed in each other, seemingly unaware that there were other people dancing within a few feet of them. And although Jessica only came up to Grant's chest, there was a symmetry between them, an unaffected grace in the way they moved together as if they were one.

"They're very sweet together, aren't they?" Janet observed.

"Yes," Karen said. "Adorable."

Janet looked sharply at her. She studied Karen's face for a moment and then said, "You're jealous of Jessica, aren't you?"

Karen turned away from her sister's scrutiny. "Don't be ridiculous," she scoffed.

"Then don't try to fool me," Janet said. "I know you, Karen. I can tell when something's bothering you. So if you're not jealous, what is it?"

Karen looked slowly around the room before bringing her eyes back to Janet. "I guess I'm a little scared," she said finally. "I've never even been a mother before—let alone a stepmother."

"Is that all of it?" Janet persisted.

"Don't you think that's enough?" Karen retorted quickly, giving her sister a pained look.

"Yes, of course," Janet said, suddenly chagrined. "I didn't—I mean I wasn't trying to dig up the past. I don't know what's the matter with me," she apologized. "I shouldn't be sitting here trying to psychoanalyze you—not on your wedding day, anyway. So forget I said anything—let's just relax and enjoy ourselves."

But what Janet had said continued to nag at Karen. Was it possible—could she really be jealous of an eleven-year-old girl?

Or maybe it wasn't jealousy, maybe it was envy—yes, that was a more acceptable word—the natural kind of envy that a woman would feel for her husband's child by another woman. Especially if that relationship was an unusually close one.

But no, the emotion she had felt watching the two of them dancing together had nothing to do with envy. It was the kind of primitive sexual jealousy she might feel if another woman tried to move in on her man.

But Jessica isn't another woman, Karen told herself. *She's only a child—and a poor motherless child at that.*

What was wrong with her—how could she react in that jealous, clutching way? Was she so apprehensive about being Jessica's new stepmother that she was reading things into the situation that just weren't there?

Thank God she and Grant would have some time alone together before she would be thrust into her new role. Maybe by the time they got back from their honeymoon she would be ready to face Jessica and her new responsibilities.

That night after the reception Karen and Grant took a late flight to Bermuda, leaving Jessica in the company of Fran and Jerry and their three boys.

They were only going to be gone ten days, but as they said their farewells Jessica clung to her father as if she were never going to see him again.

Their hotel consisted of a cluster of stately old buildings perched on a rocky cliff above the sea. They had a secluded bungalow all to themselves, hidden away from the other guests by a jungle of greenery. To Karen, it was the perfect honeymoon setting—far different from the resort hotel in the Poconos that Randy had taken her to.

It was Karen's first trip to Bermuda, and she was enchanted by the island's lush foliage and fragrant flowering bushes, pastel houses and pink beaches surrounded by an azure sea. During the day they played tennis or golf, went snorkeling or explored the island on motorbikes. At night they ate leisurely suppers, danced under the stars, and walked along the beach before returning to their bungalow, where they made love languidly for hours.

The days and nights slipped past until Karen realized that the following day would be their last in Bermuda. The thought filled her with sudden panic.

"I don't want to leave here," she told Grant.

They were lying on chaises on the beach, basking in the late afternoon sun. The sky above them was cloudless, the sea nearby a translucent turquoise and farther out a deep indigo. From somewhere behind them a steelband was softly playing.

Grant looked over at her and smiled lazily. "I know what you mean."

Karen sat up. "Not just because it's so beautiful," she said, taking off her sunglasses to give Grant a piercing look.

He gazed uncomprehendingly at her for a moment before his eyes snapped into alertness. "It's Jessica, isn't it?" he said. "You're worried about how you two are going to get along."

Karen nodded her head slowly. "I can't help it, Grant. It's a whole new role for me."

Grant sat up and swung his legs over the side of the chaise. "Then just remember one thing," he said. "It's a new role for Jessica, too. She's never had a stepmother before. So you've got to give each other time—don't rush things. And above all, be yourself. Jessica is very quick to pick up on any pretenses."

Karen listened carefully to what Grant said. He made it sound so simple. And maybe it would be—maybe the problems were all in her own mind.

But returning to New York, they quickly discovered that Jessica was going to make life more trying for them than even Karen had feared.

They took a cab home from Kennedy Airport, stopping along the way to pick up Jessica. Her welcome was reserved, her kisses and hugs nothing more than perfunctory.

Grant tried to draw her out as they rode the final few blocks to the apartment, but he couldn't get anything more than listless replies to his questions about what she had done while they were away.

When they reached the building and had all the luggage unloaded from the cab, Karen noticed that

Jessica held back, clutching her small suitcase tightly in both hands.

"Jessica," Grant called out to her, "please don't dawdle. Karen and I are tired—we want to get upstairs."

Jessica came along slowly, trailing after them as they got into a waiting elevator. Grant unlocked the door to the apartment and let Jessica pass inside, but blocked Karen's way. "Just a second," he said, setting the luggage down inside the door. Then in one swift movement he swooped Karen up in his arms and carried her across the threshold.

Giggling, Karen started to say, "Grant, you romantic fool—" but broke off as she caught sight of Jessica. The child was standing in the middle of the foyer, staring at them, her eyes wide and her mouth gaping. The suitcase fell from her hands, and when it hit the floor, she turned and ran from the room.

Grant set Karen down and they exchanged puzzled glances. "What in the world was that all about?" Karen said, more than a little annoyed that her homecoming was being spoiled by Jessica's petulance.

"I don't know," Grant said. "I'd better go after her."

He walked to the closed door of Jessica's room and knocked on it. "Jessica, it's Daddy," he said. "Can I come in?"

Karen saw him open the door and shut it behind him. For a moment she felt like a neglected guest, standing there in the foyer—but no, this was *her* home now, too. So she picked up her suitcase, thinking she might as well unpack.

She went into the master bedroom, set her suitcase down, and opened it up. One bureau had been set aside for her, and she began to put her things in it. She was nearly finished unpacking when Grant came into the room.

"I'm sorry about that little incident with Jessica," he said. "I know it's hardly the kind of welcome-home reception you wanted."

"It doesn't matter," Karen said, not wanting him to know that she had been offended by Jessica's behavior.

"Are you sure?" Grant said, coming to stand next to her at the bureau. "I thought that was the kind of reaction you were so worried about."

Karen studied his face in the mirror over the bureau. "I think I can handle it," she said with more conviction than she felt. Then she decided that now was a good time to bring up something that had been bothering her. "But what does worry me," she added thoughtfully, "is these vague lapses of Jessica's. She seems to stare so blankly. Sort of like a trance. Why haven't you told me about them before this?"

Grant went blank. "Trance?"

Karen turned to face him. "Don't tell me you don't know she has them. What do you call what happened just now out there in the foyer?"

Grant laughed. "You mean when Jessica was gawking at us as I carried you over the threshold?"

Karen nodded, wondering why Grant was trying to deny something that was so blatantly obvious to her.

"That was no 'trance,'" Grant said, giving the last word a slightly sarcastic edge. "She was simply surprised, maybe a little taken aback to see us acting like a couple of kids."

Karen looked at him without saying anything for several seconds. Then she shook her head in disbelief. "This isn't the Middle Ages, Grant," she said. "If Jessica has something like epilepsy, I wish you'd tell me. It's nothing to be ashamed of. Is that what's wrong with her?"

Grant turned away from her, making a scoffing noise deep in his throat. "There's nothing 'wrong' with Jessica," he said somewhat heatedly. "You must be imagining things." Then he marched out of the bedroom.

Karen walked over to the bed and sank down onto it. Here she was, not more than half an hour in her new home, and she and Grant had already had their first fight and—not surprisingly—it had been over Jessica. She had the feeling that it was a subject over which she and Grant would disagree for some time to come.

CHAPTER SIX

Karen's first few days in her new home were an odd mixture of bliss and bewilderment. When she and Grant were alone together, he couldn't have been more loving and affectionate. But the moment Jessica entered the room, Karen could sense a change in Grant. He became defensive, watchful, even suspicious.

Karen guessed that he was simply exhibiting a form of parental protectiveness. Since in his mind she had made what amounted to a slur against his offspring, he was now on guard against any further attacks. She pictured him as a kind of Mama Bear, prowling the forest, sniffing the wind for any scent of danger to her young cub.

But there was something else that caused the change in Grant, something that Karen couldn't put her finger on. Some deep-seated fear that showed in his eyes. But fear of what? That she and Jessica wouldn't get along? No, it was more than that, she was sure—and it was also quite obviously something Grant wanted to keep secret from her.

She did her best to ignore her feelings of being

shut out and told herself that time would take care of a lot of difficulties in this new three-way relationship.

And time was on her side, for soon it would be September, and Jessica would be going back to school, freeing Karen of the responsibility of watching over her during the day.

Karen had set up her studio in the small room at the end of the hall. The room was painted a stark white and was nearly bare of furniture before Karen moved her drawing board and taboret in. She hoped that someday they would be using it for a nursery and hadn't given much thought to what the room might have been used for—until one morning when Jessica came to watch her unpack her art equipment.

The child stood for a long while leaning against the doorjamb, silently observing Karen organizing her pens and brushes atop the taboret.

Karen vainly tried to keep up a stream of conversation to which Jessica had little response until she suddenly blurted out, "Know what room this used to be?"

"No," Karen said, shaking her head. "What?"

"It was Sarah's," Jessica said, her blue eyes boring significantly into Karen's. "This is where Mommy and Sarah were."

Karen shivered involuntarily. "I didn't know," she said softly, tearing her eyes away from Jessica's and letting them drift slowly about the room—as if expecting to see some reminder of that grim day.

"Daddy had the room repainted," Jessica said. "And he gave away Sarah's crib and all the other furniture." She paused before adding, "Actually, he had almost the whole apartment redone and he gave away all of Mommy's and Sarah's things."

Karen wanted to show the child that she understood what her mother's and sister's deaths had put her through. "Does it bother you to talk about that, Jessica?" she asked gently.

Jessica stared dull-eyed at her for a moment; then her eyes turned wary. "Yes," she said flatly. "But I thought you ought to know about the room." Then she turned and was gone.

Karen had not realized until they got home from the honeymoon just how nervous she would be making love with Grant with Jessica sleeping in the next room. Every night when they turned out the lights and Grant reached for her, Karen tried to respond to the increasing passion of his kisses—but a part of her remained detached, observant, conscious of every sound they made.

Then one night, from somewhere close by, she heard a soft mewling sound.

"Grant," she said, pulling her lips away from his. "What was that? I thought I heard a cry."

Grant went on kissing Karen for a moment longer, and then suddenly he released his grip on her and slipped out of bed.

"Where are you going?" Karen asked as in the dim light she saw Grant crossing to the door. "Was that Jessica?"

"Yes," he answered curtly. Then he pulled open their door and disappeared into the blackness of the hall.

Karen lay in the dark for several minutes waiting for Grant to return. When it became apparent that he was not coming back immediately, she sat up, switched on the light, and reached for a book on the bedside table.

Every few minutes she would glance at the time on the clock radio, wondering what was keeping Grant so long in Jessica's room. Fifteen minutes went by, then twenty. Karen thought about going to see if anything was wrong, but something held her back.

She would be an intruder if she went into that room now. She would be violating the intimacy of Grant's relationship with his daughter. So she tried to concentrate on the pages in front of her, willing her eyes not to glance at the clock.

Grant returned after forty minutes, silently opening the door and then blinking rapidly as his eyes focused on Karen. "What are you doing up?" he asked.

"Waiting for you," Karen replied. "Is everything all right with Jessica?"

"She's okay now," Grant said, climbing back into bed. "She had a nightmare. I had to calm her down."

"Does this happen very often?" There was an edge of annoyance in her voice that even surprised Karen when she heard it. *Now why did she have to go and do that*, she groaned inwardly. She really ought to make an effort to keep her negative feelings about Jessica to herself.

Grant's eyes flicked over her face. "I'm sorry if it inconveniences you," he said defensively. "But yes, Jessica does have these nightmares occasionally. They're very frightening to her—she wakes up crying and screaming. I suppose you think I'm coddling her by comforting her instead of letting her cry herself back to sleep."

Karen turned away from the anger in his eyes. "I'm sorry," she said. "I didn't realize."

"Well, now you do," Grant said, rolling over so that his back was to her. "So maybe you can try being a little more understanding of Jessica." He pulled the covers up around his shoulders. "Now if you don't mind, I'd like to get some sleep."

Karen stared forlornly at his back before she reached over to turn out the light. It was the first night since they'd been married that they hadn't made love.

From that night on Karen did make an effort to be more sensitive to Jessica's feelings, to give her the benefit of the doubt, to go out of her way to include the child in activities. And sometimes she thought she was making progress.

Jessica seemed to be fascinated by Karen's work. She was back in school now, but very often, when she came home from school and found Karen in her studio, she would stand and watch over Karen's shoulder, occasionally asking questions.

At first Karen had found the child's attention flattering, but it grew to be more and more annoying to her. She found it increasingly difficult to concentrate in Jessica's presence, but at the same time she didn't dare tell her not to bother her; the child's insecurity would probably interpret it as a rejection—not as a reasonable demand for privacy.

So Karen gritted her teeth and tried to get most of her work done when Jessica was in school. And then berated herself time and time again for being so one-sided in her criticism. Sometimes, she swore, she went out of her own way to be annoyed by the child.

Karen's work was no less important to her than it had been before her marriage, but now that the economic pressures were gone she was driven more by artistic ones. She felt free to pick and choose her assignments and to select those that represented a challenge to her creativity.

Grant went along with her continuing to work—or so he said—although Karen sometimes wondered if he considered it an indulgence. But it didn't really matter what Grant or anybody else thought about her work, she determined; she would keep on doing it— even if they should have a baby.

One afternoon when she was having a particularly unproductive day at the drawing board, she decided that she would at least be creative in the kitchen—she would fix them an elaborate Chinese meal for dinner.

Standing over the chopping board with her back to the kitchen door, she was humming softly to herself and didn't hear the front door open and close.

Suddenly, Jessica's voice rang out: "What are you making?"

Karen jumped and whirled around. "Oh, Jessica," she mumbled, trying to cover up her surprise with an ingratiating smile. "I didn't hear you come in."

Jessica shrugged. "I thought you knew I was here."

"No, I didn't," Karen said. "You have such a light step." Then she asked cheerily, "How was school today?"

"Just okay."

"Sounds pretty boring."

"Uh-huh."

"Nothing unusual happened?"

Jessica pursed her lips as she thought. "Oh, yeah," she said finally. "Miss Bell fainted in English class. Everybody said it was because she was pregnant, but I don't believe that."

"Why not?"

"Because she's too ugly."

Karen was pondering the meaning of this statement when Jessica nonchalantly pointed to the cutting board. "You're bleeding," she said in a voice that was mechanical and detached.

Karen's eyes dropped to the cutting board. A bright red rivulet of blood was flowing from her left index finger onto the pale green stalks of celery she had been chopping up.

For a second Karen stared dully at the wound; then she dropped the knife and grabbed a kitchen towel to wrap around her finger. She expected Jessica to volunteer some assistance, but the child just stood there, gazing indifferently at Karen's efforts to stanch the bleeding.

Then Karen realized that Jessica was not simply standing there; her eyes were glazed over as she stared at the spots of blood soaking into the wood of the cutting board.

Karen had a sudden overwhelming desire to take the child and shake her, to jolt her back to reality. But instead she turned quickly and hurried to the bathroom, where she washed the finger and inspected the wound. It was fairly deep, but already the bleeding had nearly stopped. She wrapped a Band-Aid around it and prepared to forget about it.

But what she couldn't forget was the expression on Jessica's face as she had pointed at the wound and said, "You're bleeding." Surely, Jessica had seen immediately that Karen had cut herself, so why had she waited to tell her?

Karen wondered what kind of excuse Grant would come up with when she told him about his daughter's behavior. Then she realized that she couldn't tell him anything more than that she had cut herself chopping celery. Whatever else she might add would only sound as if she were blaming Jessica for her own carelessness.

And perhaps he'd be right; perhaps she *was* too quick to jump to the conclusion that Jessica disliked her—maybe she was even projecting her own feelings onto the child. After all, it was far easier to think that Jessica was hostile to her than to deal with her own ambivalence toward Grant's child by another woman.

CHAPTER SEVEN

Jessica looked up from her bowl of cereal and grinned at her father. "Guess what, Daddy," she said brightly. "I'm going to be captain of my volleyball team again this year."

"That's great, honey," Grant responded without looking at her. "When did that happen?"

"Oh, the election's not until today," Jessica said blithely. "But I'm sure to be chosen."

Grant glanced sideways at his daughter. "What makes you so positive they'll elect you?"

"Because I'm the best player on the team. And besides, I was captain last year."

"Well, I hope you're right, kitten. But try not to be too disappointed if they don't pick you. Okay?"

Jessica shook her head in mock exasperation. "Oh, Daddy," she sighed. "You just don't have any faith in me."

Grant looked at her and laughed. Then he reached over and tousled her blond curls. "You little minx," he said, chuckling. "Sometimes I think you're too smart for your own good."

"All right," the gym teacher intoned. "Everybody

who wants Jessica Cameron for team captain, raise your hands."

Jessica lifted her own hand a few modest inches over her head and glanced around. Only one other hand was raised: that of her best friend, Patty Blake.

"All right now," Ms. Olson continued. "Everybody who wants Carole Parr, raise your hands."

As if in a single motion all the rest of the hands shot up.

"Carole Parr is the new team captain," Ms. Olson announced.

Carole, a tall, slender girl with saucerlike brown eyes, sent a smirking glance in Jessica's direction as all her friends crowded around to congratulate her.

"How could they pick her? She can't play worth a darn," Jessica said out of the corner of her mouth to Patty.

"Oh, Jess—don't feel too bad," Patty sympathized. "You know that group—they're like glue. They all stick together."

"Who needs them anyway?" Jessica shrugged. "Not me."

Patty's eyes were full of admiration as she gazed at her friend. "You don't let anything get to you, do you?" she said. Then she sighed. "Boy, I wish I could be like you."

"Oh, Patty, you're such a child," Jessica said, smiling at her tolerantly. "When will you ever learn?"

Just then Ms. Olson blew sharply on her whistle. "All right, girls, you can stop your gabbing," she shouted. "We're here to play volleyball, not to stand around gossiping. Now I want the captains to get their teams into position. Then you can volley for serve."

Carole Parr left her group of friends and strode over to Jessica and Patty. "I think I'll break you two up," she said with a note of newfound authority in her voice. "Patty, you go in the front row between Beth and Samantha. And you"—she smiled haughtily at Jessica—"you come in the back row with me—where I can watch you."

Jessica returned Carole's smile with one of her own. "Anything you say, Carole. You're the boss now."

The game began and their team won the first serve, but the score seesawed back and forth until it was fourteen to thirteen in their favor. Their next point would win the game.

Both teams managed to keep the volley going until suddenly the ball shot like a missile over the net, appearing as if it might drop right between Carole and Jessica. Both girls went up in the air for it, and Carole, being the taller one, got her hands on it first, but Jessica had a better position on it, and she was the one who actually managed to get the shot off, sending it back over the net. A member of the other team made a valiant dive for it, but the ball fell just beyond her reach.

While their team was rejoicing over its victory, Carole and Jessica were disentangling themselves from the heap they had fallen into on the floor as they crashed into each other. Jessica stood up first, but Carole stayed on the floor, hunched over, her right hand clutching at her face.

Then, one by one, Carole's friends noticed that she was still down, and they came to bend over her.

"Ms. Olson!" someone called out. "Come quick. Carole's hurt."

The gym teacher arrived on the scene just as Carole was being helped to her feet. "What is it?" she demanded. "What's the matter with you?"

Carole took her hand away from her face. The tip of her nose and her upper lip were covered with blood.

Ms. Olson peered at the injured area. "It's just a nosebleed," she said. "Nothing to get upset about."

"But it hurts," Carole whimpered.

"Then go to the nurse," Ms. Olson said peremptorily. "She'll put an icepack on it for you. The rest of you get back to the game."

Carole's friends murmured sympathetically among themselves as they watched Carole leave the gym, blood streaming onto the front of her white T-shirt. Then one of them looked at Jessica and said something in a low tone.

Jessica was standing with her head bowed, staring at two large spots of red blood on the thickly varnished surface of the gymnasium floor. Her mouth was open, and she seemed completely unaware of the whispered buzzing of Carole's friends.

"Jess." Patty came over to her. "Watch out. They're going to do something."

Jessica jumped at the sound of Patty's voice. "What?" she said, looking around her in obvious confusion.

An overweight girl with frizzy blond hair broke out of the group and came rushing toward Jessica. "You did that to Carole on purpose!" she shouted.

Jessica put her hands up as if to fend the girl off. "I did not!" she said, getting angry herself.

"You—you were out to get Carole," Samantha sputtered, "because you wanted to be captain of the team!"

The rest of Carole's friends had come to stand alongside Samantha. Their eyes were fixed menacingly on Jessica.

Not in the least bit intimidated, Jessica held her ground, staring defiantly at them.

"We'll get you for this, Jessica," someone said, and another voice echoed, "Don't think you can get away with what you did to Carole."

"Break it up, girls!" It was Ms. Olson's voice, and she was bearing down on them. "If you don't get back to volleyball in the next thirty seconds, I'm going to give this whole team demerits."

"It's all Jessica's fault, Ms. Olson," Samantha piped up. "She deliberately hit Carole in the nose, so she's the one who should get the demerits."

Jessica said nothing, but gave Samantha a look that would have withered a statue.

Ms. Olson regarded Samantha a moment, then turned to Jessica. "Well, what about it, Jessica?" she asked. "Is there any truth to what Samantha says?"

Jessica looked up at the gym teacher, her blue eyes glittering with sincerity. "It was an accident," she said. "It was my ball—Carole got in the way."

"Did you hit her deliberately?" Ms. Olson persisted.

Jessica shook her head. "Of course not."

Ms. Olson fingered the whistle hanging around her neck. "All right," she said. "I hope that settles it. I don't want to hear any more about this incident. Now, get back to your game." And she walked off to the other end of the gym.

Carole's group of friends grumbled—but broke up and went back to their positions.

"Tell me the truth—did you deliberately hit Carole?" Patty whispered to Jessica.

"Nah," Jessica said, shaking her head. "She's nothing but a crybaby." She threw a contemptuous glance in the direction of Carole's friends. "They made a big deal of it just to make me look bad. They want to make it look like *I'm* the troublemaker."

Several days later Karen accompanied Grant to Parents' Night at the school. She had been surprised that he wanted her to go, thinking that perhaps he considered his daughter's education his exclusive province.

But she had not set foot in a school since her teaching days, and she did not want to go, knowing that it would bring back some painful memories. When she told Grant he'd better go alone, he seemed quite put out and began pressing her for her reasons. So rather than make an issue of it, she gritted her teeth and went with him.

Grant proudly introduced her to each of Jessica's teachers, but as she sat listening to their reports of how bright Jessica was and what a good student she was, Karen thought she could read something between the lines of what each teacher was saying: that Jessica was perhaps *too* good a student. Having been a teacher herself, Karen knew the type—the student who was always a step ahead of the rest of the class and who, as a result, was often bored. Sometimes these precocious children were lonely, too, because they were resented by the other students.

"Tell me," Karen asked one of the teachers. "How does Jessica get along with her classmates?"

Grant and the teacher both looked sharply at Karen, who had not spoken up until that time.

"Well," the teacher began hesitantly. "I'm afraid that's the only area where Jessica has some problems of, uh, adjustment."

Grant pounced on this. "What do you mean by that?"

"She has very few close friends," the teacher said almost apologetically.

"That's because she's particular in her choice of friends," Grant said, barely bothering to hide his irritation.

Karen could see that the young woman was intimidated by Grant and was clearly afraid to venture another opinion. "Is there something else?" Karen asked her.

The teacher nodded her head gratefully. "I don't

know how to put this," she said, pausing to take a deep breath, "except to say that Jessica seems to have more than her share of, well, disagreements with the other students."

Grant frowned. "Disagreements? What sort of disagreements?"

The teacher looked distinctly uncomfortable. "Please understand," she said. "Jessica never seems to start anything—and yet, whenever there's a fight or an altercation of some sort, she always just happens to be in the middle of it."

"Do you mean to say that the other kids pick on her?" Grant asked.

"Oh, no," the teacher said quickly. "I don't think it's anything like that—" She looked helplessly at Karen. "I guess I really don't know how to explain it."

"Well, *try*," Grant said, his voice full of exasperation.

The young teacher looked thoughtful for a moment. "Well, you see, it's not as if Jessica's a troublemaker—it's more that things just seem to *happen* around her." She glanced at Karen as if hoping to find support.

Karen was sure she understood. She had felt the same way about Jessica herself. But she kept her eyes downcast and said nothing.

Grant, on the other hand, continued to stare at the teacher. "You're new here, aren't you?" he said finally.

"Yes," she responded. "This is my first year."

"Then you haven't had that much of an opportunity to observe my daughter as closely as you seem to think you have," Grant said. His tone was provocative, and Karen could see in the set of his jaw that he was barely restraining his anger.

"Grant, I think we've already taken up more than

our share of time here," Karen said, getting to her feet. She put her hand on his arm and gave it a purposeful tug.

Grant looked at her, the anger apparent in his eyes, but he got out of his chair.

Karen exchanged farewells with the young teacher—who was visibly relieved to see them go.

Outside in the corridor, Grant vented some of his wrath. "What an officious little bitch!" he growled, shaking a clenched fist. "I wish you had let me tell her what I thought of her and her half-assed ideas."

Karen watched him for a moment and then said thoughtfully, "I don't quite understand what you're so angry about. That teacher was simply trying to be helpful."

"You call that helpful?" Grant scoffed.

Karen realized that she was treading on dangerous ground, but she had held back for so long that she couldn't stop herself now. "Why are you so overly protective of Jessica?" she plunged on. "Why do you become so angry and defensive whenever anyone so much as suggests that there's the least little thing wrong with her?"

For a second, Karen thought that Grant was going to strike her—right there in the corridor with teachers and other parents milling about. His whole body was tensed and his right hand came up, but then he brought it to the back of his neck and rubbed it in a gesture of frustration. The anger in his eyes had been replaced by fear, and it puzzled her.

"Grant," she said softly, reaching for his arm. "What are you afraid of?"

He shook her off. "Afraid? What makes you think I'm afraid of anything?"

"I can see it in your face."

He turned away from her. "Then you're mistaken. I'm not afraid—I'm annoyed with you for your insensitivity and lack of perception when it comes to anything having to do with Jessica."

"Am I, Grant?" Karen said calmly. "Am I really? Or is it just that you're overly sensitive on the subject?"

Grant gave her an icy glare. "Come on, let's get out of here," he said. "I've had enough of teachers for tonight."

CHAPTER EIGHT

Sitting at her drawing board the next morning, Karen was unable to work. Over and over she kept replaying the scene with Grant, regretting the impetuous words that had upset him so and had turned his anger against her. She had known how he would react; why had she found it necessary to goad him?

He had remained distant to her for the rest of the evening, shutting himself up in his study when they got home. Just before Jessica's bedtime he had let her come in, and Karen had heard them laughing and talking behind the closed door.

She had gone to bed ahead of Grant and had pretended to be asleep when he came in, listening to the sounds of him undressing: the familiar, methodical way he emptied his pockets, carefully muffling the clink of coins as he placed them in a tray on top of his bureau, the soft thud of his shoes, the rattle of wooden hangers. Then she could feel him getting into bed, and she waited, hoping he would reach for her. But he settled the covers around him and then lay very still. His breathing became increasingly deep and regular—he was falling asleep.

Karen was stunned. How could he do that? How could he just go to sleep as if nothing had happened? She was tempted to shake him, make him wake up and deal with her. But no, if he could go to sleep with things unsettled between them, so could she.

Instead, she lay awake half the night. And in the morning she stayed in bed until both Grant and Jessica had left, avoiding any further confrontation.

Now she listlessly picked up a pen and began to doodle on a blank piece of paper, and as she did she remembered the interview she and Grant had had with Jessica's art teacher the night before—something she had forgotten in the ensuing conflict.

The woman had shown them several of Jessica's pictures, and then both she and Grant had looked expectantly at Karen, waiting for her evaluation.

Karen had cocked an appraising eye at them and said, "They're very promising."

The teacher nodded approvingly. "I'm glad you think so," she said. "You know, Jessica has told me so much about you," she went on chattily. "When she came back to school this year, that was the only thing she talked about—that her father had remarried and that her new stepmother was an artist. She seemed very proud and excited about it, and even hinted to me that she might like to follow in your footsteps when she grows up."

Karen had been dumbfounded by this revelation, but then she realized that it was only her own shortsightedness that prevented her from seeing the signs of Jessica's interest in art. Instead of being annoyed with the child for hanging around her studio, she should have been flattered. She should have encouraged her, not pushed her away.

Feeling ashamed of herself, Karen realized that if she was wrong about Jessica's motives in this instance she could have very seriously misinterpreted the child's behavior at other times, too.

But perhaps she could make it up to Jessica—and get back in Grant's good graces simultaneously—by showing the child that she did appreciate her interest.

Later that afternoon when Karen heard Jessica come in from school she called out and asked her to come into the studio.

Jessica only came as far as the door. "What is it?" she asked, her blue eyes skeptical and guarded.

Oh, Jessica, what have I done to make you so suspicious of me? Karen thought as she saw the look on the child's face. Out loud she said, "I learned something very interesting about you last night at school."

The eyes became wary, defensive. "What?"

Karen smiled benignly. "Your art teacher showed me some of your pictures. I thought they were very good."

Jessica took a tentative step into the room. "Really?"

"*Really*," Karen said. "I had no idea you were so talented."

Jessica fairly beamed.

"As a matter of fact," Karen went on, "you show a lot of promise, and I'd like to help you develop it. How about it? Would you like to work with me?"

"You mean you'd teach me how to draw like you?" Jessica asked, wide-eyed.

"Of course. We could set up an area for you—maybe on that table over there—and you can draw or paint or do whatever you like, and I'll show you some of the techniques I've learned."

"Wow!" Jessica said. "That's fantastic!"

Karen was gratified by the child's enthusiasm and felt that she had just taken a tremendous first step toward winning her over.

When Grant came in later, the two of them were

hard at work, bent over their respective drawing boards. "Hey, what's going on here?" he asked. "Don't I even get a hello?"

Karen and Jessica both looked at him and then exchanged glances. "Why don't you tell your father what you're doing, Jessica," Karen suggested.

"Karen's helping me with my drawing," Jessica said proudly.

Grant came and peered over his daughter's shoulder. "I can see that," he said, kissing the top of her head. "You're getting better already."

"Oh, *Daddy*," Jessica moaned, grinning immodestly.

"I'm afraid you're going to have to take us out for dinner tonight," Karen said. "We were so engrossed that I completely forgot about cooking."

"I don't mind a bit," Grant said. He gave Karen a lingering kiss on the cheek. "Not when I see my two girls together, having such a good time."

Things went along happily for the next several weeks. Jessica was an eager and diligent pupil, listening raptly to Karen's every word, her eyes intelligent and alert and full of admiration as she watched Karen demonstrate whatever it was she was teaching.

Sometimes Karen would gaze at the child working so industriously on the fine points of a drawing, and she would marvel at the change that had come over Jessica—and herself, too, she realized. The two of them were more at ease together, and they seemed to have a lot more to talk about—sometimes they even managed to find a few things to laugh about. Karen found herself looking forward to these afternoon sessions and realized that she was actually growing fond of the child.

She could feel Jessica beginning to open up to her, too, and yet sensed that there was still a deep and hidden part of her that she was holding back. In that way she was very much like her father. But Karen hoped that she was gaining Jessica's trust and that in time the child might even come to love her—not as she loved her father, of course, or her real mother—but in a warm and special kind of closeness. Karen knew it might take time before she and Jessica fully trusted each other—but a start had been made.

Grant acted as if he himself had thought up the idea of the art lessons. "I *knew* it was just a matter of time before you two found something in common," he repeatedly told Karen. "And I think it's terrific."

The household began to fall into a comfortable routine. Karen tried to make sure that the art sessions were over by dinnertime. Then after dinner she and Grant would usually relax and talk, while Jessica went off to her room to do her homework. When Jessica was finished, she would come out and join them. Sometimes the three of them would watch television or play cards or a game, but whatever they did Grant would always make a point of spending some time alone with Jessica.

The weeks went by and then suddenly the routine was disrupted: Grant began bringing home work from the office and shutting himself up in his study after dinner. Karen didn't mind too much because Grant had explained to her that it was a special report he needed to write and that it shouldn't take him more than a few nights of work—if he was left alone and allowed to concentrate on it.

But although Grant had explained this to Jessica, she did not seem to understand that this meant he would not be able to spend their usual time together in the evenings.

She managed to find any number of excuses to knock on his study door: a problem with her math homework, a reference book she needed from his library, his opinion on a composition she had written.

Grant was patient with her at first, but with each interruption, even his long-suffering tolerance began to wear thin. Finally, he simply said, "Jessica, please don't bother me anymore. I can't work with you knocking on the door every ten minutes. If you have any questions, go to Karen with them—*don't come to me*. Do you understand?"

To this, Jessica sullenly nodded her head. "Yes, Daddy. I'll leave you alone." And she went slinking off to her room, slamming the door behind her.

Karen was relieved to see that Jessica seemed to have recovered her cheerfulness by the next afternoon when she got home from school. Karen was in the kitchen when Jessica came in, but told her to go into the studio and get started without her.

By the time Karen got into the studio, Jessica was working feverishly and had already completed a small stack of drawings. "My goodness, Jessica," Karen laughed, "you certainly are in a hurry today, aren't you?"

Jessica turned her head to look at Karen and gave her an inscrutable smile.

"Well, let's see what you've got here," Karen said, picking up a finished drawing from the pile. It was a badly proportioned picture of a horse, and Karen was disappointed, for she had seen Jessica do much better. Then, as she held the drawing up to the light, Karen noticed that there seemed to be writing on the back of the paper. She turned it over and couldn't make sense of the words for a moment until it suddenly hit her—this was a page from Grant's report. "Where did you get this, Jessica?" she asked, holding back the suspicion in her voice because it was possible the child had scavenged it out of Grant's wastebasket.

"From Daddy's desk," Jessica said defiantly. She

spread her hands to reveal the rest of the report, all covered with scribbles.

"Oh, *Jessica*," Karen cried. "Your father is going to be very upset with you."

"I don't care," Jessica sulked. "It serves him right for spending all his time working on this stupid report when he should have been paying attention to *me*."

Karen gathered up all the pages of the report. "You'd better go to your room and get started on your homework," she said sternly. "I'll put this back on your father's desk—maybe it can be salvaged."

Jessica eyed her warily. "Are you going to tell Daddy?"

Karen threw up her hands in exasperation. "Don't be ridiculous, Jessica! What do you expect me to do? Tell him *I* did this?"

Jessica thrust her chin haughtily in the air. "I don't care what you tell him," she said, flouncing out of the room.

When Grant came home, Karen called him into the study and showed him what Jessica had done. "Please don't be too upset with her," Karen pleaded. "I'm sure she didn't realize what she was doing."

"I'm sure she didn't," Grant said coldly. "But where were you? Why weren't you keeping an eye on her?"

"Are you saying that it's *my* fault?" Karen asked incredulously.

"More yours than hers," Grant insisted. "Didn't you check on her? Didn't you see what she was doing?"

"I don't believe this!" Karen strode to the door and shot Grant a look of fury. "Your dinner's in the oven," she said. "You can get it yourself." With that she marched across the living room and down the hall to her studio, shutting the door firmly behind her.

It wasn't more than ten minutes before she heard a muffled knock on the door. "It's Grant. Can I come in?"

Karen grumbled a reluctant assent.

He opened the door, grinning sheepishly. "I've come to apologize."

"Oh?"

"It was stupid of me—I shouldn't have gotten angry with you like that."

"Then why did you?"

Grant frowned. "You know why, Karen."

"Do I?"

"Of course you do." Grant spread his hands helplessly. "I realize it isn't fair to you, Karen—but what can I do? Obviously, Jessica ruined the report because she was afraid it had become more important to me than she was."

"What about the report? Can it be fixed?"

"Yes, I think so. It'll just take me a little longer."

"And what about Jessica? What are you going to do about her?"

"Talk to her, reassure her." He turned to go. "I think I'd better do that right now."

And how about reassuring *me*, Karen raged silently as she watched Grant walk down the hall to Jessica's room and knock on the door. Don't *my* feelings count? Or is your precious daughter the only one who's allowed to have them? Sometimes, she thought, this marriage would be happier if there were only the two of them.

CHAPTER NINE

Jessica tugged at Patty's arm. "Hurry up, slowpoke," she said. "I don't want to hang around here all day."

A heavy textbook fell out of Patty's hand and onto the floor of her locker. "Now look what you made me do," she whined.

"Not me—you're the klutz," Jessica said. She took a step backward. "If you don't come this instant, I'm leaving without you."

Patty threw a couple of books into her knapsack. "I'm coming, I'm coming," she muttered, slamming her locker door shut and giving the combination lock a quick turn.

"Well, it's about time," Jessica groaned. "I can't believe how slow you are."

"What in the world is the matter with you?" Patty asked sharply. "You've been in a crummy mood all day."

They were at the entrance to the school. Jessica didn't say anything until they had pushed through the doors and had taken several steps down the sidewalk. Then she turned to Patty. "Do you think your mom will ever get married again?"

Patty's parents had been divorced since she was three. "I dunno," she said. "I overheard her talking to one of her boyfriends once—she said she didn't want to get married again 'cause then she'd have to give up all the alimony my father pays her."

"Then you're lucky," Jessica said bitterly. "You'll never have to live with a stepmother."

Patty looked closely at Jessica. "Gee, is it that bad having a stepmother?" she asked innocently. "I always thought yours was pretty nice."

"I don't want to talk about it," Jessica said, walking faster. After a while she slowed down and looked at Patty. "Want to come home with me today?"

"Okay. Maybe for a little while. My mom's not going to be home, anyway."

"Good. I can show you the pictures I've been doing with Karen."

"That's really nice of her to help you like that," Patty said.

"Yeah, I guess so."

"What's the matter? Don't you like her anymore?"

"She's okay."

"But I thought you were getting along a lot better with her. . . ."

"I *was*," Jessica said. Then she sighed. "But she doesn't like me—I can tell. I think she wishes I weren't around. Then she could have my father all to herself."

Patty nodded sympathetically. "I know what you mean."

Karen was surprised to see that Jessica had brought a friend home from school with her. She had met Patty Blake only briefly once before, but even then had noted what a sweet, shy little thing she was. As far as Karen knew, Patty was the only close friend Jessica had.

Karen accompanied the girls into the studio, where Jessica proudly showed Patty some of her latest drawings.

Then Jessica suggested to Patty that they go into her room and listen to some of her new records.

Karen watched as Patty dutifully followed Jessica down the hall. She wondered if Patty always did exactly as Jessica told her.

Karen worked in her studio for another half an hour and then decided to take the girls some cider and cookies. Putting them on a tray, she carried them to the door of Jessica's room. She was about to knock when she caught a snatch of their conversation—and it made her smile. The girls were talking about sex, and she remembered her own fascination with the same subject when she was their age.

Suddenly, she heard Jessica's voice ringing out: "Well, my daddy wouldn't do that—he doesn't want another baby." And then in a softer tone she added, "Besides, Karen's too *old* to have a baby."

Karen shrank back involuntarily from the harsh words—which had struck much too close to home. She longed for a child, one to share in her love for Grant: she had assumed that he would want one too. In confusion she turned away from the door and carried the tray back to the kitchen, set it down on the table, and sank into a chair.

She tried to calm herself, to tell herself that the child didn't know what she was talking about, but that didn't help because she knew that Jessica had voiced something that just might be true: maybe she *was* too old to have a baby; she already had had two miscarriages and her first husband had left her because she had lost their child; maybe it was wrong for her to want to bring another baby into a household where a baby brought so much tragedy; maybe Grant really didn't want to have a baby—and Jessica knew this. The questions went spinning around in Karen's mind until she didn't know what to think anymore.

She was still lost in thought when Jessica came into the kitchen. "I want to get something to eat for Patty and me," she explained.

"Here, take this." Karen gestured at the tray. "I was just bringing it to you."

"Thanks." Jessica picked up the tray and gave Karen an inquisitive look. But when Karen did not meet her gaze, she turned and left.

Grant was on the verge of drifting off to sleep, when he heard Karen sigh deeply beside him. His bone-tired, half-conscious body told him to roll over and ignore it, but another little voice inside him told him to stop being so selfish and to find out what was wrong with Karen. Begrudgingly, he listened to the second voice.

"Karen?" he asked, feeling for her in the darkness. "Is anything the matter?"

She came into his arms, and he could feel her body quivering. "What is it?" he asked, puzzled because Karen usually contained her emotions so well. "Are you crying?"

Her response was a muffled sob.

"Sweetheart, what's wrong?" he said, holding her tighter. "Have I done something to upset you?"

"N-no," Karen managed to gasp out. "It's n-not you."

"Jessica then," he said resignedly. "Did she do something?"

This brought on a fresh new wave of sobs, so Grant sat up, turned on the light, and reached for the box of tissues on the nightstand. "Here," he said, offering Karen a handful of tissues. "Dry your eyes and tell me what happened."

He waited patiently while Karen wiped away the

tears from her eyes and blew her nose. Her face was all red and puffy, and he had to turn away momentarily to keep himself from chuckling at the sight of it. God forbid she should think he was laughing at her.

When she had apparently calmed down, he said, "Will you please talk to me now?"

"I'll try," she sniffed, in a voice still quavering with emotion.

"All right. What happened?"

She looked at him dubiously. "You'll think it's stupid...."

"I promise I won't."

She took a deep breath and let it out slowly. "I overheard Jessica say something today—something that hurt me."

Oh God, what has Jessica done now? "What was it?" he asked because he knew the question was expected—not because he wanted to hear the answer.

Then Karen described the scene outside Jessica's door: how she had not really meant to listen in but had just happened to catch a snippet of the girls' conversation and had thought it rather touching and amusing that they were discussing sex.

"I was just about to knock on the door," she went on, "when I heard Jessica say—very clearly, so I couldn't be mistaken about it—that you don't want another baby and that I'm too old to have one."

Relieved that it was nothing more serious, Grant burst out laughing—but he was quickly silenced by a pained look from Karen.

"It's not funny, Grant," she said. "For all I know, it's true."

"What's true? That I don't want a baby or that you're too old to have one?"

"Both," Karen said grimly.

"Now wait a minute," Grant said. "Give me a chance to defend myself."

"Well, do you want one?"

Oh boy, there's nothing like being put on the spot. "I don't know," Grant said, shrugging his shoulders. "I know we've talked about it, but . . ."

Karen's lower lip trembled. "Then think about it—*please.*"

Grant looked at her for a long moment before he said, "I didn't realize that having a baby was that important to you."

Karen nodded mutely. There were fresh tears shining at the corners of her eyes.

"Please don't cry anymore," Grant said, slipping his arms around her. "I can't stand it."

Karen dabbed at her eyes with a tissue. "I'll try not to," she mumbled.

"That's better," Grant said. "Now tell me where this sudden desire to have a baby came from."

"It's not sudden. I've wanted to for a long time."

Grant studied her face. "But you never spoke about it so strongly to me."

"I guess I was afraid to."

"But why?"

"I don't know. I suppose I thought you'd be angry—or think I was being foolish or . . ." Her voice faded away.

"Or what?"

Karen hesitated a moment before saying, "Or that it would upset you because it would remind you of Sarah—and Emily."

Grant nodded. "It might." It would. Of course, it would. There would always be *something* to remind him of Emily and Sarah. But that didn't mean he should stop living.

Karen turned her face away from him. "I knew it."

Grant put his hand under her jaw and gently, but firmly, pulled her face around until she was forced to look at him. "You're being very unfair to me, you know," he said.

"In what way?"

"You just *presume* what kind of reaction I'm going to have—without giving me a chance to speak for myself."

"All right," Karen said, pulling away from him. "I'm giving you your chance now." There was a hint of challenge in her voice. "How do you feel about having a baby?"

Grant sighed. "I'm not sure I can give you a definitive answer."

"I didn't ask you for logic," Karen said. "I want to know your *feelings*."

"My feelings," Grant mused. "Well, that's another story." He gazed pensively at Karen, and as he did an image sprang into his mind: of her cradling a child in her arms, *his* baby. It filled him with an overwhelming feeling of tenderness—and pain, too. Pain at the memory of the other child and woman that he had lost. He had to turn away from Karen for a moment so that she would not see the combination of emotions that crossed his face.

"Grant?" Karen touched his arm. "Is something wrong?"

He turned to look at her and suddenly realized that he had never loved her more—or needed her more—than he did at this moment. "Karen," he said, his fingers reaching out to trace the shape of her tear-stained cheek. "I—yes, let's have a baby."

Karen blinked at him. "You mean it?"

Grant couldn't help grinning at her. "Yes, you silly. I said so, didn't I?"

"But are you sure?"

"What is this, a cross-examination?" Grant laughed. "Can't you just take what I said at face value?"

"Well, yes, but—"

"But what?"

"Well, I hope you're not just saying you want to have a baby—just so you can keep me happy."

"Believe me—I'm not. I really do want one."

"Oh, Grant, that's wonderful. I'm so happy." Karen hugged him. Then he felt her body tense.

"What's wrong now?" he asked.

"I just remembered Jessica," Karen said. "How do you think she'll react to the news?"

Grant wondered about that himself. "It'll probably be a shock to her at first," he said. "But I'm sure that once she gets used to the idea she'll love it."

"Tell me," Karen said thoughtfully, "did she accept Sarah when she was born?"

Grant frowned. "She never really got a chance to. Emily was so fiercely protective of that baby—she would hardly let Jessica or anyone anywhere near her."

"That must have been very hard on Jessica," Karen said. "She probably felt shut out."

"You're right," Grant said, suddenly feeling very hopeful. Perhaps Karen was beginning to understand Jessica—at least she was obviously trying to.

"Well, we'll just have to see that that doesn't happen with *our* baby," Karen said.

Grant looked at her and felt love—and desire, too—welling up inside him. Marrying Karen had been good for him; it had helped him forget some of the horror of the past. And having a baby would be good, too—or would it? Could it be just a little bit too much happiness to ask for? Would the gods or whoever was up there keeping track of such things see this and be jealous and strike him down again?

He was not a superstitious man, but he suddenly shivered—as if someone with chilly breath were breathing down his neck.

The next day Karen happily made an appointment with her gynecologist. As she hung up the phone she noticed that Jessica was standing in the kitchen doorway.

"Why are you going to the doctor?" Jessica asked. "Are you sick?"

"No," Karen said, smiling in spite of herself. "This is the kind of doctor women go to when they want to have a baby."

Jessica stared at her. "Are you going to have a baby?"

"Not yet," Karen responded. "But your father and I both want one."

"Oh," Jessica said meekly, distress clouding her face.

"What's the matter?" Karen asked. "Don't you want to have a little brother or sister?"

"I don't know," Jessica said in an uncharacteristically childish tone. "Babies make people do bad things."

Karen felt a rush of sympathy for the child. "Oh, but that's not true," she said, wanting to take Jessica in her arms and comfort her. "Babies make most people happy. What happened to your mother was an exception. . . ." Her voice trailed off as she noticed that the moment she mentioned Jessica's mother the child had stiffened and her face had gone blank, and Karen realized that she was not getting through to her.

Jessica started to back away from Karen. "I'd better go," she said. "I've got lots of homework to do." Then she seemed to remember something and stopped. "Please don't tell Daddy what I said about the baby," she said gravely.

Karen restrained herself from smiling at the seriousness of the child's tone. "I understand," she said. "And I promise not to tell him."

CHAPTER TEN

Karen went to her doctor and was assured that there was no reason for her not to get pregnant—even in spite of her history of miscarriages. She left the doctor's office grinning from ear to ear, and even when strangers turned to stare at her in the street, she couldn't stop smiling.

It was a lovely fall day, so she decided to walk home up Madison Avenue, one of her favorite routes for window shopping. Strolling along, she kept glancing at her reflection in store windows, marveling at the happiness that was so apparent on her face.

She passed a shop for chic maternity wear and stopped to look at its window display. On one mannequin was a fire-engine-red jersey dress—obviously designed to show off a pregnancy rather than hide it. Karen stared at the dress, admiring the audacity of it. Suddenly, on an impulse she went into the shop and asked to try it on.

As she stood in front of the mirror, trying to imagine what she would look like seven or eight months pregnant, a saleswoman approached her. "Oh, that dress is perfect for you," she said. "And it'll look even better when you start to show."

Karen nodded. "Mmm. I think you're right."

"Tell me, if you don't mind my asking," the saleswoman said conversationally, "how far along are you?"

Karen looked at her and without even batting an eye said, "Two months. I just found out today." It seemed a harmless enough lie, a sort of projecting into the future when she *would* be able to announce to people that she was pregnant. Besides, she would be too embarrassed to admit to the truth now. She was in too deeply, and she would look ridiculous if she admitted she really wasn't pregnant at all. *Just hoping to be,* she reminded herself gaily. *Anyway, this is really just a game—it can't hurt anyone.*

"Oh, how wonderful," the saleswoman cooed. "You must be very happy. Is this your first baby?"

"Yes," Karen said, her voice sounding wistful to her own ears. "I've waited a long time for it."

"I know how you feel," the saleswoman said. "I was past thirty-five before I had my son. It makes them even more special."

"Yes, I suppose it does," Karen mused, staring down at the dress and the way the ample folds of material fell across her flat belly. Suddenly she shivered, aware of a cold, nameless dread somewhere deep inside her. She had no right to play games. She had already lost two children. . . . God, she was acting positively unstable. She recoiled in horrified embarrassment from her image in the mirror. It seemed to be laughing at her, showing her how ridiculous she looked wearing this dress, pretending to be pregnant. "I've decided I don't want the dress," she mumbled as she spun around and headed back to the dressing room.

She hastily pulled her own clothes back on and

then rushed out of the store, her eyes averted from the saleswoman as she passed her. She kept up a rapid pace until she was at least a block and a half away. Then she stopped to catch her breath—and to puzzle out why she had reacted so strongly.

It had something to do with fear, of that much she was certain. But fear of what? Fear of loss? Of being hurt again? She realized now how very desperately she wanted the child she had yet to conceive. But too many things had already gone wrong. Her miscarriages, her divorce, the gruesome deaths of Grant's first wife and baby, that one incident in the school. . . . Karen shook her head as if to deny her numbing fears. She wanted a child, and she would have one, she swore mutely.

Suddenly she wanted a drink. She looked around and spotted a bar on the next block and began to walk toward it.

What am I doing? she asked herself as she was reaching for the polished brass door handle at the bar's entrance. *This isn't like me.* She didn't even like to drink much, let alone go into bars by herself—especially in the middle of the day.

But she still wanted that drink, so she pulled open the door and went inside.

A few curious faces turned around to look at her as she slipped into the first booth inside the door, but when she did not meet their eyes, they turned back to their drinks.

A lank-haired young waitress came over to take her order.

"White wine," Karen said automatically, then for no reason changed her mind. "No, make that Scotch—on the rocks."

Scotch? Whatever made her order that? She had had Scotch perhaps one other time in her life—and had not particularly liked its musty, smoky flavor then. But when the drink was placed in front of her, she discovered she liked its taste. When the first one was gone and she was feeling calmer, she ordered another one.

By the time she was halfway through the second one, she began to face the real reason why she had run out of the maternity boutique: something about the situation had reminded her too much of the past.

The first time she found out she was pregnant she had gone into a department store and tried on maternity outfits. Shortly after that she had lost the baby. Now, ten years later, she was afraid of the same thing happening.

What was I so afraid for? she asked herself. *I can't lose a baby I haven't even conceived yet.*

Yes, another nagging voice said, *but what if you can't conceive?*

Then I'll die.

Karen started and looked around her. Had she been talking to herself? Time to get out of here. The alcohol was obviously going to her head.

Unused to drinking Scotch in the afternoon—and so quickly, too—Karen stumbled and dropped her keys. She opened the door of the quiet, empty apartment and was struck by the oddest feeling of loneliness—almost complete isolation and desolation. She tried to shrug off the depressing feelings, attributing them all to her drinking in the afternoon. But it didn't seem to help. She felt so undeniably alone—as if Jessica—even Grant—weren't with her anymore. She was all alone—weeping soundlessly for the child she wasn't sure she could conceive. Wandering through the rooms, she saw, couldn't ease the black tension grinding in her chest.

Somehow she felt herself drawn to the studio, and

here the feeling grew, became almost palpable—as if there were another presence in the room with her.

"My God, Karen, calm down, stop imagining things," she said out loud, trying to make the sound of her own voice break the spell.

But the resounding silence only mocked her.

Karen sucked in her breath. She whirled around suddenly, arms swinging. She stumbled and as she was losing her balance, she grabbed at the small table where Jessica kept her artwork, upsetting a stack of sketches. They fell to the floor—except for one lying on the bottom.

With both hands Karen leaned against the table, steadying herself as she bent over the sketch.

She picked it up and held it to the light. It was the figure of a woman—a woman obviously in the last months of pregnancy. The sight of it sent an icy finger down Karen's spine.

Don't touch my baby, her anguished cry beat against her mind.

But then the figure began to blur and the room began to spin around. She felt herself slipping away.

Sometime later she heard a small insistent voice urging her to wake up. "Please," it said. "Please open your eyes. I don't know what to do."

"Do?" Karen said thickly. "Do about what?"

The small voice let out a long sigh of relief.

Karen opened her eyes. Jessica was kneeling over her. "What happened?" Karen asked.

Jessica shook her head. "I don't know. I guess you fainted."

"Fainted!" Karen raised herself on an elbow. "But I've never done that in my life."

"Maybe you hit your head," Jessica suggested.

"I don't think so," Karen said, gazing around her. She was lying on the floor in the middle of the studio and scattered randomly about the floor were at least half a dozen pieces of sketching paper.

"Are those your sketches?" Karen asked, sitting up, groggily tasting Scotch in the back of her throat.

Jessica nodded. "You must have bumped against my drawing table," she said.

"Yes, I guess I did," Karen muttered, rubbing her hand across her forehead, trying to grasp at a memory that was just out of reach.

"What is it?" Jessica asked. "What's wrong?"

Karen drew her hand away from her eyes and looked at the child blankly. "I don't know," she said. "I can't remember what happened."

Jessica's eyes were no longer on hers. They were staring at something lying on the floor near Karen's feet. Suddenly she reached for it, and Karen saw that it was one of Jessica's sketches.

Something began to buzz in Karen's mind. "What's that?" she asked Jessica.

"Nothing." The child shrugged. "I just thought I'd start picking up these drawings."

Karen held out her hand. "May I see it, please?"

Jessica shook her head. "You weren't supposed to see this one—it's not very good. I don't know how it got into the pile with the others."

"I'd still like to see it," Karen insisted. "May I?"

Jessica's eyes hardened to a steely blue. "All right," she said, a slight quiver of defiance in her voice as she placed the drawing in Karen's outstretched hand.

Karen stared at the sketch, and suddenly shuddered. It reminded her so vividly of something she would rather forget: a classroom, another little girl, children laughing cruelly at her, herself reaching out ... and then nothing.

Karen shook herself, and the vision went away. She drew in a deep breath. "Tell me, Jessica," she said, tapping the paper with her finger. "Who is this? Is it a real person—or did you make it up?"

Jessica's eyes slid away from hers. "It's nobody you know," she mumbled.

"I don't care about that," Karen said impatiently. "Who is it?"

Jessica's hand flew to her mouth, and she began to gnaw on her fingernails—something Karen had never seen her do before.

"Take your hand away from your mouth," Karen snapped, desperate to make sense of her feelings.

Jessica dropped her hands into her lap and intertwined them in a ladylike gesture. "It's just a stupid picture," she said, her lower lip curling into a pout. "I don't know why you're so interested in it."

Karen sighed. "Never mind, Jessica. Just tell me who it is."

Jessica's small body seemed to sag. "It's my mother," she said dully.

Karen was sure she had misunderstood the child. "Your mother?" she echoed. She stared at the sketch dumbly, remembering the words she'd heard screaming in her mind just before she fainted.

Don't touch my baby.

She felt weak and the hand holding the sketch began to tremble.

"Are you all right?" Jessica asked. "You're not going to faint again, are you?"

Karen gazed at the child in some confusion. What was happening to her? What was causing her bizarre behavior? She was all right. She knew she was. They told her she was. Perhaps it was the Scotch—or the excitement of planning to have a baby. Yes, that must be it. She was so agitated that she wasn't quite in control of herself.

But whatever it was, Grant must not hear of it. He

might change his mind about the baby. This time she had to have her baby. Her own baby.

"Will you promise me something, Jessica?" Karen asked cautiously.

"What?"

"Promise not to tell your father that I fainted."

Jessica's eyes were guarded. "I don't know," she said. "I don't like to hide things from Daddy."

Who are you trying to kid? Karen thought to herself. Out loud she said, "But there are some things he's just better off not knowing, Jessica."

"You mean it would upset him?"

"Yes."

"Well, okay," the child said with great reluctance. "I promise not to tell Daddy."

CHAPTER ELEVEN

"Oh, Fran, I'm so glad to see you," Karen said, opening the door. "Thanks for coming over."

Fran put a smooth, sweet-smelling cheek forward for a kiss and then wafted through the door in her usual breezy style. "Well, what else are friends for?" she said, doffing the billowing cape that suited her so well. She cocked an appraising eyebrow at Karen. "So what is it? What's bothering you? Tell old Fran all about it."

Karen pointed in the direction of the living room. "Go on in and sit down. Do you want coffee?"

"Oh, God, yes," Fran moaned, fluttering her eyelashes theatrically. "I can't make it through the morning without a gallon of the stuff."

Karen laughed. "All right, I've got a fresh pot on. You sit down, and I'll bring it right out."

When Karen entered the living room carrying a tray with coffee and some Danish pastries on it, Fran was seated on the loveseat, her head tilted to one side. She was deep in thought and didn't notice as Karen put down the tray and sat on the sofa.

"Here's your coffee," Karen said, pouring a cup and offering it to her.

Fran shook herself. "Sorry," she said. "Guess I wandered off for a little while."

Karen poured herself a cup of coffee. "What were you thinking about? Anything special?"

Fran fixed her with a penetrating gaze. "As a matter of fact, I was thinking about Emily."

"Emily?" she repeated faintly. "What made you think of her?"

Fran settled herself back against the cushions of the loveseat and sipped slowly at her coffee. "I remembered one of the last times I saw her: I came over here for coffee—just like today."

"When was this?"

"Mmm, well, I saw her a lot, but I suppose that time couldn't have been more than a few days before the baby was born. She was, as they say, 'great with child.'" Fran suddenly stopped and looked sharply at Karen. "You don't want to hear about this, do you? So I'll just shut up, and you can tell me what you called me over here to talk about."

Karen laughed mirthlessly. "You're not going to believe this, Fran, but that's what I wanted to talk to you about—Emily."

Fran's eyebrows shot up. "Really? Why?"

Karen stared at her friend for a moment; then she jumped up from the couch. "Wait a minute," she said. "I want to show you something." She went into the studio, found the sketch that Jessica had drawn, and brought it back to Fran. "What do you think of this?" she asked.

"It looks like a blimp in a dress."

"It's a pregnant woman," Karen explained.

Fran laughed. "Oh."

"Doesn't it remind you of anyone?"

"No. Should it?"

"It's Emily. Jessica drew it."

Fran reached for the sketch, peering closer at it. "That's strange. When did she draw this?"

Karen shrugged. "I'm not sure. Probably within the last couple of weeks."

Fran's brow knitted together in puzzlement. "More to the point, I wonder *why* she drew it."

"What do you mean?"

"Well, haven't you noticed, darling? There isn't a single picture of Emily *anywhere* in this apartment."

Karen frowned. "Are you sure?"

"Oh, yes. Because *I'm* the one who went through all the photo albums and the framed portraits. I took out every picture of her and got rid of them—Grant asked me to."

"What did you do with them?"

"I burned them—Grant made me. There were a couple I wanted to keep for Jerry and me, but Grant insisted that I throw everything into the fire. He was so adamant about it, and at the time I remember thinking it was a little odd."

Karen picked up the sketch from Fran's lap. "You know," she said tentatively, "I had a very strange experience yesterday afternoon."

"Really?" Fran said, her eyes suddenly watchful. "Tell me what happened."

Then, not really sure why she was telling her, Karen described for Fran the events of the previous afternoon: how she felt so totally deserted in the lonely apartment and was drawn to the studio where usually she felt most comfortable; there she found the sketch, and then passed out. But she left out her visit to the doctor's office, the irrational fear that caused her flight from the maternity boutique, and her subsequent foray into the bar. For some strange reason, she did not want Fran to know about these things.

"Do you have any idea how long you were unconscious?" Fran asked when Karen was finished.

"I don't know. Maybe fifteen, twenty minutes. Maybe longer."

Fran clucked sympathetically. "Nothing like this has ever happened to you before?"

"Never."

For one of the few times since Karen had known her, Fran seemed uneasy. "I don't know what to think," she said, shaking her head slowly from side to side. "It sounds—God, I hate to say this—but it sounds like some kind of delirium."

Karen winced. "Don't say that."

Fran gave her a piercing look. "Well, doesn't it?"

Karen met her gaze head-on. "What are you trying to say, Fran? That I've gone ga-ga?"

"Nothing of the kind, and don't go getting defensive on me. I'm on your side, remember?"

Karen nodded mutely.

"What I meant," Fran went on, "was that there didn't *appear* to be any logical reason for what happened—"

"You know, maybe it's that room," Karen suddenly blurted out.

"The room?"

"Yes, I think I've felt a little strange about it ever since Jessica told me what had happened there. Most of the time I manage to forget about it, but every once in a while when I'm sitting at the drawing board I think about Emily and the baby, and I practically gag at the thought that I might be sitting in the very place where—where—" She broke off, looking helplessly at Fran.

"I understand," Fran said, her eyes full of compassion. Then she added softly, "And I think I see something else—something that you're possibly not aware of."

"What?"

"That you might feel a little guilty that you've taken over Emily's place, that her tragedy has brought about your happiness. Is that possible?"

"I-I never thought about it," Karen said in some confusion. "I suppose you could be right."

"Maybe this experience of yours was a way of identifying with Emily so you wouldn't have to feel so guilty about her."

Karen laughed self-consciously. "What is this? Are you turning into a shrink now, Fran?"

"Sorry," Fran said. "I guess I have a tendency to come on a little too strong. It must be all those years of analysis I had."

"I didn't know you'd had analysis."

"Sure. Six whole years of it—five days a week."

"My God."

"Exactly. But I really needed it at the time. It changed my life." Fran let out a deep sigh. "I wish I'd been able to get Emily to go."

"Do you think it would have helped her?"

"It's hard to say. You see, what happened to Emily was so sudden—of course, it must have been building up for years, but the final breakdown seemed to happen practically overnight. So I'm not sure that a psychiatrist would have been able to help her."

Karen refilled both their cups with coffee. "Tell me about her, Fran," she said, handing Fran her cup. In a morbid sort of way, she shivered, she was eager to hear everything about the woman who had lived in this very room—and died so bloody a death in the room at the end of the hall.

Fran drank her coffee, considering; then she said reflectively, "Emily was perhaps the gentlest person I ever knew."

"Gentle?" Karen said in some surprise.

"Yes. Ironic, isn't it? That the gentlest person I

knew should come to such a violent end. What changed her, I don't know."

"She didn't talk to you, then? Tell you what was troubling her?"

"No. I don't think she talked to anybody. From what Grant says, she wouldn't even talk to him. God, I wish she had—even if it was just for his sake so that he wouldn't have felt so responsible."

"Why do you think she did it, Fran?"

Fran's eyes glazed over. "I'm not sure, but I've thought about it a lot. I think she got very confused about who she was and what she was—it just overwhelmed her, and she couldn't take it anymore."

"But why did she kill the baby, too?"

"She probably felt she had to. The baby must have seemed like part of herself."

Karen shook her head. "I don't understand it. I don't understand how she could do it."

"I do," Fran said almost bitterly.

Karen stared at her friend in puzzlement. "What do you mean?"

"Not everybody should have children. Not if the person is unstable. I don't think Emily was cut out to be a mother—and she knew it. She only had her children out of a sense of duty, and once they were born she hated the responsibility of raising them. She was really quite indifferent to Jessica, and I don't think Grant was aware of it because she put on a good act with Jessica for his sake whenever he was around."

"But Jessica knew, didn't she?"

"Of course. Children aren't stupid. They can tell when someone really cares about them—or is just pretending to. Oh, Jessica knew all right—and she turned to her father. Maybe Grant knew, too—without being aware of it—and he tried to make it up to Jessica."

"You know, I'm not trying to make excuses for

Emily," Karen said almost apologetically, "but Jessica is not an easy child to love."

"I know. She's always been standoffish. I'm quite fond of her now—but that's mostly because I've known her for so long. And also because I know what she's been through, and I can't help feeling sorry for her."

Karen frowned. *Poor little Jessica. Poor little Jessica—she's been through so much. I feel so sorry for her.* Karen was getting very, very tired of hearing that same old refrain. She decided to change the subject. "Who does Jessica look like?" she asked. "Emily?"

"Oh, yes. She's got Emily's coloring, and she does resemble her quite a bit. But their personalities are completely different."

"How? What was Emily like?"

"Well, like I said, she was gentle. I don't think I ever saw Emily really angry in all the years I knew her. Actually, I thought she was a little too passive. She adapted herself to other people much too readily and never really stood up for what *she* wanted."

"A lot of men like that in women," Karen observed, her thoughts flitting back to her first marriage.

"Yes, well I think that Grant may have liked that about her when he was younger, but as he matured I think he wanted Emily to become somewhat more of her own woman."

Somewhat reticently Karen asked, "Do you think he loved her?"

Fran was thoughtful for a moment. "Yes, I suppose he did—but not the way he loves you. He loved her because she was there, because she was his wife, and maybe most of all because she was Jessica's mother."

"Has he always been so crazy about Jessica?"

"From the moment she was born. I never saw a man so crazy about a baby. I think he spent more time with her than Emily did. He was always holding her and rocking her, talking to her and telling her how beautiful she was and how much he loved her."

"Maybe that was part of the problem," Karen suggested. "Maybe Emily felt shut out because Grant was so devoted to Jessica."

Fran eyed her quizzically. "Do I detect a note of projection there?"

"What?"

"It sounds like *you* might be the one feeling shut out. Am I right?"

Karen stared into her coffee cup. "Sometimes," she said. "They *are* awfully close, you know."

Fran gave her a reproving look. "Yes, and I also know that it makes life a lot easier if you can blame all your problems on being the odd man out."

"I don't think I know what you mean by that," Karen said somewhat huffily.

"Oh, yes, you do." Fran's voice became brusque and authoritative. "I'm your friend, Karen, and because I am, I'm going to tell you something: you're making this situation more difficult than it really is. Jessica is only a child, but you're making her into your rival for Grant's affection. That child needs a *mother*, Karen, but I don't think you've given her half a chance."

Without waiting for Karen to respond, Fran put down her coffee cup and stood up. "All right, I've said my piece, and I can see you're probably very angry with me so I'll be going. But I hope you think about what I said." And with that she picked up her things and left quickly.

Karen watched Fran's abrupt departure, glad to see her go. She was tired of listening to the kind of holier-than-thou, officious crap that Fran handed out so readily. She didn't live with Jessica—how did she know what it was really like. Might as well write off that entire friendship, she thought hotly. Yet . . . was there the slightest possibility that Fran was right?

Karen was in the kitchen waiting for Jessica when she got home from school. "Oh, Jessica, come on in," she called out invitingly. "You're right on time. I just got finished baking some chocolate chip cookies."

"Yes, I can smell them," Jessica said, appearing in the doorway. "Why'd you bake those?"

"Because they're your favorites," Karen said, walking over and giving the child an affectionate squeeze.

Jessica pulled away and eyed her suspiciously. "I didn't know you liked to bake."

"Well, I do sometimes," Karen said, giving her arm a gentle tug. "Now, come on over to the table, and we'll sit down and have some cookies together. We can talk."

Jessica dutifully sat down at the table. "What do you want to talk about?" she asked before popping a still-warm cookie into her mouth.

"Oh, nothing in particular," Karen said nonchalantly. "Whatever interests you."

Once again a suspicious gleam came into Jessica's eyes. "I can't think of anything," she said.

"Well, maybe you can explain something to me then, Jessica," Karen suggested.

"What?"

"Tell me why you drew that portrait of your mother."

Jessica was reaching for another cookie, but her hand was arrested in mid-air. "Why do you want to know that?" she asked, her eyes narrowing.

"Because I'm curious, that's why," Karen said, trying to make her voice sound reasonable and matter-of-fact. "I'd like to know more about her. Wouldn't you if you were in my position?"

Jessica thought for a moment. "I suppose so," she said grudgingly.

"You see," Karen went on, "your father has told me so little about your mother. I guess it's difficult for him to talk about her. And you obviously don't like to talk about her either—so I was surprised to see that you'd drawn a picture of her. And I wondered why."

Jessica shrugged her shoulders. "I don't know. I just felt like it."

"Why did you make her pregnant in the picture?"

Jessica's eyebrows came together in concentration. "I guess because you had talked about having a baby. It made me remember Mommy when she was like that."

"She was all right then, wasn't she?" Karen asked. "It wasn't until later—after your sister was born—that she became sick."

Jessica picked up another cookie and studied it intently. "She was okay before Sarah was born," she said. "She couldn't get around very well, and Daddy and I had to wait on her. But she was kind of funny then— she used to laugh and call herself 'The Fat Lady.'"

"That's interesting," Karen said. "Tell me some more about her."

Jessica took several bites out of the cookie and swallowed them before she spoke. "There's nothing to tell," she said, her voice betraying no emotion. "She's dead."

Karen gaped at the child. "Jessica! She was your *mother*!"

Jessica's face still wore a mask of indifference.

"Don't you care?" Karen said, prodding for some kind of reaction, pushing farther than perhaps she had any right to go. "Don't you care that she killed your sister—and then she killed herself?"

"Is that what Daddy told you?" Jessica said. "That Mommy killed herself?"

"Well, *yes*," Karen replied. "Isn't that what happened?"

Jessica appeared to retreat behind some invisible barrier. "You'd better ask Daddy," she said cryptically. Then she picked up a handful of cookies and walked out of the kitchen, leaving Karen, shocked and confused, staring after her.

CHAPTER TWELVE

The conversation at the dinner table that evening was hardly sparkling. In fact Grant felt that he was the only one making any attempt to be sociable.

Whenever he spoke to Karen, she would nod or make some ambiguous response that showed she wasn't paying attention. Whatever was on her mind, Grant decided, would have to wait until the two of them were alone.

Jessica vainly tried to be polite, but it was evident that she was interested in neither the conversation nor the cuisine.

"Jessica, what's the matter with you?" Grant asked impatiently. "You've hardly touched your food."

"I don't know, Daddy." Jessica sighed. "I guess I'm just not very hungry tonight. May I please be excused?"

Grant frowned. "What did you do—stuff yourself with snacks after school?"

"I'm afraid it's my fault, Grant," Karen suddenly broke in. "I baked a batch of cookies this afternoon, and I think Jessica may have eaten a few too many."

"All right, Miss Piggy," Grant said teasingly to his

daughter, relieved that the silence hadn't been caused this time by a disagreement between Jessica and Karen. "You can leave the table. But I want you to get cracking on your homework, understand?"

"Yes, Daddy." Jessica put down her napkin and pushed back her chair. "I'll do it right away."

As Jessica left the room Grant glanced at Karen, but her eyes were fixed on her fork as she listlessly pushed her food around on her plate.

"What's the matter?" Grant kidded, hoping to draw her out. "You eat too many cookies, too?"

"What?" Karen said, startled. "What did you say? I didn't hear you."

"Never mind. It wasn't important."

Silence fell between them as Grant finished off the rest of his meal and Karen nibbled at a few more bites.

Then Grant put down his napkin. "All right, Karen," he said firmly. "Let's have it. What's bothering you?"

Karen's green eyes stared at him blankly. "I don't know what you're talking about," she said, quickly getting to her feet and stacking the dinner dishes.

Grant pushed his plate toward her. "What do you want me to do, wheedle it out of you?"

Karen responded to this with a scornful glance.

"Then have it your way," Grant said. He got up, collected the glasses from the table, and carried them into the kitchen.

He hated what was happening to them, the distance that was growing between them—but he felt helpless to stop it. He was not the kind of man who found it easy to go to a woman. Let her come to him. But would she? Or would she be like Emily and keep it all inside her? No, Karen wasn't like that. He hoped to God she wasn't like that.

But she was acting differently, wasn't she? Somehow, in small ways, she wasn't quite like the same person he married. She seemed, well, just different, he thought. Distracted, vague, bothered by something. He wondered briefly just how well he knew his own wife, and then just as quickly brushed away such a foolish, indulgent thought.

Karen had followed him into the kitchen and went to the sink, where she started scraping the dishes and rinsing them before loading them in the dishwasher. Her back was to him, and he could see the rigidity with which she was holding herself. *Damn stubborn woman. Well, two could play at that game.*

Suddenly, Karen's shoulders collapsed, and she turned to face him. "I don't know why I bother trying to hide something from you," she conceded grudgingly.

"I don't either," he responded, trying to add a little levity to the situation.

She attempted a smile, but only managed to twitch the corners of her mouth. Then she sucked in a deep breath. "There's something I've got to ask you."

"What is it?"

"Not here," she said, hastily drying her hands on a dish towel. "Let's go into your study."

Puzzled, Grant followed her into the study and closed the door behind them. "Well?"

Karen sat down gingerly on the Chesterfield. Her hands gripping her knees, she didn't look at Grant but gazed resolutely at a sailing-ship lithograph hanging on the wall behind the desk. "Grant," she said, a perceptible quiver in her voice, "what really happened to Emily?"

Grant did not trust himself to speak right away, so he made a show of going to his desk and casually perching on the edge of it. Then he allowed himself to look into Karen's eyes while he feigned mild surprise. "What do you mean?" he asked.

Karen stared back at him unblinkingly. "How did she really die?"

This time Grant couldn't hide his reaction. He swallowed hard. "That's a rather pointless question, isn't it?" he stalled. "You know the answer."

Karen's eyes were suddenly sad, as if she regretted what she was doing, but she had to know and plunged on. "Do I?" she said. "Do I know the real answer?"

Grant jerked off his glasses and rubbed the bridge of his nose. "I don't know what you're talking about," he said defensively. "Where did you get this crazy idea in the first place?"

Karen bit at her lip for several seconds before she said, "From Jessica."

"What?" Grant put his glasses back on. "You talked to Jessica about her mother?"

Karen nodded meekly. "It just slipped out—I didn't mean to. But it didn't seem to bother her."

"How would *you* know whether it bothered her or not?" Grant said sarcastically.

Karen's eyes flashed. "I *told* you it was unintentional—"

"All right, all right," Grant said. "Now, just what did Jessica say to you about her mother that's made you so curious?"

Karen looked down at her hands in her lap. "She told me to ask you if Emily really killed herself."

Grant stopped breathing for a moment. "What?" he said, his voice barely a whisper.

Karen looked up at him, her eyes full of concern. "You look awful," she said. "Have I upset you?"

"No, no. I'm fine," he said, rubbing a hand across his forehead.

"Are you sure?"

Grant stood up and slowly walked around his desk. "I can't believe she said that," he muttered, more to himself than to Karen. Then suddenly he stopped pacing and looked sharply at Karen. "I should have known this would happen," he said.

Karen stared at him. "What are you talking about?"

Grant sagged into the leather swivel chair behind his desk. "Maybe it's better that you know." He sighed. "Maybe it'll help you to understand Jessica better—maybe."

"Grant, you're not making sense," Karen said, frustration written on her face. "Will you *please* just tell me what this is all about?"

Karen made it sound so simple, he thought pensively, as if the words once spoken would make everything fall into place. But he knew better. The words would make everything worse. They were harsh, indelible labels that once spoken could never be forgotten.

For three years he had kept the secret, watched over it night and day, ever alert to dangers within and without. He had never doubted for a moment that he had done the right thing, but it had been a terrible burden for him to carry alone.

"Grant?"

Karen's voice jerked him back to reality. "I—all right, I'll tell you," he said weakly. "Jessica's aroused your suspicions, so I suppose I have to tell you the rest." He gazed off into space for a moment and then began to speak in a soft monotone: "I had to protect her. She was only eight years old—she hardly knew what had happened. It wasn't right that she should be made to suffer anymore for what her mother had done to her. You see," he said, pausing to look directly at Karen, "Emily didn't kill herself—Jessica did."

Karen winced as if she had been slapped. "Oh, my God," she breathed.

"It was self-defense, of course," Grant went on, willing his voice to be toneless, unemotional. "Emily had already killed Sarah and then she came after Jessica with the knife. But she was drunk and Jessica managed to fight her off—and then Jessica said that Mommy suddenly fell down and the knife was sticking out of her chest, and she didn't know how it got there, but Mommy wasn't moving anymore. Even so, she was still afraid that Emily would come after her, so she ran and locked herself in the bathroom and stayed there until I got home."

Karen shook her head sadly. "How horrible for her."

"It took me a while to get what had happened out of her," Grant said in a rush of words. "She was in an extreme state of shock. But right away I knew I had to protect her, so I made her change her clothes because they had blood all over them, and I made sure that the only fingerprints on the knife were Emily's. Then when the police came I simply told them that Emily had killed Sarah and then herself and that Jessica had found them when she came home from school. That explained the deep shock Jessica was in. The police were very sympathetic, and there was no reason not to believe the story that I told them."

"I think I understand now," Karen said gently. "I understand why you watch over Jessica the way you do."

Grant frowned. "I thought she had forgotten. I thought that she didn't remember that day, that she had accepted my version of the truth. But obviously she hasn't."

"You mean you thought she really didn't know?"

"Yes, but it's been so long since we talked about it, I just assumed that she didn't know."

"Or want to know."

"Yes. That too."

Karen spread her hands helplessly across her lap. "I'm sorry if I raked it all up for you—it must be very painful."

"The pain is a little duller now, thank God," Grant said. "The worst part is worrying about Jessica—hoping that she won't remember, living in fear that the truth will come out someday, that someone will point a finger at her and say, 'She killed her own mother.'"

"But who would ever do such a thing?" Karen asked incredulously.

"Anybody," Grant said harshly. "Anybody who knew the truth."

"Yes. I suppose you're right."

"You know you mustn't ever tell anybody that I told you this," Grant said warily. "Not even Jessica."

"I won't. I promise."

"But I'm glad you know," Grant said, relief flooding through him. "It makes it a little easier for me; now I don't have to be on guard against you."

"I'm glad you told me, too," Karen said, getting up off the couch and coming to put her arms around him. "It makes me feel that you trust me, and it makes me feel a lot closer to Jessica."

Grant shut his eyes and gave himself up to the warmth of Karen's embrace. The secret had been revealed, the words had been said. He had been wrong to keep it from Karen. He had been wrong to doubt her. She did love him—and Jessica. She was trying to be a better mother to Jessica than Emily had ever been. It was good that Karen knew the truth.

CHAPTER THIRTEEN

Fran waited until after dinner, when the boys were in their rooms—supposedly doing their homework—before suggesting to Jerry that they go out for a walk.

He knew her so well. "What's the matter?" he asked. "Something on your mind?"

"It's Grant," she said, knowing him equally well—knowing that the mere mention of his friend's name was enough to get Jerry up from his easy chair and heading to the closet for his sheepskin jacket.

Outside, they turned up Fifth Avenue. Across the street was the grandiose, four-block-long presence of the Metropolitan Museum of Art, its exhibition banners gently flapping in the cold December night. Fran linked her arm through Jerry's as they strolled past one magnificent address after another.

Finally, Jerry broke the silence. "What's this about Grant?" he asked. "Is there something going on I don't know about?"

Fran sighed. "It's Karen, actually. She's been so strange lately."

"Don't tell me you're having second thoughts about

bringing them together," Jerry said sourly. "It's a little late for that now."

"We've had sort of a disagreement and I don't know what to do," Fran said bluntly, brushing away a strand of hair the wind had blown across her face. "If it was just Grant, I wouldn't be so worried, but it's really Jessica I'm concerned about."

"Jessica?" Jerry said sharply. "Why Jessica?"

"I don't know," Fran said. "I guess I really don't understand Karen, but I get this feeling from her that she really doesn't like Jessica—in fact, I think she detests her."

Jerry suddenly stopped walking. "What do you mean? You don't think she'd do anything *physical* to her, do you? That would just about destroy Grant."

Fran gazed up at her husband. "I don't know."

Fran began walking again, and Jerry fell into step beside her. "I think something odd happened to Karen once," she said cryptically and then fell silent.

"Has she ever spoken to you about her teaching?" she asked abruptly. Jerry shook his head, and Fran continued, tapping her forefinger on her lip as she spoke. "She always gets a strange tone in her voice whenever the subject comes up, and then she'll hurry on to something else. Several times I wanted to ask her about it, but she always manages to steer the conversation away from herself."

"So what are you going to do now—how are you going to pin her down if it's something she doesn't want to tell you? Anyway, maybe you're reading more into the situation than actually exists?" Jerry asked skeptically.

"Ah, but I wouldn't talk to Karen," Fran continued. "I hope to have another source."

"Who?"

"Her sister, Janet. You remember her from the wedding, don't you?"

"Of course. But what makes you think that Karen's sister would be willing to talk to you about Karen? Wouldn't Karen have told her that you two have had a falling out?"

"Probably. Maybe I'll call her up and ask her if I can come out to New Jersey because I want to talk to her about Karen. That I'm worried about her—and Jessica."

Jerry looked at her dubiously. "You'd better not lay it on too thick—or she might not let you in the door."

"Oh, don't worry—I'll know what to say. Maybe there isn't anything at all, and I'm just acting like a worrywart." Fran shivered from the cold and pressed herself close against the warmth of Jerry's body. "But I've got to do something," she said. "I feel like I'm responsible for that marriage."

"You *are*," Jerry said, but his tone was more gently teasing than reproachful.

"I don't really think Karen is a *violent* person," Fran said. Then, frowning, she added pensively, "But we didn't think that about Emily either, did we?"

Jerry said nothing, but shook his head slowly in the darkness. Then they turned around and went home.

On the wall in her studio Karen had hung a calendar with the expected date of her next menstrual period circled in red. As that day approached, she found herself glancing more and more at that circle and saying an anxious prayer: "Please dear God, let me be pregnant. *Please.*"

Finally, the day arrived, and there was no sign of her period. *Don't get your hopes up just yet,* Karen warned herself. *It could still be a false alarm—your period has been a day or two late before.*

Two days later she got her period. It sent her into an emotional tailspin. And as if fate had decided to add insult to injury, she was beset by a bad case of abdominal cramps. So, depressed and aching, she stayed in bed most of the day, feeling quite justifiably sorry for herself.

When Grant called her in the middle of the afternoon, she told him the bad news.

"I can tell how disappointed you are; we'll just have to hope that you do get pregnant soon," he said. "Maybe the play tonight will cheer you up."

"Play?" Karen echoed. "What play?"

"Don't you remember? We've got tickets for the new Neil Simon play tonight."

"Oh, no," Karen groaned.

"What's the matter?" Grant asked solicitously. "Don't you feel up to going?"

"I don't feel like getting out of bed, let alone getting dressed up and going to see a play," Karen said. "But I've got an idea. Why don't you take Jessica?"

"Oh, I don't know," Grant wavered. "I don't think I want to go out and have a good time when you're feeling so miserable."

"Don't be silly," Karen said. "I'd be really lousy company for you tonight. And as a matter of fact I'd prefer being alone. So why don't you take Jessica? You know she'd love it—just the two of you going out on the town together."

"Well, it is Friday and she doesn't have school tomorrow. So maybe I will. You know, that was a very thoughtful suggestion on your part, Karen," Grant said tenderly. "I'm going to make sure that Jessica knows that tonight was your idea."

"You do that," Karen said. *That ought to be worth at least a couple of Brownie points.*

When Karen watched the two of them go out the door for their evening together, she felt an unexpected twinge of envy.

Jessica had been so caught up in her father and in

her eager expectations for what lay ahead that she had barely mumbled a good-bye to Karen, while Grant had seemed torn between his attentions to his daughter and his guilt at leaving Karen alone.

"Don't you worry about me," Karen had insisted as she gave him a gentle push out the door. "I'll be fine. You two just go ahead and have a good time."

But when she closed the door behind them, Karen let out a long, pensive sigh. Why did she have to suggest he take Jessica tonight? He could have gotten rid of the tickets easily enough. Then he would have stayed home—with her. Overwhelmingly depressed about not getting pregnant right away, she would have liked his sympathy, his company that evening. *He should be with me,* she thought, *he's my husband.*

As the evening wore on she found herself growing more and more irritable.

As she was fixing herself a sandwich with some cold leftover ham, she envisioned Grant and Jessica in some elegant French restaurant, dining on haute cuisine. It made the ham taste like cardboard.

When she finished the sandwich, she fixed herself a drink to wash the taste of the ham out of her mouth. She turned on the TV and tried to concentrate on the silly comedy that was on, but she kept seeing images of Grant and Jessica in their orchestra seats, laughing uproariously at the play.

She expected them home around eleven o'clock. When they hadn't returned by eleven thirty, she started pacing the floor. At a few minutes before midnight, when she heard Grant's key in the door, she flung herself down on the couch and picked up a magazine, pretending to be engrossed in it when Grant and Jessica walked into the living room.

"Hi, honey. Feeling better?" Grant asked brightly.

"A little," Karen replied, peering at him over the top of the magazine.

"Guess where Daddy took me to dinner," Jessica said eagerly.

"I don't want to guess, Jessica," Karen said, putting down the magazine with exaggerated reluctance. "So why don't you tell me?"

Jessica's enthusiasm was not at all dampened by Karen's response. " '21' " she said, glancing up at her father, her eyes shining. "That's where Patty's father takes her whenever he comes to town. Now I can tell her that *I've* been there, too."

"How nice," Karen said curtly. Looking pointedly at Grant, she asked, "How was the play?"

"Oh, it was good," he said. "Didn't you think so, Jessica?"

"I thought it was wonderful," she exclaimed. "There's this really funny scene where—"

"Jessica, aren't you tired?" Karen cut in sharply. "It's way past your bedtime, and I think it's time you got some sleep."

Jessica seemed to wilt. "I'm really not tired," she murmured, but all the life had gone out of her voice.

"Sweetheart, it *is* pretty late," Grant said, going to his daughter and putting his arm around her sagging shoulders. "Maybe you ought to go to bed." He shot Karen a meaningful glance. "You can tell Karen all about the play tomorrow."

When Jessica had said her good nights and had gone off to her room, Grant turned back to Karen. "Don't you ever do that to her again!" he said, his voice low but seething with fury.

"Do what?" Karen replied coolly.

Grant strode across the living room until he was standing over Karen, who was still lying on the couch. "You had to spoil it for her, didn't you?" he said. "You couldn't stand seeing her so happy—just because you're miserable you think everybody else should be, too!"

"That's not fair, Grant," Karen retorted. "Wasn't I the one who suggested you take her in the first place?"

"You're right. And I can't tell you how pleased that made me. But you had to ruin it for her, didn't you?"

"That's right, make me the villain," Karen said peevishly. "It doesn't seem to matter to you how bad *I* feel."

"Don't pull that line on me," Grant said. "I know that you've got your period and that you're depressed because you didn't get pregnant right away, but that's still no excuse for tearing into Jessica the way you did."

"I didn't *tear* into her," Karen said vehemently. "She was jabbering on about the play, and I really didn't feel like hearing about it just then."

"I didn't like the tone you took with her," Grant said. "As if what she had to say was of no importance to you."

"But it was just childish prattle—"

"What *my* daughter has to say is *never* childish prattle," Grant said firmly, his jaw clenched and his hands working into fists. "Jessica knows that I respect her opinions and that I will always listen to them. And I want her to expect the same from you." With that, he turned on his heel and began to walk from the room. Over his shoulder he said, "I'm going to bed now. Good night."

Karen felt like throwing something at his retreating back, and she rolled up the magazine but then let it fall to her lap. No, that was being too childish, and she didn't want to give Grant the satisfaction of being able to accuse her of that.

Fuming, she lay on the couch, replaying the entire conversation in her mind and trying to think of suitable rejoinders to Grant's allegations. All she could come up with was, "Well, if your daughter is so perfect and so wonderful, what do you need me around here for?"

But she could answer that question herself, and it only made her more depressed.

What was wrong with her? Why did she have to keep picking these fights with Grant? She loved him so much, and yet she was always at odds with him. She'd better be careful and learn to control her vicious tongue or Grant would end up divorcing her the way Randy had. . . . If only she could have a child of her own everything would be all right. She would do *anything*, if only she were pregnant. . . .

She ended up crying herself to sleep and spending the night on the couch.

In the morning Karen woke up with a start, wondering where she was. As she looked around and realized that she was in the living room, the scene with Grant and Jessica came rushing back.

God, what have I done now? she thought, sick with shame. *They must both hate me.*

As she sat up she could hear the soft buzz of voices coming from the direction of the kitchen. Grant and Jessica must be having breakfast. She didn't want to face them, couldn't stand the hurt, accusing looks in their eyes.

What was the matter with her? Ever since Grant had told her the truth about Emily's death, she had actually felt *less* sympathy for Jessica, not more. Was it because now that she knew the real reason for Grant's overprotectiveness she couldn't tolerate the fact that Jessica's needs were quite clearly greater than her own—and that Grant would always defer to Jessica's?

She got up, her body stiff from the too-soft cushions of the couch, and went into the bathroom, where she splashed her face with water. Last night's tears had left her eyes puffy, so she put on a little makeup. It didn't seem to help much, and she stared at herself in the mirror. She looked old and tired, drained. *What was it someone had said? By the time you're forty you have the face you deserve....*

Well, here she was, not even forty yet, and look what havoc jealousy and petulance had already drawn on her face.

She'd have to make it up to Grant and Jessica for her behavior last night. There must be something she could do to show them how sorry she was.

Then she remembered something that Jessica had mentioned a few days before; it seemed like a good idea, so she squared her shoulders and marched into the kitchen. "Good morning," she said in her cheeriest voice.

Grant looked up from his scrambled eggs. "Morning," he said gruffly. "How did you sleep?"

"Not too well," Karen admitted. "That couch wasn't exactly designed for sleeping."

Jessica had given Karen only the briefest of glances as she walked into the room and then had resumed eating her eggs. Now Karen walked over to her and put her hand on the child's back. There was no response.

"Jessica," Karen said, staring at the top of her head. "I want to apologize to you for being so short with you last night. It was very thoughtless of me, and I'd be very interested in hearing whatever you have to say about the play—or any other subject."

Jessica tilted her face up toward Karen. "That's all right," she said tonelessly.

"No, it's not," Karen insisted. "And I want to make it up to you." She looked to Grant for his approval. "How about the three of us going ice skating today?"

Jessica started to jump out of her chair. "Oh, Daddy," she squealed. "Can we?"

"I thought you didn't know how to skate," Grant said pointedly to Karen.

"I don't," she responded gaily, determined to make amends for last night's harsh words. "But that doesn't mean I'm not willing to give it a try."

"Please say yes, Daddy," Jessica persisted. "Please, *please*. I haven't been ice skating in such a long time."

"You make it sound like it's been *years*, Jessica." Grant chuckled. "It's only been since last winter."

"Well, can we go, Daddy?" Jessica asked.

"Oh, come on, say yes," Karen chimed in. "It'll do us good to get out in the fresh air."

"I don't know," Grant said, obviously teasing them now. "I haven't been on skates in a while. I might fall down and hurt myself. What would you do then?"

Karen looked at Jessica and gave her a wink. "We'd push your wheelchair," she said blithely.

"Okay, I give up." Grant laughed. "Where do you want to go—Central Park?"

"Actually, I thought we could go to the Rockefeller Center rink," Karen said. "A lot of the Christmas decorations are up already, and it's so festive there."

"Is that all right with you, Jessica?" Grant asked.

Jessica nodded her head enthusiastically. "It's fantastic!"

Karen grinned. She felt well on the way toward making retribution for her selfish behavior.

Rockefeller Center was like a winter carnival. Lights were strung from every potted shrub, Christmas carols reverberated off the walls of skyscrapers, the golden figure of Prometheus shimmered in the rosy glow of the late afternoon sunlight, and over it all towered a splendid green giant of a Christmas tree.

Karen stood with Grant on the edge of the rink, taking it all in. The air was crisp and clear, and as the skaters whizzed by she could hear the soft crunch of the ice.

"Are you ready yet?" Grant asked, reaching for her hand, which was tightly gripping the railing surrounding the rink.

"No, wait a minute." Karen stalled for time. "I want to watch Jessica."

Grant seemed to think that this was a legitimate excuse, so he turned his attention to the center of the rink, where Jessica was executing some fairly respectable spins.

"Where did she ever learn to skate like that?" Karen asked enviously.

"Oh, she's had a few lessons," Grant responded. "She went through a phase when she wanted to be a figure skater." He looked back at Karen. "You know you're never going to get anywhere hanging onto the railing like that." He extended his hand to her. "Come on, lean on me and give it a turn."

Karen looked at him dubiously but put her hand in his. "Well, here goes nothing," she said, a note of bravado in her voice as she put one tentative foot out onto the ice. She transferred her weight to it and—surprisingly—didn't fall down. She brought her other foot forward and immediately began to slide. "Grant!" she cried and clutched at his arm.

"Whoa." He laughed. "Don't panic like that or you'll pull us both down."

Delighted to find that she was still standing up, Karen asked breathlessly, "What do I do next?"

"We'll take some short, gliding steps," Grant said. "Do you think you can manage that?"

"I'll try," Karen said, gritting her teeth in determination.

Grant moved forward slowly, and Karen followed, faltering, slipping, but somehow managing to stay on her feet. With every step her confidence increased. "I can't believe I'm really doing this," she exclaimed to Grant. "I think I may even grow to like this sport."

"Jessica would love that," he said. "The two of you could go skating together in the afternoons."

"I wouldn't be able to keep up with her," Karen said. "Besides, if I get pregnant soon, that will put an end to my ice-skating career."

"Yes—well, what about skiing?" Grant asked. "I thought we were going to go skiing after the holidays."

"Who's going skiing?" Jessica suddenly piped up. She had skated up behind them, and neither Grant nor Karen was aware that she was there.

Grant looked over his shoulder at her. "Never you mind, Little Miss Eavesdropper," he said in a mock disdainful manner. "Karen and I were having a private conversation—and it doesn't concern you."

"Sorry," Jessica said quickly and skated off.

"Grant, I think she took you seriously," Karen said. "Maybe she got the idea that we're not going to take her on the skiing trip."

"Don't be ridiculous," Grant said. "I'm sure she knows I wouldn't do something like that without her."

"If you say so," Karen replied, suddenly realizing that she had been skating along quite easily the whole time they were talking.

"Grant," she said impulsively. "Let me try skating on my own for a while. I think I've got the hang of it now."

Grant looked skeptically at her, but he released her

hand. "Do you want me to follow along behind you?" he asked. "Just in case?"

"Just in case I fall down?" Karen laughed. "No, no, you go ahead. If I do fall down, I'll just have to find some way of getting up again."

"All right, I'll keep an eye on you," Grant said, pushing off. He quickly picked up speed as he threaded his way through the other skaters.

Karen watched him and sighed wistfully. Well, she'd never learn to keep up with him just standing here. Frowning in concentration, she began taking tiny steps forward, little by little adding a glide to the end of each step. Within minutes she was gliding smoothly from one foot to the other.

There was a mirror in the glass wall of the cafe next to the rink, and as Karen passed it she caught sight of herself. Her arms were flapping jerkily like a pair of graceless wings, her shoulders were hunched up nearly to her ears, and she was pitched forward in an effort to balance herself—but she was *skating*.

It was no small triumph for Karen. For she had spent most of her life sitting on the sidelines watching others compete, cheering as they performed some extraordinary athletic feat, secretly wishing that it was *she* out there dazzling the crowd. Skiing was the only sport she had ever come close to mastering, and that was simply because Randy had forced her to. He had been a fanatic skier, and even in the early days of their relationship, he had insisted that she learn to ski. She had been terrified at first and was sure that every time she fell—which was frequently—she would break her leg. But miraculously, she had learned how to conquer the slopes, and in spite of everything else, she would always be grateful to Randy for introducing her to the joys of skiing.

Now as she circled the rink she had visions of herself executing intricate turns and leaps, the audience standing and applauding her, throwing bouquets of roses out onto the ice. . . .

Suddenly, she saw Jessica, skating backward, coming rapidly toward her. "Jessica! Watch out!" Karen cried, attempting to come to a wobbly stop to avoid a collision.

"Don't worry," Jessica laughed, grinding to a graceful, abrupt stop only inches away from Karen. But it was too close for Karen's precarious balance, and she toppled over, flat on her back, onto the ice.

Karen was torn between laughing at the ridiculousness of her position and crying at the loss of her dignity. But she did neither and, raising herself onto her elbow, looked helplessly up at Jessica.

"Are you okay?" Jessica asked, reaching down to her with both hands. "Let me help you up."

"I'm fine," Karen said, grasping the child's hands and pulling herself up. "I hardly felt a thing. I'm pretty well padded there, you know."

Jessica smiled uneasily. "I'm sorry I stopped so sharply. I guess I didn't gauge the distance very well."

"No, no," Karen said, brushing off the back of her pants. "It wasn't your fault. I was off-balance."

Jessica opened her mouth as if to speak, but at that moment her father skated up. "What happened?" he asked. "Did you have a bad fall?"

Karen suddenly saw an opportunity to cast Jessica as the bad guy, and her words were spoken before thinking twice. "It was nothing," she said in a tone that implied she was being bravely forbearing. "Jessica just ran into me, that's all." It wasn't exactly the truth, but close enough.

Grant looked accusingly at Jessica. "What did you do that for? You're a better skater than that."

Jessica's eyes were downcast. "It was an accident," she said grudgingly. "I didn't mean to do it."

"I'm sure you didn't," Grant said. "But it was still

pretty careless on your part." He looked solicitously at Karen and took her by the hand. "Have you had enough skating for the day?"

"Yes, I think so," she replied.

"Fine. We'll go then. Jessica, you can take one more turn around the ice, and then I want you to take off your skates. We're going home."

"Oh, Daddy," Jessica wailed.

"You heard me," Grant said. "And if you don't stop that whining, I'm going to make you get off the ice right now. Do you understand?"

"Yes, Daddy." Jessica pushed off, her shoulders slumping dejectedly as she skated around the rink.

Grant put his arm around Karen's waist and held tightly to her as he escorted her off the ice. Karen leaned uncertainly against him, a hidden, unexpectedly primitive streak of perversity making her glad that for once she had been able to turn the tables on sweet, darling little Jessica.

CHAPTER FOURTEEN

Grant was particularly attentive to Karen throughout the rest of the afternoon and evening, and when it was time for bed, she was certain that he would make lingering, passionate love to her.

She was right. The moment she got into bed his arms were around her, his lips pressing hungrily against hers. She responded immediately, straining her body against his, enjoying the ecstasy of the moment...

Then it happened. She felt Grant's embrace suddenly go slack, and he pulled his lips away from hers. "What's wrong?" she asked, clinging to him.

"Shh," he whispered. "I thought I heard something."

There was a soft but distinct noise nearby.

"It's Jessica," Grant said.

"I didn't hear anything," Karen lied, trying to keep him from leaving her.

"I'll be right back," Grant said, slipping out of bed.

"Grant, wait," Karen called in the darkness. But he was already gone.

Karen fell back against the pillows, cursing Jessica's

timing, for she was certain that Grant had heard Jessica.

"How could she know?" Karen said out loud. Was it possible that she could hear them through the wall? An image of Jessica, her ear glued to the wall, listening intently to the sounds of their lovemaking, sprang into Karen's mind. It made Karen cringe. But she somehow wouldn't put it past Jessica.

She sat up and turned on the light. How ridiculous! Her imagination was running away with her again. Jessica was only a child, hardly capable of something so scheming. Anyway, *she* was the one who was behaving childishly, begrudging Jessica any special attention from her father.

Karen's fit of pique at Jessica's interruption of their lovemaking began to wane, so she settled herself back against the pillows, picked up a book, and started to read.

She became engrossed in the book and was surprised to see when she looked up at the clock that at least half an hour had passed since she turned on the light—which meant that Grant had been gone even longer than that.

She slammed shut the book. Where the hell was he? It couldn't be taking *all* this time to calm Jessica down and get her back to sleep.

Karen threw back the covers and got out of bed. Soundlessly, she eased open the door to their room and tiptoed to Jessica's door. It was ajar by a couple of inches, so she pressed it open with her fingertips.

There, lying on her bed, his arms tenderly cradling his daughter, was Grant. He appeared to be asleep.

The sight of the two of them together like that was too much for Karen. She pulled shut the door with a violent wrench, letting it bang loudly, and stomped into the living room in a blind rage.

She stood in the dark for a moment, waiting to see

if Grant would wake up and come after her. When there was no sign of him, she switched on the light. Shaking with her pent-up fury, she headed for the dining room and the liquor cabinet.

A drink would calm her down. She got out the Scotch and poured herself a strong drink, not even bothering with ice.

Putting the bottle on the dining room table, she sat down. She managed to get the Scotch down in several large, throat-burning gulps. But it made her feel relaxed, pleasantly warm. So she poured herself another one.

She was in the midst of the second drink when Grant appeared. "What's going on here?" he asked brusquely.

"I'm having a little nightcap," Karen replied, hoping her voice sounded as nonchalant as she intended it to be.

Grant advanced into the room. "I've never seen you do that in the middle of the night before," he said, gesturing toward the drink in her hand.

"There are a lot of things you don't know about me," Karen said. Then she added pointedly, "Anyway, I never had a reason to before."

"What is that supposed to mean?"

Without thinking, Karen blurted out, "It means that I'm tired of you leaving me so you can go running to your precious daughter's bedside every time she even sneezes!"

Grant's eyes narrowed and the muscles around his jaw visibly tightened. "I should have known you would react like this," he said between clenched teeth. Then he spun on his heel and marched stiffly out of the room.

Karen gulped down the rest of her drink. Damn him! He wasn't going to walk out on her like that when she had things left to say to him!

She fortified herself with another fingerful of Scotch and then followed Grant into the bedroom. Snapping on the light, Karen saw that Grant had gone back to bed. He glared at her, his eyes blinking furiously as they accustomed themselves to the light.

"What do you want now?" he asked sullenly.

"I want to talk to you!" Karen cried, her voice so high-pitched that she was nearly shouting.

"Then shut the door—quietly. I had a hard enough time getting Jessica back to sleep when you slammed the door before."

"That's just too damn bad!" Karen said, flinging the door shut, hoping it would make a resounding noise. But it brushed over the carpet and swung into the door frame with only a muffled thud. Karen looked disappointedly at it and then walked over to the foot of the bed.

"Are you going to tell me what's eating you?" Grant asked, sitting up and propping himself against the pillows.

Karen paced back and forth. "There are a lot of things," she said. "I have a whole list."

"Well, don't keep me in suspense," Grant said, his tone heavy with sarcasm.

Karen ignored him. "Tonight was the last straw," she said. "I can't take it anymore."

"Take what?"

Karen stopped pacing and looked at Grant. "That I always end up playing second fiddle to Jessica."

"Don't be absurd," Grant sneered.

"It's true," Karen insisted. "You *left* me, right in the middle of making love." There were tears in her eyes. "You left me—to go to Jessica because she had a bad *dream*."

Grant looked somewhat chagrined. "I didn't think I'd be gone so long."

"That's not the point. What matters is that Jessica seems to be more important to you than I am."

Grant studied her for a moment. Then he said, "You're jealous of Jessica, aren't you?"

Karen's nostrils flared in anger. "Well, if I am, I've got good reason to be," she said defiantly.

"I don't think we'd better carry on this conversation anymore tonight," Grant said suddenly. "You've been drinking and you might say something you'll regret later."

"You mean I might say something that *you* don't want to hear!"

"Karen," Grant said darkly. "I'm warning you."

"I don't care!" Karen cried. "I don't care what you say. I'm going to tell you just how sick I think the relationship is between you and your darling daughter—"

"Sick?" Grant said incredulously.

"You know what I'm saying. I think it's sick the way you fawn over her, the way she hangs on you—"

"I don't have to listen to this!" Grant said, leaping out of bed.

"You don't want to listen to it because it's the truth!" Karen said, nearly hysterical now.

"Shut up!" Grant yelled. "Just shut up!"

Suddenly, Karen put her finger to her lips. "Shh," she said in an exaggerated whisper. She pointed to the door. "Jessica's out there. She's listening to us."

Grant stared at her, his eyes wide in disbelief. Then he went to the door and jerked it open. The hall was empty. He shut the door and came back to Karen. "My God," he said, shaking his head as if to deny what was happening. "First the drinking, and now *this*." His voice cracked as he said, "You—you're beginning to act just like Emily."

Karen let out a gasp, but quickly recovered herself. "Well, if I am," she said bitterly, "then maybe I can understand why she did what she did." The moment the words were out of her mouth she regretted saying them.

"Just what are you implying?" Grant said in a chilling voice. "That *I* drove her to it?"

"No, *no!*" Karen sobbed. "I'm sorry, darling. I didn't mean it—I don't know what made me say that."

Grant stared at her, but it was as if he were seeing through her. "It's all right," he said bleakly. "It's nothing that I haven't thought of myself."

CHAPTER FIFTEEN

More than anything, Karen wished she could take back her angry words, for they seemed to have destroyed something inside Grant. Perhaps they would even destroy the marriage itself.

It pained her to even look at Grant. Once again, there was the same sad, haunted look in his eyes that she had seen when she first met him. And she had put it back there—with her vicious, drunken invective.

And yet for all her self-flagellating contrition, she realized that there was a kernel of truth in her harsh accusation: not that Grant had driven Emily to her murderous breakdown, but that there might have been something in the emotional environment that contributed to Emily's neurosis *because it seemed to be having a similar effect on Karen.*

Or was she imagining it? Was she looking for an excuse for her own mercurial moods, something to blame them on?

Wracked by these doubts—and knowing that she was doing exactly what Emily had done but unable to stop herself—Karen took to having an occasional drink or two to help her get through the day and sometimes another in the early evening to fortify herself before Grant got home.

Although she never drank in front of Jessica, she had a feeling that the child knew. But there was nothing unusual in that; Karen was sure that Jessica knew everything that went on in that household.

After the fight Grant had begun coming home late from the office, pleading an end-of-the-year business rush. Often he missed dinner altogether. Karen was almost relieved; it spared her the agony of having to sit and make pleasant, polite conversation with him for Jessica's sake. When the child wasn't around, they barely spoke to each other.

Not that Karen hadn't tried. But neither reason nor tears moved him. So she had decided to leave it alone, to let Grant approach her when he had had enough of the silence.

All the while Jessica seemed unaffected, even unaware of the tension between Karen and Grant. Karen wondered what effect this strained and uneasy truce was going to have on their skiing plans. Originally, she and Grant had talked about the three of them going up to the family's house in Vermont near Mount Snow during Jessica's mid-winter break in January.

Christmas came and went on the same unhappy note; then it was a new year, and Jessica began to chatter more and more excitedly about the upcoming trip. But Karen wasn't at all sure any of them was going anywhere. Not with the way things were between her and Grant.

One afternoon in the studio, while Jessica was experimenting with various brushes and pens and Karen was pretending to work, Jessica began talking idly about the ski trip.

Karen was only half listening to her. The talk about travel made her think back to her honeymoon with Grant, and she felt a sudden pang as she remembered the happiness of that trip. How she wished she could recapture that feeling with Grant. . . .

These wistful thoughts were interrupted by the phone. It was Janet.

Karen wanted to talk to Janet in privacy, so she hung up the extension in the studio and went into the master bedroom.

"How are things?" Janet asked. "Any better?" Karen had confided in Janet about the fight with Grant—although she'd been deliberately vague about the details—and had kept her up to date on the subsequent strain in their relationship.

"Wish I could say they were, but they're not." Karen sighed. "I'm just about at my wits' end."

"I'm sure Grant will come around," Janet said hopefully. "Just give him time."

"He's had plenty of that."

"Well, maybe when you're up in Vermont together things may be different."

"Grant and I really ought to go up there alone," Karen said. Then she thought she heard a click on the telephone. "What was that?" she asked.

"I didn't hear anything."

"It must have been static," Karen said. "Anyway," she went on, "something like that is out of the question since Jessica is counting on the three of us going up to Vermont."

"And you know Grant wouldn't dream of letting her down," Janet said positively.

"Neither would I," Karen said, knowing that Janet wouldn't fail to notice the slight trace of irony in her voice.

They talked for several more minutes, mostly rehashing the situation. But Janet always made Karen feel better, so when she hung up she was definitely in a better mood.

It didn't last long. For when she walked back into

the studio, she was greeted by a sight that froze her where she stood while she took in the horror of it.

Jessica was standing by her drawing board, and both she and the board were dripping with blood.

Then in one swift movement, Karen leaped across the room and grabbed the child. "Jessica!" she cried. "What have you done?"

Jessica was ghostly pale. She held out her left hand to Karen. In the center of the palm was what appeared to be a puncture wound. Blood was steadily seeping out of it, running down the child's arm, making vivid splashes on the floor. "I stuck myself with one of your mat knives," Jessica said calmly. "I don't know how it happened."

Fighting her own queasiness at the sight of all the blood, Karen pressed a finger down on the wound, then clasped Jessica around the wrist and pulled her down the hall to the bathroom.

She washed the wound out with soap and water and checked to make sure that the wound was clean. "There," she said comfortingly to Jessica. "It's not so bad as it looks."

Jessica smiled at her.

The wound had started to close up, so Karen put an antiseptic on and then dressed it with a gauze pad and tape. "I hope it doesn't hurt too much," she said.

Jessica shook her head. "It's not too bad."

"Really?" Karen said, surprised that Jessica had not cried out or even winced when she was cleaning out the wound. "But it must have hurt like crazy when you did it."

"No," Jessica said. "I hardly even felt it."

Karen studied Jessica's face for a moment before she asked, "How do you suppose it happened?"

Jessica shrugged, looking vaguely over Karen's shoulder. "I was putting a knife back on your drawing board, and I guess I tripped."

Karen felt uneasy. She had warned Jessica not to handle the sharp-edged instruments, especially when she wasn't in the room. But there were more urgent things to do than to stand here questioning the child. "Do you know when you had your last tetanus shot?" she asked, putting aside her questions for later.

Jessica thought briefly. "No. But Daddy would know."

Up until that moment Karen had forgotten about Grant. Now she realized that she'd have to call him—and once again he'd probably blame *her* for not supervising Jessica more closely. But damn it, she thought, it wasn't my fault. Jessica was old enough to know not to fool around with something sharp like knives—yet would Grant ever admit that?

"Well," Karen said with a sigh. "I guess I'd better call your father."

She went into the master bedroom and dialed Grant's office.

"Yes?" he said gruffly after his secretary had put Karen through. "What is it? I'm very busy. I've got a client in my office."

"Then don't let me keep you," Karen said, unable to keep the snideness out of her voice. "All I wanted to know is when Jessica had her last tetanus shot."

There was an abrupt shift in Grant's tone. "Why? What's happened?" he asked anxiously.

"She hurt her hand. Her palm, actually. But it's a puncture wound and it's fairly deep, so I wanted to make sure that—"

"How in hell did that happen?" Grant interrupted angrily.

"Well, I'm not exactly sure," Karen hedged. "But it seems she tripped and stuck herself with a knife."

"Where was this? At school?"

Karen swallowed. "No. It was here. In the studio."

"Where were you?"

"I was on the phone in the bedroom—talking to Janet."

There was an eloquent silence on the other end. Karen could well imagine what Grant was thinking, what he would be saying to her if he didn't have a client sitting in his office.

"I know you're angry with me," Karen said quickly. "But that can wait until you get home. Right now, I need to know about the tetanus shot."

"You'll have to check with Jessica's doctor, Dr. Tripp. His number's in the address book in my desk."

"Fine. I'll call him," Karen said. She was about to hang up when she heard a *click!* It was the same sound that she had heard earlier when she was talking to Janet. Suddenly, it occurred to her that Jessica had been listening in on one of the extensions.

Why, that nasty little busybody! Karen thought indignantly. *I ought to turn her over my knee and paddle her bottom. . . .*

But she could never do that. Grant would probably divorce her if she ever laid a hand on Jessica.

So she stifled her outrage and went into Grant's study to call Jessica's doctor. It turned out that Jessica recently had had a booster shot, so she was still immunized against tetanus. Karen told Jessica what the doctor had said and then sent her to her room to lie down.

Grant came home earlier than usual that evening. He gave Karen the barest, perfunctory greeting and then went straight to Jessica's room.

When he came out, half an hour later, his mouth was set in a thin, pinched line. Without looking at Karen, he motioned for her to follow him into the study.

Karen obeyed. There was no way she could avoid this confrontation. It had been coming for a long time, she thought bleakly.

She walked into the study, shut the door, and sat on the couch. Grant was pacing back and forth between his desk and the windows, his hands clasped behind his back. Then he stopped and turned, his eyes unreadable behind his glasses. "Where did Jessica get the idea that you and I were going to Vermont without her?" he asked, his voice cold and relentless.

Karen was taken aback. "What?"

"Do I have to repeat the question?" he said disdainfully.

Karen shook her head mutely.

"Then do I take it that *you* told her that?"

"No. I think she overheard it," Karen said slowly, controlling her fury as she started to put all the pieces together. "I was on the phone with Janet, and I happened to mention that it might help if you and I could spend some time alone together." She kept her eyes from meeting his and rushed on: "I'm pretty sure that Jessica was listening in on another phone. In fact, I know she was."

Grant made a scoffing sound deep in his throat. "Jessica doesn't do things like that," he said.

Karen gave him an incredulous look, but it was lost on him. He had turned his back to her and was walking to the desk.

"Well, that's not important," he said, easing himself down on the edge of the desk.

"You don't think it's important that your daughter's in the habit of eavesdropping on me?" Karen burst out resentfully.

Grant gave her a patronizing shake of the head. "I think that's mostly your paranoia, Karen."

"*My* paranoia!" Karen groaned. "Why won't you ever give *me* the benefit of the doubt?"

"Because you're a grown woman," Grant said, although his tone clearly implied that she was not.

"You're not an eleven-year-old child. You can take care of yourself."

"And in the meantime, you let *her* manipulate you to get everything she wants," Karen sputtered. "Like this accident today. I'm sure she did it deliberately. To make sure she had your attention. To make sure you were on her side. She just set you up so you wouldn't even think to leave her behind while we go to Vermont."

Grant regarded her levelly. "You may be right."

Karen's mouth fell open. "What?" Was Grant actually admitting that his darling daughter could be devious?

"That doesn't mean I think she did it consciously," Grant mediated.

"No." Karen sighed hopelessly realizing that Grant had conceded nothing about Jessica. "How could you?"

"Anyway, that doesn't matter," Grant said, waving his hand through the air as if he were erasing some trivial scribblings from an invisible slate. "The question is, what *are* we going to do about this trip?"

"Are you asking me?" Karen said, a little flippantly. "Or is that strictly a rhetorical question?"

Grant gave her a stern look. "I'm trying to be serious, Karen. We've got a touchy situation here with Jessica. Now, I have an idea. You may not want to go along with it—"

Oh, no, Karen thought. *He's going to suggest that he go to Vermont alone with Jessica—leaving me here, bored and miserable. What'll I do?*

"I'm not going to be able to get away as soon as I'd hoped," Grant was saying. "But that's no reason you and Jessica should have to stay in the city. So why don't you two go up as soon as she gets out of school?"

So that's his plan, Karen thought sullenly. *He wants to get rid of me.*

"Karen?" Grant asked. "Are you listening to me?"

"I hear you," Karen said dully. "You're sending me away."

"I'm not doing anything of the sort," Grant protested, shaking his head sadly as if he wished Karen would not be so quick to jump to negative conclusions. "I see this as an opportunity for you and Jessica to spend some time alone together—someplace other than this apartment. Get a fresh start. And maybe if I'm not around, you two will be forced to get to know each other better." He gave Karen a long, hopeful look.

"Well, since you put it that way," Karen admitted, somewhat mollified by Grant's apparent logic, "it does sound like a reasonable idea."

"You see?" Grant said, sure that the issue was settled now, satisfied that he had brought it to what seemed to him like a sensible solution. "I can tell. By the time I get up there, you two will have grown to love each other."

Either that, Karen thought sardonically, *or we'll have killed each other.* Then she realized the significance of her frivolous words. *God forbid that should happen,* she added superstitiously, *because it would be nothing new for Jessica.*

CHAPTER SIXTEEN

The first hour driving out of the city Jessica was strangely quiet, and Karen was too busy concentrating on making her way through the heavy urban traffic and finding their route amidst a confusion of signs and arrows and exit numbers to try and make conversation with the child.

But once they were well on their way along the New England Thruway, Karen glanced sideways at Jessica, determined to draw the child out since this trip was going to be her best opportunity yet to break down the barriers between them. Bring them together, and then begin to work on the problems in her relationship with Grant. Maybe she shouldn't storm the barricades just yet, but she could at least show Jessica that *she* was going to make an effort to be pleasant. She *could* be a good stepmother, a good mother. . . .

"How long has it been since you've been to your house in Vermont?" she asked casually.

"Years," Jessica replied, her eyes fixed on the road ahead.

"Are you looking forward to it?" Karen said. Then she added brightly, "I know I am."

Jessica looked directly at her. "Why?"

"Well, I'm curious to see the house, that's why," Karen said. "But of course, I'm mostly looking forward to skiing."

Jessica's interest suddenly picked up. "Are you a good skier?" she asked.

Karen laughed. "I'm a better skier than I am an ice skater, that's for sure."

A smile broke across Jessica's face. "That's good."

"Why? Were you worried that I'd embarrass you on the slopes?"

Jessica wrinkled up her nose ingenuously. "Well, maybe just a little."

Karen shot her a quick glance. "Then I'm surprised that you agreed to come up here alone with me."

Solemnly, Jessica said, "I think Daddy needs to spend some time by himself."

Was this the child's way of letting her know that she was aware of the problems between her and Grant? Karen took another swift look at Jessica, but she was staring resolutely out the side window.

Again, silence prevailed until the road signs showed that they were practically in New Haven, where they would turn north.

"New Haven," Jessica said, spotting a sign and becoming suddenly animated. "That's where Yale is, isn't it?"

"Uh-huh," Karen answered, her eyes watching the road for the turn-off.

"That's where Daddy went to school," Jessica said with unconcealed pride.

Don't you think I know that? Karen had been tempted to retort, but instead she said simply, "Did he?" Why was she always so impatient with the child?

Because the child made her feel like an outsider to her own marriage, she thought grimly.

"I want to go there, too, when I'm ready to go to college," Jessica continued.

"That's nice." *Like father, like daughter. So what else is new, Karen old girl? And you're the mother. You just have to learn to deal with this child. Don't let her get the best of you,* she cautioned herself.

"But I haven't decided what I want to study yet."

"Well, there's no real rush, you know," Karen said, inadvertently allowing a trace of facetiousness to creep into her voice. "You've got plenty of time." *Go slowly. She's just a child; she's almost your child.*

Several seconds passed and then Jessica suddenly asked, "Do you think I could be an artist?"

"Well, of course you can. If that's what you want." *That's it—bring her to you,* Karen encouraged herself.

But Jessica was not reassured. "I mean," she said earnestly, "do you really think I have talent?"

Something in the child's tone made Karen glance at her. A desperate need for approval was written all over her face. It was unusual for Jessica to display such intensity, let alone vulnerability. Perhaps it was a good sign.

"Jessica, I think you're a very talented young lady," Karen said quite sincerely. "So talented that you could do anything you put your mind to."

Jessica grinned. She seemed to have heard exactly what she wanted to hear. Still smiling, she settled back in her seat, eyes front, and began humming some unrecognizable tune.

Karen found the humming annoying and looked sharply at Jessica, but the child paid her no attention. After a few minutes, Karen snapped on the radio and twisted the dial until she found a station playing soothing pop music. Jessica stopped humming immediately.

The road north took them through Hartford and then on up into Massachusetts. They began seeing patches of snow on the ground, and the terrain steepened as they passed through the edges of the Berkshires. It was lovely, lonely country, and there were few other cars on the road.

Years before, Karen had traveled this same route with Randy many times. Throughout their marriage, they had always taken winter shares in ski houses in Vermont. One season, their house had even been near Mount Snow.

Since the divorce, she had not been back to Vermont. Instead, she had indulged her appetite for skiing with trips to resorts in Colorado and Utah. Then, she had been sure that she would never go to Vermont again.

Now, the memories of those winters with Randy were fading. They were souvenirs from another lifetime, something that no longer had significance for her. And no power to hurt her anymore.

Only Grant could do that now.

Oh, Grant, I love you so much, she thought suddenly. *Please don't let me lose you, too. I've lost so much already. Oh, God, give us our own child to bring us together.*

The road blurred as her eyes misted over, and she quickly grabbed a tissue out of her purse.

"What's wrong?" Jessica asked as Karen dabbed at her eyes.

"Nothing," Karen lied. "A speck of dust got in my eye. It's gone now."

They stopped for lunch in Northampton, and from there it wasn't far to the Vermont border. In Vermont, they turned off the interstate onto a two-lane, winding, hilly road that required all of Karen's concentration so that she barely saw any of the splendid Vermont countryside with its gentle, tree-covered heights and rugged, rock-strewn valleys.

Wilmington was the closest town to the house, and they stopped there to buy groceries. Then they turned off onto another two-lane road, and Jessica took over the directions, guiding Karen onto one back road and then a second.

"How far is it?" Karen asked, steering carefully along the narrow, gravel road.

"All the way to the end," Jessica said matter-of-factly.

Karen couldn't remember whether or not she'd seen any houses along the way. "Do you have any neighbors?" she asked.

"Only a couple," Jessica said. "Unless somebody's built since we were up here last."

Karen had wanted to get away from it all, but she wasn't sure that she wanted to get this *far* away. "Doesn't it get lonely out here?" she said.

"Sometimes."

"What made you choose this place?"

"It belonged to Mommy's family. They've been coming here for years."

That explained a lot of things, Karen thought. Especially why Grant had not been up here since Emily's death. It was odd that he hadn't told her the house was really Emily's—but perhaps he had thought it better that she not know.

The road widened into a cul-de-sac, and there, among the trees, its brownish gray weathered siding nearly blending into them, was the house.

Karen pulled up in front of it and gazed at it through the windshield. It was not quite what she had pictured; it was larger and older and looked more like a small farmhouse than a cabin in the woods. Although it appeared to be well maintained, it had a lonely, vacant look to it; it was evident that the house had been empty for a very long time.

Jessica was already out of the car. "Come on," she said, nearly jumping up and down with excitement. "Let's go inside."

Karen decided that the luggage could wait. She was curious to see the interior of the house and followed Jessica onto a low porch, protected by an overhanging eave.

Karen unlocked the front door with the key Grant had given her, thinking to herself that she hoped the caretaker had been there.

Apparently he had. The house was warm, and Karen could hear the whir of the furnace as they walked through the door. Just inside was a large foyer with a bare, scraped floor. "This is where we leave all our equipment and wet clothes," Jessica explained. "So we don't track it into the house."

"I see," Karen said, touched by the child's enthusiasm. She smiled warmly but she kept quiet and let Jessica go on showing her around the house.

"This is the living room," Jessica said, her hand gesturing around a large room dotted with braided rugs, several comfortable chairs, and a sofa. In one wall was a huge fieldstone fireplace, and stacked alongside it was a pile of firewood and kindling. Obviously, the caretaker had seen to that.

While Jessica darted into another room, Karen gazed dreamily at the fireplace. For the first time she began to feel happy about this trip. She could see a cheerful fire burning in its grate and lying on the rug in front of it two bodies, hers and Grant's, passionately intertwined, making love . . . then, with a start, she realized that the two bodies in front of the fire could just as easily be Grant's and Emily's. Perhaps they had lain together on the very rug she was standing on. . . .

It was funny that she seldom thought of Emily in the New York apartment. All traces of her had been destroyed and buried long before Karen moved in. Everything there was fresh, new—antiseptic. But somehow this old house had been overlooked. Somehow images of Emily came alive here.

Her earlier enthusiasm dimmed, Karen wondered if she would ever be able to feel at home here. She felt more like a stranger in this house than she ever had at the apartment in the city. Emily's presence was everywhere. . . . Unbidden glimpses of Grant's bloodied wife and child filled her mind, and then she turned quickly, following Jessica on her tour of the downstairs of the house.

She caught up to Jessica in the kitchen, a spacious and surprisingly modern room. There was even a garbage disposal and a dishwasher and in one corner a washer and drier. Seizing on something ordinary, to help forget the gruesome death images, Karen commented lightly, "I didn't expect to find those up here."

"It was all done over a few years ago," Jessica said, opening up a cupboard door to show Karen some of the dishes. "Mommy designed all of it herself," she said, her voice so low that Karen bent to hear her words.

Karen looked quickly at the child's face, but the tension was broken; Jessica was already leading the way up the steep, enclosed stairs to the second floor.

"There are four bedrooms up here." Jessica continued the tour, leading Karen along a narrow hall and opening doors as they went. "There's one bathroom up here and another one downstairs." She pointed to a door at the end of the hall. "I guess that'll be your room."

"Which one is yours?" Karen asked.

Jessica gestured toward a door at the top of the stairs at the opposite end of the hall.

"I really like this house," Karen said as they walked down the stairs. "It has a lot of character."

Jessica looked at her quizzically. "I didn't know houses could have character."

Karen smiled, relieved of the strange anxiety she had felt earlier. She had forgotten the literal-mindedness of a child of eleven. "It's just a figure of speech," she said. "Shall we unpack the car?"

It took them several trips to unload their suitcases, ski boots, and other paraphernalia. Karen decided not to leave the skis and poles in the car rack overnight, so she brought them into the foyer and hung them from hooks on the wall, designed for that purpose. "By the way, Jessica," she asked, "where are your father's skis?"

"In there." Jessica pointed to a closet just off the foyer.

Karen opened the closet door. Inside were several pairs of downhill skis and boots, along with some cross-country equipment. Karen picked up a pair of downhill skis; they had a name etched on them: *Emily Cameron.*

Upstairs, in the room that Jessica had assigned to her, Karen put her suitcase on the double bed and began to unpack it. There were two small chests of drawers in the room, and she took one for her things. As she was hanging some clothes in the closet, she noticed a woman's ski outfit pushed to one side. It was a brilliant turquoise color, and Karen couldn't help thinking that it would go well with her eyes. She took the outfit out and looked at the label; it was European but appeared to be approximately her size.

Karen knew it had to be Emily's. Another reminder

that she had once been flesh and blood instead of the shadowy wraith that seemed to linger on.

But Emily *was* dead, and the jumpsuit was so pretty, so much like something Karen would have picked for herself. She couldn't resist it.

Walking over to the mirror atop one of the dressers, she held the jumpsuit against her body to see if it might fit.

The turquoise made her eyes look like the sultry green sea of the tropics. She had to try the outfit on.

She slipped into it and then stood admiring herself in the mirror, liking the way the slick fabric emphasized the curve of her waist and hips.

Then, reflected in the mirror, she saw Jessica's face, staring at her from the hall. The child's eyes were wide and glazed.

Karen cringed. She wished she could hide under the bed. She spun around. "I'm sorry," she said, but the sound of her voice startled Jessica, and she ran away like a frightened deer.

Karen quickly took off the outfit, put her own clothes back on, and went down the hall to Jessica's room. The child was in there, busily putting her things away in drawers. When Karen tapped on the open door, she turned around slowly.

"Jessica, I . . ." Karen began, still feeling foolish.

The child wasn't making it any easier. She just stared at Karen, her face blank.

"Was that your mother's?" Karen asked. "The jumpsuit, I mean?"

Jessica nodded.

"I'm sorry. I know I shouldn't have tried it on," Karen apologized. "But it was such a pretty color—one of my favorites. I didn't mean any harm."

Jessica shrugged. "It's no big deal."

Karen made a sudden decision. This trip was an

opportunity to break down the walls between them—but only if they were honest with each other. As the adult, it was up to her to make the first move.

"I don't believe that, Jessica," she said, taking a step into the room. "Why won't you admit to me that it upset you to see me wearing your mother's clothes?"

Jessica's blue eyes grew wide and her mouth gaped open. Then she shut it quickly—as if she were afraid she might say something she would regret.

"I wish you would stop pretending with me," Karen went on calmly. "I don't know how you and I can get to be friends unless we tell each other the truth."

Jessica lowered her eyes. "I wasn't upset—honest," she said grudgingly. "I was just surprised to see you in Mommy's ski outfit. From the back you looked just like Mommy."

No wonder the child had turned and run away, Karen realized. She must have imagined for a minute that her mother had come back. As Karen turned to leave the child to her unpacking, she noticed a group of framed pictures hanging on the wall just inside the door. Curious, she moved forward for a closer look.

Most of the pictures were of Jessica—a younger Jessica—tumbling in the snow, cavorting on skis, her cheeks rosy-pink, her eyes shining with laughter. Grant was in a few of the pictures with her, his face less lined, his hair a shade darker. Then Karen's eye zeroed in on one of the pictures of Jessica, for in the background was the out-of-focus figure of a woman wearing the turquoise ski outfit.

Karen turned to Jessica. "Who's that?" she asked, pointing to the picture.

Jessica stepped closer. She studied the photograph a moment before saying in a peculiar, hollow voice, "That's Mommy."

Somehow Karen knew it would be Jessica's mother. This was the first picture of Emily she had ever seen. Curious, she peered intently at the woman's face, trying to make out her features: she appeared to be quite pretty, with soft, laughing eyes and a beautiful, shy smile. If there was a resemblance to Jessica, it wasn't apparent in the photo.

"Do you know when this was taken?" Karen asked.

Jessica's brow knit in concentration. "It must have been the last winter we were up here."

Only months before the tragedy. Karen gazed thoughtfully at that lovely, radiant face and wondered what had happened to change Emily into a woman who would kill her own children.

CHAPTER SEVENTEEN

After calling Grant to tell him they had arrived safely, Karen and Jessica went to bed early that first night, both eager to get a good start on the morning's skiing. As weary as she was from the long hours of driving, Karen had thought she would fall off to sleep immediately. But instead she lay in the dark, listening to the creaks and groans of the house and the gusts of wind through the trees outside, thinking about the woman who had slept in the bed before her.

Emily's presence was stronger here than it was in the New York apartment. Everywhere there were reminders of her: the skis, the jumpsuit, the photograph, books with her name in them. Everything seemed precisely as she had left it, and Karen could easily imagine the house lying empty for all those years, waiting for its mistress to return....

Carried along by the meandering current of these thoughts, Karen eventually managed to drift off to sleep.

She couldn't tell how long she'd been asleep when she suddenly awoke, aware of a new sound that had been added to the noises of the night.

It sounded like the bleating of a lamb. It rose and fell, as if the wind swirling around it alternately drowned it out and then magnified it.

Karen listened intently, her ears straining to locate the sound. At first she was sure that it came from outside—an animal caught in a trap. Then she realized that it was from inside the house.

Jessica!

Karen threw on her bathrobe and fumbled around on the cold floor for her bedroom slippers. Bumping into furniture and walls, she managed to find her way to the door of the unfamiliar room. Turning on the light, she pulled open the door and dashed down the narrow hall to Jessica's door and pushed it open.

"Jessica, are you all right?" she cried, feeling around for the light switch.

A sleepy, indistinct response came out of the dark.

Karen found the switch that turned on the overhead fixture. It bathed the room in a wash of yellow light.

Jessica sat up in bed, her eyes squinting against the brightness. "Who's there?" she mumbled drowsily.

"It's Karen. I thought I heard you cry out."

Jessica blinked as her eyes tried to focus on Karen's face. "Well, it wasn't me," she said defensively. "I was asleep."

Karen moved to the edge of the bed. "Are you sure? Maybe you were having a bad dream."

Jessica thought for a moment and then shook her head forcefully. "No. I was having a good dream. Daddy was here. We were skiing together."

Karen stared thoughtfully at the child. Why would she lie about such a simple thing? And the answer was that there was no reason for Jessica to lie—Karen must have imagined what she heard.

Karen shrugged. "I guess it must have been the wind playing tricks on my ears."

Jessica nodded sleepily as she lay her head back down on the pillow. "G'night."

"Good night, Jessica. Sleep tight." Karen turned off the light and tiptoed back down the hall to her own room. She turned off the light and slipped back into bed, but lay in the dark, her ears alert for the sound she had heard before. But there was nothing there except the wail of the wind.

The morning dawned bright and clear, one of those special diamond-edged days that turn the winter sky an azure blue and the snow a pristine white, and the disquiet of the day before was gone.

As they drove into the parking lot at Mount Snow, Karen felt that old familiar flutter in the pit of her stomach: it was part excitement, part fear.

The lodge seemed to have been added on to since the last time she was there, and there seemed to be more lifts than she remembered. But the mountain remained the same, a breathtaking rise of white magnificence, crisscrossed with a spiderweb of ski trails.

She stopped the car and got out, turning to gaze up the mountain to the broad white gashes in its side. She could see no darker gray patches against the white—that would be ice, and she hated ice. The only time she had ever injured herself skiing had been on ice. She had fallen and had kept sliding until she was completely turned around and hit herself in the head with her own skis.

Now, as she remembered the incident, she chuckled to herself.

Jessica was busy unloading her gear from the car. "What's so funny?" she asked.

Karen related the story, and they both laughed. "You must have looked pretty silly," Jessica said. "All upside down and tangled up like that."

"At the time I didn't think so," Karen said. "I was glad there was no one around to see me."

"But you were hit on the head," Jessica said. "You could have been knocked unconscious."

Karen shrugged. "All I got out of it was a bump on the head and a headache." She reached up and began undoing the ski rack on top of the car. "Well, enough of this reminiscing—let's get all this stuff unloaded and then we can hit those slopes!"

"You bet!" Jessica agreed enthusiastically.

Jessica's eagerness warmed Karen's heart and made her feel a bit like a child again herself. The two of them were making progress—she was sure of it.

Between the two of them they carried both sets of skis, boots, and poles across the parking lot, bought their lift tickets, and headed for the area outside the sprawling lodge complex. Here, skiers milled about, looking for friends, adjusting their equipment, exchanging information about where the best skiing was that day.

As Karen glanced around, taking in all the skiers in their brilliantly hued parkas, she spotted a man standing with a woman and two small children. He had his back to her, but from twenty feet away he looked just like Randy. The shape of the head, the color of the hair, the tall, slightly stocky build—they were all the way she remembered them.

Karen held her breath, waiting for the man to turn so that she could see his face. It *could* be Randy. They had skied Mount Snow together when they were married, so why shouldn't he come back here with his new wife? And those two children, a boy and a girl—had his second wife been able to give him what she never could?

Then the man turned, laughing, and caught Karen staring at him. He gave her a quick, puzzled look and then turned back to his family. It was not Randy.

Karen let out a long sigh.

"What's the matter?" Jessica piped up.

"Why?" Karen looked blankly at the child.

"You look as if you've seen a ghost," Jessica said, her eyes alertly searching Karen's face.

"Do I?" Karen laughed self-consciously. *God, from now on she'd better watch herself—Jessica didn't miss a thing.* "It was nothing. Somebody I thought I knew—I was mistaken." She shrugged her shoulders, dismissing the entire incident.

But Jessica was not to be put off. "Who was it?" she asked.

Karen looked sharply at her. "You're being rude, Jessica. I thought you knew better than that."

Jessica looked properly chagrined. "Sorry," she mumbled, then bent over her skis, fastening the safety straps.

Karen suddenly regretted her harsh words. Surely Grant had told Jessica that she had been married before, so why should she try to hide anything from the child?

She put her gloved hand on the small of Jessica's back as she straightened up. "I'm sorry I sounded so short-tempered before," she apologized. "I realize you weren't being rude—just curious."

Jessica nodded without looking at her. "That's okay."

Very matter-of-factly, Karen said, "I thought I saw my ex-husband."

Jessica didn't say anything. Her eyes appeared to be riveted on something in the snow under the tips of her skis.

"You knew that I was married before, didn't you?" Karen asked.

Jessica's head bobbed up and down, but she still said nothing, and her eyes remained where they were.

"Well," Karen said, a little too heartily. "What are we standing around here for? Let's get going!"

They took the gondola chairlift to the top of the mountain, and Karen found herself quivering excitedly as they neared the end of the long ride. She was surprised that Jessica, sitting right next to her, did not remark on the tremors that were going through her body.

Every season she was always like this the first time out. Awed by the mountain, and a little afraid of it, too. Afraid that she had forgotten how to master it, afraid that the mountain would break her.

They were at the top. A young, bearded lift operator opened the gondola, and they slipped out, moving quickly out of the large barn where the gondolas were turned around and sent empty back down to the bottom of the mountain.

They slid away from the barn, away from the warming house with skiers loitering nearby, away from the rumble of machinery and the clank of the gondolas into a sheltered trail and a strange, soundless world of white.

"Listen!" Karen cried, coming to a sudden stop.

Jessica drew up beside her. "What is it?"

Karen said breathlessly, "Silence. Absolute silence."

Jessica cocked her head and listened. Then a broad grin spread itself across her face. "It's incredible," she whispered. "I can't hear a thing."

Fresh-fallen snow lay deep and cottony around them, weighing heavily on the trees that protected the trail, absorbing all sound.

Karen and Jessica exchanged a silent, smiling glance and then moved forward again, slowly—as if they were afraid to make a noise and violate this enchanted place.

The trail came out on the top of a wide slope, and

they stopped again, gaping at the sight that lay at their feet.

Spread out below them was a valley embraced by a circle of rolling hills. It was a broad expanse of white, shadowed only by patches of trees looking like gray hatch marks against the glaring purity of the snow.

From where they stood, the valley seemed to stretch all the way to the horizon, where the sky rose above it, a flawless jeweled dome of sapphire blue.

Neither of them spoke, but then as if by a prearranged signal, they both began to ski down the face of the slope. Karen's first turns were wide, sweeping arcs, but as she gained confidence she tightened the turns until she was moving easily and quickly from one into the next.

This was what it was all about, Karen thought joyously. The feeling of freedom, the wind rushing in her face as she flew daringly down the mountain, skis and body moving together effortlessly. She was so carried away that she was only dimly aware of Jessica skiing just off to her side.

Halfway down the slope, Jessica halted, and Karen swished to a stop beside her. "Isn't this great?" Karen cried, her voice ringing out with delight.

Jessica smiled back at her, but behind her dark gray ski goggles it was hard to see if the smile extended to her eyes. "I was watching you ski," she said noncommittally.

Karen chuckled. "I hope I didn't look *too* bad. Remember, it *is* the first day."

"No, you're really good," Jessica said. There was just the tiniest note of envy in her voice.

"Well," Karen said because she knew it was expected of her, "you're not so bad yourself."

"Thanks." Jessica smiled again, and this time the glimmer in her eyes shone through the goggles.

Jessica set off first down the mountain, and Karen

gazed after her almost fondly. She had gotten the distinct impression that her skiing ability had raised her a notch or two in Jessica's estimation. Now, if she could only break down that final wall of reserve surrounding the child . . . perhaps they could really be friends.

Over the next few days they did seem to be getting closer. They fell into a happy routine: skiing all day to a point close to exhaustion, then returning, blissfully weary, to the house, where they both pitched in on the evening meal, and when that was out of the way, they sat in front of the fire until bedtime, sometimes talking idly, sometimes simply sharing the afterglow of the day.

Each night after dinner Grant would call to hear about their day. He was almost finished with his project, but he was taking his time wrapping it up. He was relieved to hear Karen's and Jessica's easy chatter as they described skiing, long walks in the woods, and shared cooking chores. They both sounded eager to have him join them, but for the first time they sounded comfortable with each other. He wanted to give them a little more time alone together.

Maybe everything would straighten out, as he hoped it would. Surprised that Karen said nothing to him about it, he had been startled to learn from Jerry that Karen and Fran had had a falling out. He didn't know what their argument had been about, and Jerry didn't say. But Karen had covered it up fairly well; Grant had never guessed. Something silly, he had assumed. She would patch things up with Fran.

Karen had been on edge because she was so impatient to get pregnant. Perhaps when she gets back from Vermont . . . then they *would* be one happy family.

Karen was sitting by the hearth one night after

Grant's call, gazing dreamily into the crackling fire and nursing a glass of red wine she had left over from dinner. Jessica was in the kitchen, putting away the last of the dinner dishes. "Do you want some more wine?" she called out to Karen.

"Sure," Karen answered languidly. "I guess a little more won't hurt me."

Jessica brought in the bottle and filled Karen's glass. "I don't suppose you'd let me have a little," she said with a sigh.

"Not on your life," Karen laughed. "Your father would kill me if he found out."

"*I* won't tell him."

Karen shook her head. "No, my dear. The answer is still no."

Jessica stuck her lower lip out a fraction of an inch. "Patty gets to drink wine. . . ."

"I don't care," Karen said with finality. "That's another family. In this family your father sets the rules."

Jessica put the bottle down on the coffee table and plopped herself, belly down, onto the hearth rug. "Why do grownups like to drink, anyway?" she asked, leaning on her elbows and staring lazily into the fire.

Karen took a sip of wine before she answered, wondering if this was a reference to her own recent drinking. "Because," she said, "it makes them feel good. It helps them to relax."

"Well, it didn't make my mommy feel good," Jessica argued. "It made her act funny."

"Funny?" Karen echoed, surprised that for the first time Jessica was volunteering information about her mother. "What do you mean 'funny'?"

"Oh, you know. She cried a lot, and she said weird things."

Karen was suddenly very curious. "What kind of weird things?"

Jessica's face was in profile to Karen, and she grew very still for a moment as she gazed into the leaping flames.

"What things?" Karen repeated.

In a faraway voice Jessica said slowly, "She was mean to him. She didn't have any reason to be mean to Daddy."

Karen fell silent for a moment. Did she dare bring up the subject of that final day? Should she let the child know that Grant had told her the truth? Perhaps she should let Jessica decide how much to tell.

Her voice full of sympathy, she asked, "Was your mother ever mean to you?"

Jessica briefly pursed her perfect little cupid's bow mouth. "Sometimes."

Karen knew she was entering on very shaky ground. "She was mean to you that last day, wasn't she?" she said softly.

Jessica seemed not to have heard her. There was no reaction.

Karen hated to repeat the question. She waited. Finally, she said gently, "Jessica?"

"What?" The child turned her head to look straight into Karen's eyes.

"I guess you don't want to talk about that day," Karen said quietly.

There was a momentary flash in Jessica's eyes, and then she turned back to the fire. "It doesn't bother me," she said, her voice betraying no emotion.

What a cool little cookie, Karen thought to herself. They might almost be discussing the weather. But the subject was obviously closed—for Jessica, at least.

CHAPTER EIGHTEEN

The next morning a storm lay brooding far off in the western sky. Karen could see its angry black clouds through the treetops as she parted the curtains and stood, sleepy-eyed, at her window. *Great,* she thought, *more snow.* It would be good for skiing.

She could hear that Jessica was already up and stirring, so she began to get dressed. She was just stepping into the bottom half of her thermal underwear when there was a tentative knock on the door.

"Come on in, Jessica," she called out.

The door opened and Jessica's blond head peeked around it. "Oh, good," she said. "I wasn't sure you were up."

"Well, I'm not awake yet," Karen said with exaggerated weariness. "But I am up."

Jessica smiled and came into the room. She was already dressed for skiing. "I think it's going to snow today," she said. "The sky is really gray and overcast."

"There's a storm coming from the west," Karen said. "You can see it from this window."

Jessica walked to the window and peered out.

"Wow, it looks really bad out there," she said. "Maybe we'll get snowbound." She turned around to face Karen. "Wouldn't that be exciting?"

"That kind of excitement I think I'll pass on," Karen said drily, pulling a cotton turtleneck over her head.

Jessica walked over to the closet. "What are you going to wear today?" she asked. "I'll get it for you."

How sweet Jessica could be at times, Karen thought. "I don't know," she said. "The navy blue, I guess."

Jessica was reaching for the navy blue ski pants and parka, when she seemed to be struck by an idea. "Why don't you wear the turquoise outfit?" she said suddenly. "It looked so nice on you."

Karen shook her head resolutely. "Oh, no, Jessica, I couldn't do that. It wouldn't be right."

"Why not?"

Karen gaped at the child. *"Because,"* she said, wondering why she should even have to explain it to her.

"It's just hanging here going to waste," Jessica persisted. "Why shouldn't you wear it?"

"Well . . . your father wouldn't like it," Karen said uncertainly.

Jessica pulled the turquoise outfit off the hanger. "We don't have to tell Daddy," she said, smiling conspiratorially. She held out the outfit to Karen. "Please wear it—for me." Her blue eyes were fixed on Karen with a poignant, beseeching gaze.

She seemed so insistent that Karen began to waver. Why not? Why shouldn't she wear it? It certainly didn't seem to arouse any bad memories in Jessica.

"All right," Karen said, reaching for the jumpsuit. "I'll wear it—just for today."

Jessica smiled, looking very pleased with herself.

Karen finished dressing, avoiding both Jessica's eyes and her own image in the mirror. She was afraid that she looked just a little too flashy—or worse: that she looked too much like Emily.

But her fears began to subside as they loaded up the car with the ski equipment and set off on the drive to Mount Snow. Her fears were completely gone by the time they arrived at the ski area, replaced by her enthusiasm for skiing.

The top of the mountain was enveloped in a dense gray mist, and few skiers were venturing all the way to the summit. Most of them were taking the shorter lifts, which served the lower slopes.

"Let's take a couple of runs down here," Karen suggested. "Maybe the fog will have lifted by then."

They made several quick runs down what Jessica referred to scornfully as a "baby" slope before she managed to talk Karen into taking the long gondola ride to the top of the mountain.

As they came out of the gondola barn, the mist sat heavily all around them and visibility was shortened to a few feet.

"We'd better go slow for a while," Karen said cautiously. "I can barely see the trail."

"Oh, pooh," Jessica scoffed. "That's no fun. I *like* not being able to see—it's like skiing in a cloud."

"Stick close to me, Jessica—" Karen started to say, but before she finished speaking, the child had taken off, vanishing into the mist.

"Jessica! Where are you?" Karen called out, angrily edging her way slowly down the trail. "Don't play games with me—it's not funny!"

There was no answer as Karen peered through the fog, straining to catch a glimpse of Jessica's blue parka. No sign of her.

It seemed impossible that Jessica had disappeared so completely—and yet she had somehow managed to.

"Damn!" Karen said under her breath. "Where could she have gotten to?" She began to pick up speed, relying on her amber ski goggles to help her discern the terrain—which was coming up much too fast for comfort now.

She hit the top of a small mogul and flew off into space for a few breathless seconds. Landing off-balance on one ski, she managed to bring her other ski down quickly enough to remain upright.

By now, she had no idea where she was, whether she was in the middle or on the edge of the slope. If she was anywhere near the trees at the edge, she could possibly be rushing headlong into disaster.

Suddenly, just up ahead, she could make out a small figure swerving right into her path—and she was going too fast to stop abruptly.

"Jessica!" Karen shouted at the top of her lungs. *"Watch out!"*

But it was too late. Jessica turned—but in the wrong direction. As Karen bore down on her, Jessica stuck out her ski pole in what looked like a gesture of self-defense.

Karen just managed to avoid hitting Jessica directly, but she crashed into the ski pole. It sent her pitching forward in a horrifying somersault of skis and poles and flailing arms and legs. Over and over she went, carrying a swirling cloud of snow with her. At last she came to a stop, barely conscious, the bright turquoise jumpsuit hidden under a clinging layer of snow.

Jessica had been knocked down when Karen hit her pole, and she had lain still as she watched Karen's spectacular fall. Now, she quickly got to her feet and began to sidestep down the slope, making her way to where Karen's crumpled body lay.

"Don't move!" she cried, her voice sounding unnaturally flat in the still, heavy air. "I'm coming—as fast as I can!"

Karen was just beginning to come around when

Jessica reached her. She had lost her goggles in the fall, and snow was sticking to her eyelashes, making her blink rapidly as she tried to open her eyes.

Jessica bent over her, wiping the snow from her face, and Karen stared at her blankly for a moment.

She didn't know where she was—she hurt all over; she couldn't move. In shock it slowly started coming to her: Jessica appearing out of nowhere right in her path, holding her ski pole at such an angle that Karen could not avoid hitting it. . . .

Then Karen's eyes hardened. "You made me fall," she wailed. "You did it intentionally—you tried to hurt me."

Jessica pulled back, her eyes hurt and wary. "No, I didn't," she muttered.

"Yes, you did," Karen said, hysteria rising in her voice. "You tried to hurt me! Get away from me!"

Jessica straightened up. "I'm leaving you now," she said calmly. "I'll see if I can find the ski patrol," she said and skied away, soon lost in large wet drops of snow.

Karen waited frantically, watching anxiously for another skier. But no one came.

Then the ski patrol was there with a toboggan to carry Karen down the mountain. Jessica hovered somewhere in the background, watching them gently lift Karen onto the toboggan and strap her in.

One of the men took Karen's poles and skis, and Jessica moved next to him. "Do you think anything's broken?" she asked uncertainly.

"Is that your mother?" the man asked.

Jessica shook her head. "She's my stepmother."

The man frowned. "Looks like her left leg's broken. It looks bad—but you'll have to wait till you get to the hospital and get her X-rayed before you'll know."

For Karen it was a strange and painful journey

down the mountain as she drifted on the edge of consciousness throughout the toboggan ride. Each bump they hit made her cry out in pain, and she wondered if the men were deliberately taking the roughest route to the bottom. She hurt all over, but the numbness in her left leg seemed to be a special pain. At one point, she deliriously thought that her leg had been chopped off below the knee.

An ambulance had been called and was waiting near the ski patrol facilities, and Karen was quickly transferred to it. Jessica sat in the back with Karen, but all during the ride to the hospital she kept her eyes carefully directed out the window.

The easy efficiency of the ambulance attendants and the familiar motion of the ride began to lull Karen. She realized that she was still in one piece and that the worst thing that had happened to her was probably a broken leg. But she had nearly forgotten about Jessica and didn't even know that the child was there.

Fran was feeling slightly foolish as she rang the bell to Janet's house in Montclair, New Jersey. She and Jerry had often discussed her concern about Karen and Grant seemed oblivious to any serious problem. Nonetheless she was concerned, but had put off until after the holidays this meeting with Janet. This whole thing would probably turn out to be a wild goose chase, *and* none of her business, she was thinking when Janet promptly opened the door.

Janet was wearing a pale blue turtleneck sweater and gray flannel pants. She looked disarmingly like Karen, although a little shorter and at least ten pounds heavier. But the eyes were that same cat's-eye green—only Janet's had a look of contentment that was missing in Karen's. Curiosity was there too. She was very obviously perplexed by the visit from a near stranger.

Containing her questions, Janet led Fran to a sunny, plant-filled room in back. Fran sat down in a wicker chair, and Janet sat opposite her. "I've got a fresh pot of coffee brewing," she said. "It'll be ready in two shakes."

Fran smiled. "Have you talked to Karen lately?" she said without preamble, sensing that Janet was edgy to hear the reason for her visit.

Janet nodded. "Well, I spoke with her before she went away. She told me that she hadn't seen you in a while."

"Yes, well, I'm sure she's probably told you why too," Fran said bluntly. "We had a fight. I said some things that maybe I shouldn't have said but that I felt needed saying, and she took offense."

"She didn't tell me what it was about," Janet said. "But I'm sure whatever it was that you two can patch it up."

"I'm not so sure," Fran said, looking Janet directly in the eye. "I've tried a few times, but she doesn't seem to want to have anything to do with me anymore. I'm really worried about her. That's why I decided to come and see you."

Janet's eyebrows knit together with concern. "What is it? I thought she was really quite happy with Grant."

"Oh, she's happy enough with Grant," Fran said. "But it's Jessica who's proved to be her nemesis. Almost everytime I spoke to Karen about her they'd been disagreeing. The two always seemed pitched for some kind of battle."

A queer, pained expression crossed Janet's face. "She hasn't *done* anything to Jessica, has she?" she asked warily.

"Now why do you say that?" Fran demanded. "Is there some reason why Karen might hurt Jessica?"

Janet chewed at her lip for a second. "I'd better get the coffee," she said, standing up suddenly and walking off toward the kitchen.

Fran was not about to be put off. She followed Janet right into the kitchen. "Janet, *please*," she said. "If you know something please tell me. Surely you know what happened with Grant's first wife—I can't stand by and see anything happen to that family again."

Janet was holding the coffeepot in her hand. She put it down and looked at Fran intensely, as if trying to gauge the depth and sincerity of the other woman's motivations. "Look," she said finally, "you're putting me in the middle of a real dilemma." She leaned against a Formica countertop and gazed out a window at the small brown patch that was their backyard.

Fran picked up the coffeepot and two cups that were sitting on the counter. "Come on," she said. "Let's go back in the other room and have a cup of coffee."

Janet followed her back to the sunporch. Fran poured out coffee for Janet and handed the cup to her and then poured one for herself. "There is something, isn't there?" she said gently to Janet. She hesitated and then said cautiously, "Was it when she was teaching?"

Janet's eyebrows shot up. "How do you know that? I'm sure Karen never told you that."

Fran nodded. "She didn't. I just guessed."

Janet let out a long sigh and put down her coffee cup. "I *told* Karen she shouldn't have hidden this from Grant. But no, she wouldn't listen to me. She never listens to anybody. She's so headstrong—it's got to be *her* way or nothing. Will she ever learn?" she said peevishly.

"You know, if you'd told me that a few months ago," Fran said, "I wouldn't have thought we were talking about the same person. But in the last few weeks I've come to realize that Karen can be quite willful—sometimes even selfish."

Janet stood up abruptly. "I think I heard Melissa," she said, excusing herself.

She was gone for several minutes, during which Fran finished her first cup of coffee and poured herself a second one, wondering how many cups she would drink before she made some sort of sense of her suspicion. If, in fact, she had any right or reason to be suspicious at all.

Then Janet returned, her face set in an expression of maternal repose. "Melissa's gone back to sleep," she said. "Poor little thing, she's so tired. I think she must be coming down with a cold."

Wistfully, Fran said, "I've often wished I had a little girl in addition to my three boys." Then she added, "But of course, Jessica is almost like a daughter to me."

This admission seemed to have hit the mark, for Janet gave her a look full of understanding and compassion. "I see," she said. "You're *really* worried about Jessica, aren't you?"

"That child has been through too much already," Fran said defensively. "And I'm not going to stand idly by and watch anything happen to her again—not if I can help it."

Janet nodded slowly, thoughtfully. "Then I suppose I'd better tell you about Karen," she said, the words pronounced with a heavy resignation.

"I'm sure you know all about Karen's divorce," Janet began. "She would have told you about that—

about Randy and his girl friend and the way he just walked out on her."

"Well, isn't that what happened?" Fran asked.

"Oh, yes. That's the way it happened," Janet said. "But there was more—later. She had a nervous breakdown—that's what my mother called it, anyway—oh, she never had to be institutionalized or anything like that. But she had to be sedated, and I kept her here for a few days." She paused and then took a deep breath and went on: "It happened when she was teaching—substituting for an art teacher at a private school in the city."

Fran wondered which school it was, but she didn't want to interrupt Janet now, so she kept silent.

"Anyway," Janet continued, "the class had been given assignments by their regular teacher to draw portraits of their families and bring them in. Karen was looking them over, and everything was going fine until she came to one little girl who had drawn a picture of a man and what looked like a balloon with arms and legs standing next to him. 'What is this supposed to be?' Karen said, and the girl told her that it was a picture of her mother. 'But you've got her all wrong,' Karen said. 'She has no shape, no form. I'm sure she doesn't look like this.' 'Well, she does *now*,' the girl answered in a kind of snippy tone, 'because she's going to have a baby.' Then the whole class started to giggle, and Karen said later that something just snapped inside her. She never remembered what happened next, but the rest of the children said that she, well, she *attacked* the girl, that she hit her and threw her to the floor and then bent over her with her hands around her neck and—well, by this time all the other kids were screaming and running out into the hall, and this brought out some other teachers, and they managed to pull Karen off the little girl before she could really hurt her.

"Karen was completely hysterical, and the school tried to call Randy to come and get her. But he wouldn't have anything to do with her—can you believe that?—so he suggested they call me. I'd just gotten married myself and moved into this house, so I had to drive all the way in from here to the East Side. By the time I got there they'd had a doctor look at Karen, and he gave her a sedative so she was asleep. The school officials assured me that the little girl was all right, that her parents had come to get her, and that they'd been persuaded not to press charges against Karen. But the officials didn't mince any words in telling me that Karen must see a psychiatrist and have his approval before she'd ever be allowed to teach again. Then they let me take her home."

Janet fell silent and Fran waited a few moments before asking, "Was Karen all right after that? Was it just that one incident?"

"Yes. Like I said, she stayed here, and she was back to her normal self in a few days. Well, as normal as you could be when your husband has just walked out on you and asked for a divorce."

"Did she see a psychiatrist?"

"Yes, of course. She went to one right here in Montclair, but she only went two or three times. I don't think she liked the idea of talking over her problems with a stranger."

"That's unfortunate," Fran said. "He might have really been able to help her."

Janet stiffened slightly. "She didn't need help. I told you, she was fine. It was just a freak thing—her doing that to that little girl. It only happened a couple of days after she got the divorce papers—and it was just the wrong combination of circumstances: her being convinced that Randy left her because she couldn't give him a child; the little girl must have seemed to Karen to be almost taunting her with that picture of her pregnant mother; and then the whole class laughing, making Karen feel like a fool. It's no wonder she cracked—almost anybody would, given the same conditions."

Fran wasn't quite convinced of that, but she didn't say anything to Janet. Of course, Karen had been under a strain when this happened, but that didn't explain everything. Why had Karen attacked the child? Why hadn't she simply dissolved into hysterics or screamed at the child? Why had she done something so physically violent? From the way Janet had described the incident, Karen had been trying to strangle the little girl—she had wanted to *kill* her.

"By the way," Fran said suddenly. "You never mentioned the child's age. How old was she?"

"Ten, I think. Or eleven. It was a fifth-grade class."

Fran felt as if a cold and clammy hand had just slithered down her spine. "That's Jessica's age," she said numbly.

"I know," Janet said. "But I don't think there's anything in that."

"No. You don't understand," Fran protested. "Karen and Jessica are supposed to go to Vermont together—in fact, you said they've already left. They're going to be all alone together for several days—in a house that's miles from the nearest neighbor."

"But I still don't see what you're getting so excited about," Janet said calmly. "Karen would never hurt Jessica. It's mere coincidence that Jessica is the same age as the child Karen attacked."

Fran stood up, preparing to leave. "I hope you're right. But I can't take that chance. Too much has happened to that child already. I've got to tell Grant—he has a right to know that Karen could possibly be dangerous to Jessica."

"I really think you're overreacting," Janet said a

little too forcefully. "Karen is not the homicidal maniac you're making her out to be."

"Then can you explain to me why she hid this from Grant?" Fran asked angrily.

Janet frowned. "I told her not to," she said. "I told her it was wrong."

"Yes, well, it's a shame your sister doesn't have your sense of decency and fair play," Fran said somberly. She picked up her purse. "Thank you for the coffee. I'm sorry our meeting couldn't end happier."

Janet showed her to the door, and they exchanged perfunctory farewells, their eyes looking sadly past each other.

In the car on the way back, driving through the suburban sprawl and then the bleak, industrialized section of New Jersey, Fran worried over how she would break the news about Karen to Grant. Finally, she decided that she would tell Jerry first and then the two of them would talk to Grant. Jerry would be calmer about it than she could be; he would know how to put things so that Grant would not get all worked up.

Oh, God, if anything happens to Jessica, it'll be my fault, Fran cried—*and I'll never forgive myself.*

At the hospital, Karen had been spirited away by the emergency room staff, and Jessica was left alone. She sat listlessly in the waiting room for what seemed like hours until a nurse came out to tell her that Karen's leg was indeed broken.

"Oh," Jessica said dully. "Will she have to stay here?"

The nurse gave her a cheerful smile. "No, dear. As soon as her cast is set she can go home."

Jessica nodded. "That's good."

"Do you have anyone to drive you?" the nurse

asked. "Your stepmother won't be in any condition to drive a car."

Jessica frowned. Their car was still in the parking lot at Mount Snow. Then she remembered the caretaker, Mr. Moffatt. Maybe he'd come and get them.

Mr. Moffatt didn't sound any too pleased when Jessica called and explained the situation to him, but he agreed to come to the hospital and drive them home.

When Karen was released and wheeled to the emergency room exit, she nodded numbly as Jessica introduced Mr. Moffatt and told her that he was going to drive them back to the house. Her eyes met Jessica's only briefly, and then they both quickly looked away.

They stretched Karen across the backseat of Mr. Moffatt's beat-up old Dodge. She was so full of painkillers that she barely said a word during the ride—even though the road to the ski house was twisted and rutted and the shock absorbers on the Dodge were obviously the original set.

"You ladies think you're gonna be all right here all alone?" Mr. Moffatt asked after he had helped Karen inside and had seen her settled on the couch.

Jessica glanced at Karen and then back to the caretaker. "I think so," she said. "But we'll have to call my father. He'll probably have to come up here tomorrow."

"There's a storm comin'," Mr. Moffatt said, the flesh around his bleary gray eyes crinkling into a latticework of wrinkles. "Yep. Could be a big one. Blizzard. S'posed to hit tonight—mebbe tomorra."

Jessica stared at the grizzled old man. "You mean we might get snowed in here?"

Mr. Moffatt thought about this for a moment, digging his hands into his pockets and rocking back on his heels. "Could be," he said. "Depends on how deep it gets 'n how long it takes the plows to get through."

"But we'll be all right here, won't we?" Karen spoke up suddenly, and they both turned to look at her.

Mr. Moffatt shrugged. "S'pose so. Long as someone knows you're here."

"Well, *you* know we're here," Karen said impatiently. "So if we get snowed in, you can just make damn sure that somebody plows us out right away."

"Sure 'nough," Mr. Moffatt said, beginning to edge his way toward the door. "I'll do m'best."

Jessica saw Mr. Moffatt off, and as she stood in the doorway watching the red tail lights of the old Dodge disappear, she could see in the bright circle of the porch light the first few flakes of the storm that Mr. Moffatt had predicted. Surely these innocent-looking snowflakes could not be the blizzard that the old man had talked about.

Jessica stared dreamily out into the night for several more minutes, softly humming a singsong tune, and then she turned out the light. The woods around the house were once again engulfed by blackness, but high above in the sky dim, gray, luminous clouds, pregnant with snow, had already begun to gather. Like secret, silent battalions they grouped, waiting for the command to attack.

CHAPTER NINETEEN

Grant opened the door to Fran and Jerry. "Come on in, you two. Come to keep a lonely man company?" He took their coats and hung them in the closet. "You sounded so mysterious on the phone, Jer, when you said you wanted to come over. What gives?"

Jerry and Fran exchanged a silent glance. "Let's go inside and sit down, Grant," Jerry said. "Fran and I have something to tell you."

Grant gave his friend a dubious look but said nothing as he followed them into the living room. They sat down on the couch, so he sat on the loveseat, looking from one to the other. "Don't tell me you're getting a divorce," he said, meaning it to be a joke—but the words came out flat and unfunny.

Jerry cleared his throat and shifted his eyes away from Grant's. "It's not us, Grant," he said ominously. "It's you."

"Me? What about me?" Grant laughed self-consciously, afraid of the tone he had heard in his friend's voice. "I swear I haven't been tinkering with the books—"

"It's Karen," Jerry broke in. "Fran found out something about her that you ought to know."

Grant looked at Fran. "Well, what is it? Tell me—come on."

Fran shot a glance at Jerry that said, *Thanks a lot for leaving it up to me*. Then she looked back at Grant. "I went to see Janet today. She told me something that I found very frightening," she said melodramatically. "Karen was forced out of teaching because she attacked and nearly killed one of her students—a little girl about Jessica's age."

"What!" Grant gaped at Fran. Then he recovered himself. "Wait a minute. Tell me again, Fran—and this time tell me exactly what Janet said. Don't extrapolate, just give me word for word what Janet said."

Fran repeated what she had heard, and when she was finished, Grant was staring hard-eyed at her. "I thought you were Karen's friend, Fran," he said. "Why are you making it sound as if she were a vicious killer? I can't believe any of that of Karen. Her relationship with Jessica hasn't been completely smooth sailing, but she's never seemed vindictive toward her. And besides, she loves children—she even wants to have a child of her own."

"Her *own*, Grant," Fran said. "That's the operative word. She doesn't want another woman's child—she doesn't want Jessica."

Grant studied their faces: Fran, looking tired and not at all glamorous with her red hair mussed and her violet eyeshadow smudged; Jerry, looking a bit like a bulldog with his chin buried in his thick neck and his top row of teeth stretched over his bottom lip and biting into the skin underneath. It was a demeanor that Grant had known for nearly thirty years and had always recognized as meaning that Jerry was brooding about something.

"Look, you two," Grant said, wondering why they were both so quick to call out the dogs on Karen. "Do you really believe that Jessica is in danger?"

Fran leaned forward, spreading her hands across her knees, palms up. "I don't know, Grant," she said. "But I *am* concerned. The idea of those two being alone up there so far away from civilization—"

"But, my God, they're not *completely* alone," Grant interrupted her. "There's the telephone—I've talked to them every day, and they both seem to be having a good time. They've been skiing every day, surrounded by hundreds of people—it's not as if they've been cooped up in that house in the woods with only each other for company."

Fran looked at Jerry out of the corner of her eye before she looked back at Grant. "Then you're not leaving for Vermont any earlier than you'd planned?"

Grant looked at Jerry. "You know I can't. I've got meetings with two different sets of clients for tomorrow and two more the day after that. I can't leave now. I'll go up in a few days."

"Maybe we could work something out," Jerry suggested. "I might be able to take over a couple of those meetings for you—the others, well, maybe we can farm them out to the staff."

Grant shook his head. "These are not the kind of people who want to work with staff. They expect to be handled by me personally."

Jerry smiled ironically. "You've always got to be indispensable, don't you, Grant? You've never learned to delegate." He seemed to be building up a head of steam as he continued. "As long as I've known you that's how you've been. You take everything on and never ask for help—even when you really need it. Maybe that was one of the problems with Emily—you never let her know you needed her."

After this speech both Grant and Fran were staring

at Jerry. It was unlike him to speak out so vehemently—especially against Grant. Then Jerry shrugged his shoulders and looked from Grant to Fran and then back again. "What's the matter," he said. "Don't you think I have the right to say something like that to you?"

"Sure, Jer," Grant said slowly. "I guess you do if anybody does—only it sounded as if you'd been holding it back a long time, and all of a sudden you couldn't wait to let me have it."

Jerry shrugged, but said nothing.

Grant looked helplessly at Fran. "Am I losing my mind, Fran—or what? First, you come in here and tell me that I may have married—for the second time, no less—a homicidal maniac who might be out to kill my daughter. Then you both seem upset that I don't quite take your news to heart and rush out and get a helicopter or dog team or whatever will get me to Vermont the fastest. Next, my best friend insults me and seems to imply that I'm a cold bastard who doesn't care about other people, and when I call him on it, he sits there and sulks. Would you please explain this to me, Fran? Am I crazy—or are you?"

Fran looked at him for a second and then lowered her eyes. "Jerry and I only have your best interests at heart, Grant," she said. "You must know that." She hesitated for a moment and then stumbled on. "I admit that Karen and I have had a falling out lately, and it has certainly colored my opinion of her—but I'm not out to make trouble in your marriage. I am simply concerned for Jessica because—because Karen may wish that she were out of the way—"

"What are you saying?" Grant asked sharply.

"Oh, Grant," Fran said, sounding apologetic. "I've seen it in her face. I've seen her be all cheerful and even laughing—and then Jessica walks in the room or her name is mentioned, and Karen suddenly looks as if she wanted to spit."

Grant shook his head forcefully. "That's just your imagination working overtime, Fran. I live with the two of them, and I've never seen anything like that."

"That's because you only see what you want to see," Fran insisted. "You want Karen to be fond of Jessica, so that's what you see when you look at the two of them together."

"Maybe," Grant said reluctantly, remembering the times he had argued with Karen over his relationship with Jessica. But he was not about to admit that there might be some problems to either Fran or Jerry.

"Well, all right," Fran said, sensing that her arguments were fruitless. "We'd better go." She nudged Jerry and stood up. Jerry cast a last concerned glance at his friend and then followed his wife to the foyer.

As Grant closed the door behind them, he wondered whether nearly thirty years of friendship had just gone down the drain. He hoped not, but why had Jerry put him in a position like that—forcing him to choose between his wife and his friends? Maybe he'd better leave Jerry alone for a few days, then try and patch things up.

But first of all, he wanted to talk to Karen's sister and find out the truth behind that story that Fran had told him. He went into his study, looked up Janet's number, and dialed, all the while wondering how he could broach the subject in the most tactful way. Maybe he should just mention Fran, see what kind of response that elicited.

Janet's line was busy. He hung up the phone and absentmindedly switched on the small black-and-white TV on the corner of his desk. He turned to a basketball game and watched the Knicks score six quick points before he dialed Janet's number again. It was still busy.

As he glanced back to the game he saw a news bulletin moving across the bottom of the screen. All he caught was the tail end of the report: "Snow warning tonight. Details after the game."

Curious, he dialed the weather information number and listened to a recording predicting that a major winter storm would blanket the Northeast in several inches of snow and would probably strike the New York area sometime during the late evening.

Grant realized quickly that any heavy snowfall might leave Karen and Jessica snowbound and that he'd better check and see if they were prepared.

It took five rings for them to answer the phone. The voice on the other end was Jessica's.

"Hi, kitten," he said easily. "How're things up there in the north woods?"

Jessica did not respond immediately, and when she spoke her voice was curiously subdued. "Something bad has happened, Daddy."

His grip tightened around the receiver. *Was it possible—could Fran have been right? Had Karen hurt Jessica?* "What?" he asked, surprised at the calmness in his voice.

"Karen took a bad fall. She broke her leg."

"What?" It was so unexpected. Something had happened to *Karen*. Now, where did that leave Fran's wild ideas? "Well, how is she? Is she in the hospital—isn't she there with you?"

"She's here. I called Mr. Moffatt and he brought us home."

"Is he still there?"

"No, he left. He said we're going to get a big storm soon—a blizzard. It's started snowing a little bit already." Jessica's voice was vibrant now, full of anticipation—as if she thought the blizzard was going to be great fun.

"Jessica," Grant said chidingly. "A blizzard is no joke. It can be a pretty scary thing. I hope you're prepared because being out where you are you can easily get snowbound. Have you got plenty of food and firewood?"

"Yes, Daddy," Jessica said in that barely tolerant tone of voice that children use whenever their parents don't give them enough credit for being able to behave sensibly. "Don't worry about us."

Then Grant heard Karen's voice in the background, calling to Jessica.

"Daddy, Karen wants to talk to you," Jessica said. "I've got to help her get to the phone. She can't walk very well by herself."

The telephone was on a wall in the dining room right next to the kitchen, and as Grant waited he could hear the sound of Karen's cast slowly thumping across the bare floorboards of the dining room. When Karen picked up the phone, she was breathing heavily. "Hello," she said, and then immediately, "are you coming up?"

Grant heard a queer sort of desperation in her voice. It puzzled him. "Are you all right?" he asked, wondering if perhaps there was more to her injuries than Jessica had said.

"Yes, yes," she said impatiently. "I'm as well as can be expected. I'm a little dopey though—the hospital gave me some painkillers." Then her voice dropped a register. "Oh, God, Grant—please come up here," she said. "Come up as fast as you can."

"Karen, what is it?" Grant said. "What's wrong?"

She started to cry. "I want you here," she sobbed. "Please—if you hurry, you'll miss the storm. *Please.*" Then she broke down.

It occurred to Grant that Karen must still be in a

state of shock from her accident. That would account for her hysterical behavior. "Karen, calm down," he said. "I'll do my best to get there as soon as possible. That's all I can promise because I don't know what the weather's going to be like. Now, put Jessica back on the phone."

He heard rustlings and Karen's voice moving away, and then Jessica came back on the line. "Yes, Daddy?" she said.

"What's the matter with Karen?" he asked.

Jessica must have cupped her hand around the mouthpiece because her voice came out low and muffled. "I don't know, Daddy," she said. "But she's been acting kind of weird."

"Was this before or after her fall?"

"Oh, after."

"Then it must be shock. You'd better take care of her. Make sure she stays warm, and try to keep her still."

"Well, I'll try. Only . . ."

"Only what?"

"Well, I don't think she *wants* me to help her."

"Why not?"

There was a moment's hesitation. "She's mad at me."

"Why? What did you do?"

"I didn't *do* anything, Daddy," Jessica said somewhat heatedly. "But she *thinks* I did—she said I made her fall."

A thrill of fright flickered in Grant's stomach. What if there *was* something to Fran's warnings about Karen? "How *did* she fall?" he asked, wanting to know the facts, hoping desperately that they would prove Fran wrong.

"It was foggy, and she was going too fast and almost ran me down. I tried to get out of her way, but she hit my pole and then she just went flying through the air. And when I went over to help her up, she just started yelling at me."

"Well, how is she now?" Grant asked.

"She keeps giving me these funny looks—like she's watching me and waiting for something to happen."

Fear took hold of him. Karen was obviously in a very precarious emotional state, and it was equally obvious that Jessica was the object of her hostilities. But what could he do to protect Jessica—without frightening her needlessly?

"Jessica, listen to me," he said calmly. "Karen is not herself. Her accident and the painkillers have made her behave strangely. She doesn't know what she's saying or doing, so you must not take her seriously. But whatever you do, don't make her mad. Do you understand me?"

"Yes, Daddy. You want me to humor her, is that it?"

Grant couldn't help but smile at the deadpan gravity of Jessica's reply. "You've hit the nail on the head, kitten," he said. "Humor her. Go along with anything she says—but don't let her get worked up. Now, where is she going to sleep tonight?"

"On the couch. She would never make it up the stairs."

"Good."

"Good?" Jessica repeated. "Why is that good, Daddy? You sound as if you're glad that Karen broke her leg."

"Do I? Well, I'm not. I know it must be very painful for her, and I'm worried about her—she seems distraught. But I don't want her taking this out on you."

"Well, she has already—"

"I know, I know—but she doesn't know what she's doing, so you're the one who has to remain calm and rational—no matter what she does. Can you do that?"

"Uh-huh."

"That's my girl. Now, I'm going to get up there just as soon as I can—"

"Why don't you rent a plane and fly up, Daddy? That way you could be here soon—"

"I might try and do that, kitten. But I have a feeling that this storm is going to ground most light planes. I'll probably have to get something with four-wheel drive."

"Gee, that sounds like fun."

Grant laughed. "Maybe. I doubt that though. I've driven through blizzards before, and I wouldn't call it a barrel of laughs."

"Then you'd better drive carefully."

"I will, sweetheart," he promised. "But I'd better get off the phone so I can get started. I have a feeling it's going to be a long night."

Karen watched and listened as Jessica talked on the phone to her father. The child was speaking in a low, subdued tone, so Karen couldn't catch every word, but she was able to gather that their main topic of conversation was the impending storm.

"Daddy says he's going to leave right away," Jessica reported when she hung up. "He's worried that we're going to get snowed in."

Karen shuddered involuntarily. She could not imagine anything much worse than being snowbound with Jessica—alone.

"I hope it snows ten feet deep," Jessica said blithely. "I'd love to get snowed in." Then she added quickly, "After Daddy gets here, of course."

Karen said nothing, but her eyes were riveted to the child's face, studying her, noting every expression, analyzing every nuance of every word, every look.

Jessica seemed oblivious to Karen's scrutiny. She sat down in a chair near the hearth and turned her face toward the fire and began humming again. She seemed almost hypnotized by the flickering glow as she stared, unblinking, into the flames. Outside, the wind began to pick up, and an occasional gust down the chimney set the fire roaring and sparking, its bright tongues flattened by the force of the wind.

But Karen never took her eyes off Jessica. She was waiting . . . waiting for the sign that would tell her she was right. For she was convinced that this afternoon she had seen the truth. In that brief second before she fell, she was sure that Jessica had purposely put her ski pole out in front of her. That meant that Jessica had deliberately attempted to hurt her—or worse.

Even as the painkillers deadened the feeling in her body, they seemed to be making her mind more lucid. For she could see it all now: how Jessica had hated her all along but had bided her time, waiting for the perfect moment to strike. Having her wear the turquoise jumpsuit must have somehow been part of Jessica's plan, too—making Karen even more like the mother who Jessica had hated. Yes, there was something there and—*my God!*—was there more? Could others have fallen victim to Jessica's evilness?

No, it wasn't possible, Karen argued with herself, her sense of morality rebelling at the possibility that such evil could exist at all, let alone in one so young. An eight-year-old child simply wasn't capable of committing cold-blooded murder.

And why not? the cynic in her countered. Little children could be exceptionally cruel; was it such a large step from cruelty to murder? And Jessica was certainly smarter and cleverer than most children; why shouldn't she be capable of plotting the deaths of her mother and sister—and carrying them out? After all, she had tried to kill Karen, a healthy, strong adult. How much simpler it would be to kill a drunken, sickly woman and a tiny, helpless baby. And most undeniably, wouldn't it be easy for her to get away with their murders since no one, least of all Grant, would dream of questioning her innocence?

Karen gazed at Jessica's angelic face, profiled against the firelight. Was that the face of a murderer?

She had to know. At last she would get the truth from Jessica.

"Jessica," Karen began, her voice studiously soft and tempered, her words jumbled from the medication. "Do you remember the day your mother died? Do you remember what happened?"

The humming stopped abruptly, but it took Jessica several moments to turn to look at Karen. When she did, her face was a small battlefield of conflicting emotions: shock, fear, suspicion. "Why . . . why do you want to know about that?" she said, faltering for just a moment before she recovered her composure.

Karen took a deep breath. "Because," she said, unable to stop her questions, "I know the truth—I know that you killed your mother."

"Who told you that?" Jessica's eyes were like tiny bits of steel, hard and accusing.

"Your father." Karen couldn't resist a tiny note of triumph in her voice.

"Oh." Jessica looked back toward the fire. "I didn't think he'd ever tell anybody," she said ruefully.

Of course not. That was your secret, your guilty hold on him, Karen thought to herself. Out loud she said, "I'd like to hear it from you."

Jessica looked at her blankly. "What?"

"What happened that day," Karen said. "The whole story."

Jessica's hands twisted in her lap. "I don't remember it very well."

Karen stared remorselessly at the child. "I think you do," she said. "I think you remember it a lot better than you let on to your father."

Jessica looked beseechingly at the fire—as if it offered sanctuary from Karen's relentless questions. "I don't remember," she mumbled. "I really don't."

Karen let several seconds go by with nothing but the sound of the fire in the room. Then in a voice that was chilling in its lack of emotion, she said softly, "You're lying."

Anger flashed briefly in Jessica's eyes, but she said nothing and continued to stare stubbornly into the fire.

Now Karen was ready for the attack. "You fought with her, didn't you?" she prodded.

No reaction.

"You told your father she tried to kill you—"

"She *did!*" Jessica burst out.

Karen ignored this. "You told him that you didn't know how the knife wound up in her chest—isn't that right?"

Jessica nodded sullenly. "She fell on it."

"Perhaps she did," Karen conceded. Then she paused before adding in a voice heavy with innuendo, "But I think she had help."

Jessica's eyes flickered, and she suddenly seemed to draw into herself.

Karen, seeing that she had struck a nerve, moved in for the coup de grace. "You *meant* to kill her, didn't you?" she said, biting off each word as if it were a weapon to hurl at Jessica.

The muscles in Jessica's face went slack, and for several seconds she appeared to go into a trance. Then she shuddered. "No," she said, shaking her head violently. "No, I didn't!"

"You killed the baby too, didn't you?" Karen taunted. "It wasn't your mother. It was *you!*"

Her hands over her ears, Jessica screamed, "Stop it! Stop it!"

Karen struggled to get up off the couch. "I won't

stop it," she said, her voice rising self-righteously. "You're the one who ought to be stopped—because you're *evil*!"

Jessica lurched to her feet. "I hate you!" she shouted, her whole body quivering. "I hate you! I hate you! You're mean! I wish Daddy had never married you!"

"I know that," Karen said, laughing spitefully. "I've known that from the beginning. That's why you tried to kill me today, isn't it?"

"I didn't!" Jessica cried; then she took a step toward Karen, her hands clenched into taut-fingered claws, her eyes glinting with a feral intensity. "I'm going to tell Daddy what you said," she snarled.

"You just do that," Karen said mockingly. "I think it's time your father heard the truth about his darling daughter—the little murderer."

Something seemed to break inside Jessica at that moment. Her hands went limp; her eyes stared unseeing at Karen. Then she whirled and fled across the living room toward the stairs.

Karen listened to her retreating footfalls and then fell back on the couch, spent.

But it was worth it; she had discovered the truth, and now she would use it to destroy that vicious little monster—all that remained was to tell Grant. He would be here by morning, and then it would all be over. She would have Grant to herself—and then they would be happy.

Now, Karen thought rather apprehensively, all she had to do was make it through the night.

CHAPTER TWENTY

Karen propped herself up on the cushions of the couch, determined to stay awake. It was much too dangerous to fall asleep with that little murderer upstairs, she grimly told herself. But after an hour or so her eyelids began to droop, and then her head began to nod; yet still she managed to shake herself awake. *Sleep means death, sleep means death,* she repeated to herself again and again, not really believing it but trying to shock herself into wakefulness—but even those words took on a hypnotic rhythm after a while. And then the combination of the painkillers and her emotional and physical exhaustion worked against her, and sometime toward midnight she fell asleep.

A loud crash awakened her several hours later, and she sat up, totally disoriented. She had left the lights on and a fire going, but now the house was in utter darkness with what sounded like a full-scale battle going on outside.

The storm had hit with its full fury while she was asleep, and now the raging winds buffeted the house, battering against the wooden walls, rattling the windows, sending shrieks and war whoops down the chimney.

Wide awake and reassured that she was alone in the room, Karen shivered and sent a glance in the direction of the fireplace. She thought she could make out a faint glow of embers where the fire should have been. If she could rebuild the fire, she could at least have heat and a little light. The crash that had awakened her had most likely been a tree falling and knocking the power out—which must be the reason there were no lights.

All the same, she reached over and flicked the switch on the nearest lamp. Nothing. She tried to remember if she'd seen a flashlight anywhere in the house—or candles, anything that would help her see in this stifling blackness.

She swung her broken leg off the couch, and the cast hit the floor with a dull thud. A brief wave of pain traveled up her leg, but she shook it off and swung her good leg onto the floor. Getting to her feet proved to be a tricky bit of balancing on her right leg and pushing herself up from the couch at the same time. Once upright, she waited a moment, catching her breath and trying to get her bearings.

Just then the howling wind died down for a few brief seconds, and she heard a sound that chilled her. It was practically inaudible, but so pathetic—like a newborn baby's whimpering cry—that she hoped it was only the wind skittering past a corner of the house. Then she heard it again.

It was coming from upstairs.

"No. Damn it, no," she swore to herself. "I'm not going up there. It's a trick—she's playing a trick on me."

But what if it wasn't a trick? What if the crash she had heard before had been a tree hitting the house.

What if it had come through the roof, crushing Jessica in her bed, leaving her barely alive?

Then let her die—and justice will be done, Karen thought bitterly.

But if Jessica were injured, and Karen let her lie up there and perhaps bleed to death, Grant would never forgive her. And then he would surely never believe her story about what Jessica had tried to do to her—and what she had succeeded in doing to her mother and sister. Jessica's death might turn Grant against her.

Karen stood there for several more minutes, wrestling with her thoughts. Then she heard the sound again—a little weaker this time, a little more anguished.

Listening intently for the sound, she stretched her arms out in front of her, feeling in the darkness for any obstacles. She took a couple of tentative steps forward—and promptly crashed into the coffee table.

Cursing loudly, she reached down and felt around until she could discern the dimensions of the table, and then sidestepped around it.

Slowly and awkwardly, she felt her way across the rest of the room, heading for where she estimated the door to the stairs should be. She missed it and had to run her hands along the wall before she found the open doorway.

The moment she stepped into the doorway she felt a chilly draft rush past her as if a window or door were open upstairs. She shivered—partially from the cold, partially from fear.

If it was possible, it was even darker in the stairwell than it had been in the living room. The dark here seemed thicker, more ominous. Karen peered blindly into the blackness above her, wondering what was waiting for her at the top of the stairs. The cold air continued to stream past her, and a chilling image popped into her mind: it was like the icy wind from an angel's wings in the doorway of Hell.

Stop it! she told herself angrily. *You're acting like a little child—afraid of the dark.* Whatever was up there, she could certainly handle it. Jessica couldn't hurt her—she knew the truth about Jessica.

She reached out for the handrail and found it, its smooth wooden surface providing her with the reassurance of something solid and familiar. She used the rail for support while she carefully lifted the heavy cast on her left leg and brought it down on the first step. That much seemed easy. But then she had to lean heavily on the handrail, balance herself on the cast, and hop up one step with the good leg. *God, did she really think she could make it all the way to the top this way?*

She started the long, laborious process again. Second step. She lifted the cast too high, and it hit the step with a painful bounce, and she winced. *Oh, God, don't do that again!* Third step. Maybe the trick was to build up a rhythm—sort of lift, swing, hop; lift, swing, hop. No, that wouldn't work—she couldn't keep it up.

Karen was so intent on climbing the stairs that she forgot to listen for more sounds. Not that she could have heard them anyway, for the clamor of the storm was now coupled with the puffs and pants of her own heavy breathing.

By the fourth step she had begun to sweat, making her grasp on the handrail slippery. She paused, wiping her hands on the flannel nightgown Jessica had helped her change into earlier. *Jessica—maybe she was dead.* The thought was like a spur to Karen.

Fifth step. It was getting harder, not easier—there was no way she could make it to the top. Sixth step. How many steps were there—was she even halfway yet? Seventh step. Her hands were wet again, and her arms were shaking from the exertion—time to stop and rest for a minute.

The storm was roaring outside again, and in the closeness of the stairwell the wind sounded like an artillery barrage as it assaulted the house again and again, causing the wooden walls to groan and protest in agony.

Karen suddenly realized with a sinking feeling that Grant would not be there by morning—not in this weather, anyway. In fact, in all probability, he had not been able to get out of New York.

She didn't hear any more noise from the blackened second floor, and feeling more alone than before, she stared anxiously up into the dark. She was a fool for climbing the stairs. She could be walking right into a trap.

But what could she do now? Turn around and hobble back down the stairs? No, she had come this far; she was almost there. She owed it to Grant to continue on the rest of the way. Grant would want her to do this—he loved his daughter; he didn't even suspect what Karen had found out about her.

She began to climb again. Eighth step, ninth, then tenth. Suddenly she ran out of handrail—she must be at the top. She stretched out her arms in front of her, completely disoriented without the handrail to guide her. She edged forward, inches at a time, terrified that she might fall and tumble down the stairs.

The sweat that she had worked up was turning to a cold, damp film all over her body, and she began to shiver in the draft that continued to sweep past her.

Suddenly she stopped, the skin at the back of her neck prickling. There was *something* there, although her grasping hands touched nothing but air. Yet she *knew*, she could sense it—she was not alone.

"Jessica?" She could barely get the words out of her dry mouth. "Are you here?"

The only response was the wail of the wind.

"I know you're here, Jessica!" Karen shouted suddenly, panic raising her voice to a shrill pitch. "Answer me!"

There was a low, muffled sound nearby—wasn't there? It seemed to come from just in front of her—no, to the right. Or was it to the left? It sounded like someone laughing—yes, a *child* laughing.

"Stop that!" Karen screamed. "Stop laughing at me!" She balled up her hand into a fist and swung her arm in a wide, reckless arc. Then she was off-balance and falling backward, her hands clutching at air.

She felt her head strike something hard, and then she saw brilliant streaks and points of light. Then they were gone, and she sank into a cloud of inky blackness.

Grant drove through the night, the snow swirling wildly about him. Sometimes visibility dropped to only a couple of yards or so in front of his headlights, and he would have to reduce his speed to a maddeningly slow ten or even five miles per hour. But for the most part he could see several hundred feet down the road, and he could keep up a fairly steady speed of twenty or thirty miles per hour.

He had managed to talk one of his clients, an auto dealer, into lending him a four-wheel-drive Blazer by telling him that it was a matter of life and death that he get to Vermont tonight. When he handed over the keys, the man had looked at him as if he were crazy. "Don't worry," Grant had promised. "If anything happens to it, I'll pay you the full market value for the Blazer."

The man had shrugged. "Then just make sure that nothing happens to you so that you're around to pay it."

He had meant it as a joke, and Grant had laughed

then, but in the last few hours he had wondered many times if he would survive this night. He had seen one really bad accident with several cars piled up on the southbound side of the road, and he had seen a number of cars stuck in deep drifts at the side of the road, where they'd skidded and been abandoned. Whenever he could tune in a radio station, he heard repeated warnings to drivers to stay off the highways, and he realized that what he was doing was madness.

Still, he kept going, driven by a fear greater than the one he faced out here alone. It was a fear he tried not to think about as he hunched over the steering wheel, peering intently into the white blur up ahead. But nevertheless, his thoughts kept returning to it.

He hadn't been able to get hold of Janet, and he couldn't believe Fran's character assassination of Karen, but what he had heard from Jessica had been enough to convince him that at least part of what Fran had said had been true: Karen resented Jessica. Perhaps it was even more than resentment—perhaps it was outright hatred. But that didn't mean that she would deliberately hurt Jessica—did it?

He remembered vividly Karen's harsh words from their last, bitter fight. She had called his relationship with Jessica "sick." He had wanted to slap her then, to wipe that sneering accusation off her face—but it wasn't in him to hit her, so he had yelled at her to shut up. And then he remembered with biting clarity what she had done next: in an overly dramatic way that he attributed to the drinks she'd had, she narrowed her lips and put her finger to her lips, whispering for him to be quiet. Then he had watched and listened in horror as she had pointed to the door and said, still in the same overwrought whisper, that Jessica was outside the door, listening to them.

It had horrified him because it was as if he were

seeing and hearing a remake of a scene he had played so many times with Emily.

Again and again when he had been in the middle of an argument with Emily—usually about her drinking—she had gotten that same peculiar expression on her face that Karen had had that night. It was as if the two of them had the same kind of sensory systems that they imagined enabled them to see and hear what he could not.

Why should two such different women share the same delusions? Why should they both fall into the same destructive behavior pattern? It could not be a coincidence—there had to be a reason. Was *he* that reason?

What was there about him? Was there something in him that attracted violent women? Or—even worse— did he do something to make them what they were? And why—why did he have this effect on the women he loved?

His hands were gripping the steering wheel so tightly that his gloves were becoming damp with perspiration. He jerked them off, and the molded plastic of the steering wheel felt cool against his clammy hands. It was surprisingly reassuring, reminding him that, at the wheel at least, he was in control.

But he was not in control of his emotions—no, not now. They were too confusing, too mixed up with the past and the present. Part of his fear came from not being able to distinguish between Karen and Emily; he could no longer separate his feelings for Karen from his feelings for Emily.

He had loved Emily—she had been the first woman he had ever loved—but after her death he had hated her more than he had thought he was capable of hating another human being. Now, the hatred had quieted and had been replaced by a kind of embittered pity. But the strongest emotion he still felt whenever he thought of her was guilt. He knew that would never go away. Because he would never know if he had driven Emily to take such final, desperate measures.

But that was the past. Now, he was married to Karen and he loved her. She had rescued him from a life of insular devotion to Jessica and his work and of forgetting that he was a man. But she had brought another set of problems with her, foremost among them her attitude toward Jessica.

He had known from the first that there was a tension between them; the polite, forced smiles that they wore didn't disguise the antagonistic glints in their eyes.

But how intense was Karen's antipathy toward Jessica? Could it take possession of her, hurtling her into some irrational act—*like Emily?*

Don't even think that! Karen was not Emily—he had to stop confusing them. It did no good for him to keep up this wild speculation; he would be much better off concentrating on driving.

His hands were clammy again, and one by one he wiped them on his pants legs and tried not to think as he drove on through the night.

When Karen opened her eyes, she was surprised that she could see. Not that she could see much, everything was gray and murky, but there was enough light to see that she was lying at the bottom of the stairwell.

The wind had gone and in its place was an eerie silence.

Karen slowly lifted her head, listening for a sound to break the unnatural quiet. But there was nothing, no wind, no stirring—either outside the house or in.

The silence seemed deafening, and for a moment she wondered whether she had lost her hearing. Then she heard the welcome pounding of her own heart and the raspy intake of her breath.

She had fallen down the stairs. Had she broken anything—her other leg or an arm?

Cautiously, she tried moving her arms, then one by one, her legs. Amazingly, everything seemed to function, and—although she was stiff and sore—she felt no pain, outside of a crushing headache.

Then she remembered: Jessica must have been waiting for her at the top of the stairs, hidden by the darkness, hoping that with one final push she could finish off what she had started earlier in the day on the ski slope.

But she had failed, Karen thought spitefully. *I'm alive.*

Yet she was still not safe—not so long as she was alone in the house with Jessica. She was helpless here, too easily trapped.

She had to get away. She had to get out of the house. Quickly—before Jessica realized she was gone.

Fighting dizziness and a sudden wave of nausea, she raised herself to her elbows, then to a sitting position. The real struggle was getting to her feet, but she made it, breathing heavily and leaning against the wall for support.

She clumped across to the hall closet, put on the first parka she grabbed, a hat, gloves, and a single boot for her right foot. Then she headed for the front door.

The door was stuck, and she had to wrench it open. Then, closing it behind her, she was struck by a vision of a transformed world.

Ice, like polished Irish crystal, crusted the trees; graceful, sculpted snowdrifts blanketed the driveway and threatened to engulf the house; the sky was a serene and incandescent blue with a warm, benevolent sun shining in it.

Karen stepped out into this unearthly, magic realm, forgetting for the moment why she was there and gazing around in wonder.

Then, as her feet crunched through more than a foot of snow down to the surface of the front porch, she realized that this beauty was nothing. She didn't know where Jessica was hiding, watching her. Karen had been too kind, too generous toward Jessica—all for Grant. But her broken leg made her helpless; she had to ignore everyone, everything else. Now she was desperately alone, and she had to get away.

Get away from the house, get away from Jessica. She stepped off the porch with her right foot, and it went sinking deep into the snow, practically up to her knee. But she stayed upright and dragged the cast up behind her. *So far, so good.* Then she had to shift her weight onto the left leg to free her right foot, and she immediately fell down. The snow was soft and fluffy, and it would have been so easy to just let herself sink back and stay there and let Jessica find her. *But no.* She wasn't going to let herself give in to that feeling. She had to pick herself up. She had to go on. She had to get as far away as possible from Jessica.

She struggled to her feet, battling dizziness and nausea, and took another step forward and then another, and kept it up until she was nearly to the edge of the road. Each step was a struggle, and she was drenched in sweat, *but she was going to make it. She was going to get away.* . . .

Flopping herself down against a snowdrift, she stopped to catch her breath, closing her eyes on the brilliance of the sun and the snow. The second she shut her eyes colors flashed, and a wave of dizziness swept over her as her equilibrium seemed to go off at a crazy tilt. Something was wrong with her head, but whatever it was she must fight it, she must keep going.

Slowly, she opened her eyes and looked back toward the house. To her horror, she saw the front door open. Jessica stepped out, carrying a pair of cross-country skis.

Karen froze for a second, blinking furiously, hoping that the sight of Jessica was only a mirage created by the sun glinting off the blinding white surface of the snow.

But no, Jessica was quite real. She quickly and deftly strapped the skis to her feet and then began gliding and poling her way across the drifts toward Karen.

With her blond hair streaming across her shoulders and the white light shimmering all around her, she looked like a young Valkyrie, Karen thought in a wild flight of fantasy as she watched Jessica, almost hypnotized by the easy, synchronized motion of her arms and legs. Then with a shock Karen remembered that in Norse legend Valkyries were the arbiters of death—death—exactly what Jessica was planning for her.

For another second Karen sat, immobilized; then adrenaline surged through her, and she began to thrash around in the snow, struggling to get to her feet. But the more she struggled, the deeper she sank.

And all the while Jessica was coming closer.

Karen started to whimper, her floundering getting her nowhere. She pulled herself into a crouch and tried to crawl, dragging herself along by her arms.

Jessica was now only a few feet away. She stopped.

"Don't you come any closer," Karen shouted at her. "You're not going to kill me like you killed your mother!" Suddenly, the snow collapsed, trapping her in a powdery, shallow pit.

Jessica's face tightened as she heard Karen's words, but she was squinting against the brightness of the sun on the snow, and it was impossible for Karen to read her eyes.

Karen lay in the pit for several long moments, staring up at Jessica, waiting to see what she would do next. Then when Jessica began to edge forward again, Karen started clawing at the snow around her, grasping for a handhold, a way of pulling herself out of this hollow that might become her grave.

Jessica's face was expressionless as she watched Karen's pitiful attempts to free herself, and all the while she was moving closer and closer.

When she was only a yard or so away, Karen began to shout wildly at her, "Get away! Get away from me!"

It was then that Jessica stopped and in a methodical, almost leisurely way began to disengage her hands from the wriststraps of her ski poles. Her mouth was set in a grim, determined line as she gazed down at Karen, who was lying virtually helpless at her feet. To Karen, it seemed that Jessica was cruelly savoring this final moment of her victory. Then, ever so slowly and deliberately, Jessica picked up one ski pole and extended it, tip first, toward Karen.

Jessica was going to stab her! "No!" Karen, screaming hysterically, thrust out her arms to ward off the deathblow. Then, mercifully, she blacked out.

CHAPTER TWENTY-ONE

So this is death, Karen thought dreamily. White lights and gentle, loving voices whispering in your ear.

One of those voices even sounded just like Grant—how amazing.

"Karen, darling," it said again. "Can you hear me?"

What a strange question. Of course, she could hear him.

The voice went away, spoke to someone else. Then it came back again. "Darling, please," it begged. "Try to open your eyes."

No, she didn't want to do that. It was much too peaceful here.

"Karen, you've got to wake up," the voice insisted.

Then it seemed to move closer and became soft and halting. "I don't know if you can hear me, but there are some things I've got to say to you." It started to talk about Fran and her being all wrong about something—which made no sense at all to Karen. Then the voice said miserably, "You've got to forgive me that I even doubted you for an instant." Again, Karen was puzzled. What was there to forgive?

"I don't want to lose you," the voice went on, "especially not now. There's too much for you to live for."

Was there? Karen wondered. Was it enough to make her want to leave this wonderful nothingness?

"Please," the voice begged. "Come back to me. I love you."

It sounded so sincere, so desperate, so *needful*—the words were not at all like Grant, but the voice . . . could it be? . . . it had to be . . . she *wanted* it to be Grant.

Karen cracked open her eyes. Yes, there was Grant, his face close to hers, his eyes worried and watchful.

"You're awake," he said eagerly. "Thank God." Then to someone else: "Doctor! She's come to."

Karen focused slowly on Grant. Then she saw another, strange face bending over her.

"Who're you?" she asked groggily.

"That's Dr. Kemper," Grant explained. "He's been taking care of you ever since they brought you in."

In? Karen looked from Grant to Dr. Kemper, then back again. "Where am I?"

"In the hospital, silly." Grant laughed, relieved that Karen was finally conscious.

Karen thought slowly, her mind just beginning to focus on something—what was it? She didn't remember coming to the hospital. The last thing she remembered was . . . *oh, my God!* "Jessica," she murmured, her thoughts clear.

"What about Jessica?" Grant asked.

Karen wondered why he was so calm. Surely he knew what Jessica had tried to do to her. "Where is she?" Karen asked, fearfully, still seeing Jessica coming at her with the ski pole.

"She's just outside," Grant said. Then he added, "You know, you really owe Jessica an enormous debt of gratitude."

Karen stared incredulously at him. "Why?" she

asked, suspicion crowding into her voice, causing it to crack.

"Because she probably saved your life," Grant said. Then a broad smile worked its way across his face. "I can't tell you how proud I am of her."

Karen closed her eyes, wishing she could retreat back into the quiet, drifting never-never land where she had been before. Out here, everything was too confusing.

"Karen, what's wrong?" Grant asked.

She opened her eyes again and looked past him. "Jessica saved my life?"

Dr. Kemper cleared his throat. "Well, I'll leave you two alone now," he said. "Got to get back to the rest of my patients. Glad to have you back with us, Mrs. Cameron."

When he was gone, Grant sat down on the edge of the bed and picked up Karen's hand in both of his own. "Sweetheart," he said, tenderly kissing her hand. "You gave us a bad scare. You've been unconscious for hours."

Karen blinked at him. "What time is it?"

Grant consulted his watch. "A little past four."

"What?" Karen tried to lift her head off the pillow. "It can't be."

Grant placed his hands on her shoulders, gently forcing her back to the pillow. "You shouldn't do that," he said. "You've got a bad concussion."

"Concussion?" Karen repeated dully. "You mean I haven't been . . . stabbed?"

Grant stared at her in puzzlement. "What makes you think you were stabbed?"

"I don't know," Karen said vaguely. "The ski pole . . . the point was coming at me. . . ."

"What are you talking about?" Grant said, gaping at her as if she were speaking another language.

Karen shifted her gaze away from his. "I'm not

sure," she said. Something was wrong. Grant's reactions were off with what she remembered. He had said that Jessica had saved her life, so it was apparent that he didn't know Jessica had tried to kill her. "Maybe it was something I dreamed when I was unconscious," she said in confusion, groping to make sense of Grant's words.

Grant nodded. "Dr. Kemper told me you were delirious when they brought you in."

"Did I say anything?"

"Nothing that made sense, he said. But he wasn't paying a lot of attention to that—he was too busy trying to find out what was wrong with you."

"What did he find?"

"The concussion, shock, quite a few bruises—but you probably got most of those when you broke your leg."

"I must have gotten some when I fell down the stairs, too," Karen said.

"What?" Grant's eyebrows arched quizzically.

"Last night—during the storm. When the lights were out."

"What were you doing on the stairs?" Grant asked; then he shook his head. "No, don't tell me. You were going up to check on Jessica, weren't you?"

Before she could explain, Grant continued speaking. "Well," he said, "that explains where you got the concussion."

"But—but didn't Jessica tell you that she—that I fell down the stairs?" Karen asked, befuddled. Naturally, Jessica's version of the story would be that Karen had simply fallen because of her clumsiness with the cast.

Grant looked blank. "She didn't mention it—I don't think she knows."

"Well, what *did* she tell you?" Karen cried out in exasperation.

Grant gave her a curious look, then said briefly: "She found you out in the snow, away from the house. You were acting very strange, yelling at her, and then you passed out. She tried to revive you, but you didn't respond. So she went back to the house, got the sled—she'd tried to phone for help, but the lines were down—and put you on the sled, bundled you up with blankets, and pulled the sled behind her on her cross-country skis until she got to the main road and found a snowplow crew. They radioed for an ambulance, and it brought you to the hospital. I only got here myself a few hours ago—it took me all night to make the drive."

Grant's words made no sense to Karen. Why should Jessica save her life? Especially when she had tried to kill Karen *twice* only a few hours earlier?

Or had she? *Was* it possible that both falls had been accidents? That Karen—out of her resentment for the child—had simply *imagined* that Jessica had tried to kill her?

Karen wracked her brain, trying to remember both falls. She could see the skiing accident again: it was foggy and she had been going too fast and Jessica seemed to appear out of nowhere. But had she thrust out her ski pole deliberately, as Karen had originally thought—or had it been an instinctive gesture of self-defense? And last night on the stairs, had Jessica really been there, waiting in the dark, ready to push Karen down, or had Karen's overactive imagination caused her to see and hear things that weren't there? In her panic had she simply lost her balance—precarious as it was—and tumbled down the stairs without any help? At the time she had been so *sure* that neither of them were accidents. But now they seemed to blur in her mind. She couldn't remember. Had she only been looking to blame Jessica with something—with anything? Perhaps she had been wrong; perhaps Jessica had had nothing to do with them.

And the child *had* saved her life. Grant said that she had. Why would he lie about it? That fact alone seemed to negate all Karen's distorted memories. Why would Jessica save her life if she had already tried at two different times to end it?

"Oh, Grant," Karen moaned.

"What's wrong now?"

Guilty tears stung Karen's eyes. "I can't tell you," she whispered. "I've been so wrong about Jessica."

Grant picked up her hand again and cradled it in his. "You're not the only one who's been wrong about a few things."

"What are you talking about?" Karen asked through her tears.

"Never mind," Grant said. "I'll explain it all to you later. But as for Jessica, well, I wouldn't worry about it. Whatever it is, I'm sure you can make it up to her."

Fighting the tears, Karen squeezed her eyes shut. *God, how could she have been so wrong—gotten so confused?*

She opened her eyes and looked pleadingly at Grant. "I've got to see Jessica right away. Please go get her. I've got to apologize to her, try and explain—"

"Hold on just a minute," Grant interrupted. "I'll go get her and then I'll leave you two alone." Then he smiled, a pleased, indulgent smile. "But first, I have something else to tell you."

Karen regarded him warily. "What?"

Grant's smile became self-satisfied, knowing. "You're pregnant," he said, his voice exultant.

"What!" Karen stared at him.

"It's true. Dr. Kemper discovered it when he examined you. Then he had the lab run a test just to make sure. They confirmed it."

Jessica forgotten for the moment, the tears began to run down Karen's cheeks. But they were no longer tears of guilt. "Oh, Grant, I'm so happy," she sobbed.

He gave her a quick, tender embrace and a fleeting kiss on the lips. "I thought you'd be." He chuckled. "I am, too."

A dark thought suddenly clouded Karen's joy: what if all the abuse her body had taken in the past couple of days caused her to miscarry?

As if he had read her mind, Grant said, "If you're worried about a miscarriage, Dr. Kemper wants to keep you here for a while. He'd probably do that anyway because of your concussion, but when I told him about your history of miscarriages, he said that the hospital was probably the best place for you right now."

Karen was reassured. "I have a feeling," she said, excitedly, "that this time I'm going to make it—I'm going to have this baby."

Grant patted her hand. "That's my girl."

Karen beamed. "Did you tell Jessica yet?"

"That you were pregnant? No, I wanted to wait until you were conscious."

"Then let me tell her, Grant. Please. It'll be something for me to share with her. Maybe it'll even get us off to a brand-new start."

Grant studied her for a moment. "Are you going to tell me what happened between you and Jessica?"

"No, it was just plain silliness on my part," Karen said, giving him an affectionate push, greatly relieved that she hadn't shared with him her terrible thoughts about his daughter. "Now you get out of here and tell Jessica to come in."

"Okay. See you in a little while," Grant said. He walked to the door and blew her a kiss.

When the door closed behind him, Karen let out a long, pensive sigh. She was so thrilled she was pregnant, and she was sure that this time she would see her child to term. She wished she could be alone for a while—mostly to savor her happiness over being pregnant, but also to sort out—and try to make sense of—everything that had happened to her in the past twenty-four hours. But Jessica had to be attended to first. The last thing she wanted to do was to face Jessica right now, but it had to be done. Somehow she had to set things right between her and Jessica—if that was still possible.

The door opened silently, and Jessica walked into the room. "Daddy said you wanted to see me," she said, her face set in its usual blank, unreadable expression.

Karen gave her a tentative smile. "Come a little closer," she said. "So I can talk to you."

Jessica crossed to the bed and stood, her blue eyes opaque and passive, staring at Karen.

"Jessica, I—" Karen began, searching for the right words. "I really don't know what to say to you. I've been such a fool, and I said such terrible things to you. Can you ever forgive me?"

Jessica opened her mouth to speak, but Karen cut her short. "No, don't answer that just yet," she said. "Let me try to explain." She paused for a moment, her forehead knit in concentration. "It was all my fault," she said heavily. "You never did or said anything, but I let my imagination run away with me. Maybe part of that I can blame on the painkillers. But still," she said, grimacing as she remembered the scene, "I should never have accused you of all those awful, awful things." She closed her eyes wearily. "Even if you can find it in your heart to forgive me, I'm not sure I can forgive myself."

Jessica shifted her weight from one foot to the

other, then back again. "It's okay," she mumbled. Then she added charitably, "I already forgot most of what you said."

Karen's eyes flew open. "Oh, you dear, sweet child! How can you be so kind to me? I really don't deserve it."

Jessica's response was to shrug her shoulders in a charming, self-deprecating way.

Karen picked up one of Jessica's hands and squeezed it affectionately. "Your father told me you saved my life," she said.

"I didn't do much," Jessica said, her eyes downcast as she discreetly withdrew her hand from Karen's. "I was scared. I was afraid you were going to die out there in the snow."

"I would have," Karen said, "if it hadn't been for you. I guess I was delirious. I didn't know what I was doing—or saying."

Jessica nodded her head diffidently. "Well, you were acting a little weird," she said. "You screamed at me to stay away from you, and when I held out my ski pole to help you up, you passed out."

Karen cringed inwardly. "I-I thought you were trying to . . ." Her voice trailed off as she shivered at the thought of the words she was too ashamed to say. *I thought you were trying to stab me.* "Oh, God," she moaned. "How you must hate me."

Jessica blinked several times. "I'm sorry I told you I hated you," she said. "I don't."

Karen gazed at her. "There's no need for you to apologize," she said. "You had good reason for saying it."

A faint, rosy blush tinged Jessica's cheeks, and she stared down at the floor.

"Well, that's all behind us now," Karen said in a resolutely cheerful voice. "We're going to forget all about our differences, and you and I are going to be great friends. And," she added dramatically, "I'm going to have to rely on you a lot in the future."

Jessica gave her a quick, inquisitive glance. "For what?"

"For help with the baby," Karen said, barely able to restrain the jubilant excitement in her voice.

"Baby?" Jessica repeated disbelievingly. "You're going to have a baby?"

"Yes! Isn't it wonderful?" Karen couldn't help bursting into a broad, silly grin. "Your father just told me."

"Then Daddy knows?" Jessica asked, seemingly unmoved by Karen's infectious happiness.

"Of course, he knows," Karen said emphatically. "And he's thrilled—just as thrilled as I am. Oh, it's so wonderful! We're going to be a family—a real family at last!"

She looked at Jessica, and for a brief moment wondered why the child was suddenly so quiet. But Karen was much too full of her own exuberance to pay Jessica much heed.

CHAPTER TWENTY-TWO

Karen went on talking, chattering on and on about what joys the future would bring, but Jessica was not listening. She couldn't keep her eyes from staring at Karen's belly, at the spot where *it* was growing.

She was remembering the last time someone told her there was going to be another baby.

It was Mommy. She had said, in that soft-spoken phony voice of hers that she always used in front of Daddy, "Jessica, dear, your father and I have something very exciting to tell you."

"I think you're really going to like it, sweetie," Daddy had said then, his eyes twinkling in a way that implied it was something special—just for her.

Jessica had wondered what it could be. It was months till her birthday, and Christmas was already past. Maybe it was a trip. Daddy had been promising to take her to Disney World for ever such a long time. . . .

Mommy had smiled then. One of those fake half-smiles where you couldn't see her teeth. "It's a baby," she announced as if it were the most important news in the whole world. "I'm going to have a baby."

Jessica just looked at her. Was *that* what all this was about? Some stupid little baby?

Jessica turned to look at Daddy. But he was smiling too. The same as Mommy—together they looked like two grinning idiots. She kept looking from one to the other, wondering what the big deal was.

"Well?" Daddy said when she didn't respond. "Cat got your tongue?"

"Huh?" Jessica wondered why Daddy was so happy; the baby didn't have anything to do with *him*.

"Are you so thrilled you're speechless?" Daddy asked again.

"Oh," Jessica said, trying to inject some enthusiasm into her tone. "Yeah. It's just—great. Really great."

"I knew you'd feel that way," Daddy said, giving Mommy a meaningful glance before he added, "The baby will be a new little playmate for you."

"I hope it's a boy," Jessica said—only because she knew she was supposed to say something like that.

"Well, we can't do anything about that, Jessica," Mommy said, laughing in a slightly condescending way. "We'll have to take what we get."

"Why do you want a brother?" Daddy asked.

"Because," Jessica explained, "I don't know many boys—not that well, anyway. And I just think it would be neat to have a brother." It was a lie, but so what—she had to say something to make them think that she cared about this dumb baby.

Lying to Mommy was no big deal. She did it all the time. But she didn't like to lie to Daddy—not unless she could help it, anyway.

Now, why did they want to go and upset everything with all this talk about a baby? Things were just fine as they were—she and Daddy had each other and Mommy was—well, *there*. She didn't interfere too much, and Jessica didn't have to pay a lot of attention to her—so she didn't really mind having Mommy around.

Of course, Daddy didn't know how Jessica felt about Mommy. He thought that Jessica loved Mommy just as much as she loved him. But Jessica and Mommy both knew better. They knew things about each other that Daddy never suspected. Like, Jessica knew that Mommy didn't really like her much, and Mommy seemed to know a lot of the times when Jessica was lying. Usually, Mommy didn't tell Daddy, though—not unless it was about something that Mommy thought was important. Then she would tell Daddy that Jessica had lied, and then Daddy would come into Jessica's room, and he'd have this real serious look on his face, and Jessica would get really scared that Mommy had told Daddy something that Jessica did that had made him stop loving her. That was the only thing she was really afraid of—losing Daddy's love—and she was pretty sure Mommy knew that.

But Jessica and Mommy both loved Daddy, and for his sake they pretty much stayed out of each other's way. But if there was going to be a baby, it looked like things were going to change. Jessica didn't like the idea of that, but she could tell that there didn't seem to be anything she could do about it—not yet, anyway.

So she had gone on pretending that she wanted the baby, and the months had gone by and Mommy had gotten bigger and fatter—and uglier. Only Daddy kept telling her how beautiful she was getting, and—strangely enough—he sounded like he meant it.

Then, one night when Jessica was fast asleep and dreaming that Daddy was a king and that she was a princess in a fairy tale, Daddy came into her room and gently shook her awake. "Jessica," he whispered. "Mommy and I have to go to the hospital now—the baby's coming. But Aunt Fran is here—she's going to stay with you tonight."

Jessica nodded sleepily, not sure what all the fuss was about.

But in the morning when she woke up Aunt Fran was there, making breakfast and looking like she would burst with self-importance.

"Oh, Jessica!" she proclaimed when Jessica, yawning, wandered into the kitchen. "It's a girl! You have a baby sister!"

Jessica thought about this for a moment before she asked, "What's her name?"

"They're going to call her Sarah—Sarah Leslie Cameron. Isn't that a lovely name?"

"Uh-huh." Jessica nodded. It was okay—nothing special. But besides Mommy, who cared? "When is Daddy coming home?" she asked.

Aunt Fran's face fell ever so slightly. "Pretty soon, I would think. He's not going to the office today—he was up all night."

"Doing what?"

Aunt Fran went blank for several seconds. Then she said, "Well, uh, he was helping your mother deliver the baby."

"I thought the doctor did that."

"He *does*. He takes care of all the medical procedures, but your father was there to give your mother moral support."

"Oh, I see," Jessica said. But she didn't—not at all. Why did Daddy want to be there with Mommy when she had *her* baby? It didn't make sense.

But then Daddy came home later, and everything was better than it had been for a long time. For the next few days it was just the two of them, and Jessica had never been so happy. Daddy came home early from work every day so that he would be there when she got out of school. He took her out to dinner nearly every night and let her order whatever she wanted, just like a grownup. He'd have to go away for a couple of hours in the evening—because he was expected to see Mommy and the baby in the hospital—and he'd leave Jessica with Aunt Fran and Uncle Jerry and their three bratty boys.

But then Daddy'd come back and they'd go home and play cards or Monopoly until bedtime. Then after she'd gotten into her pajamas, he would make hot chocolate for the two of them, and they'd sit at the kitchen table and talk. And Jessica could usually get him so involved in whatever they were discussing that he'd forget about the late hour—so she'd get to stay up way past her bedtime. Eventually, he'd look at his watch in mock horror and then teasingly scold her because he'd realized all along exactly what she'd been doing. Then she'd have to go right to bed, but Daddy would tuck her in and sit by the bed until she went to sleep.

But that wonderful time didn't last. Mommy came home—and she brought with her the ugly, noisy, scrawny little thing that they called Sarah.

From the moment they brought her through the door Jessica hated Sarah. She was all wrapped up in a fuzzy pink blanket, and you could barely see her face. But her mouth was wide open, and she was squawking at the top of her lungs. Her legs were kicking so hard that Jessica thought Mommy might drop her.

"This is your baby sister," Mommy said, bending down to let Jessica have a closer look at Sarah's face. "Isn't she beautiful?"

Was she crazy? Jessica stared at that scrunched-up, splotchy pink face with the gaping and screeching hole in its center—how could anyone call that beautiful? "I can't tell," she said diplomatically. "She's crying too much."

"She probably needs to be changed," Mommy said. "I think I'll take her into the nursery."

When Mommy and her raucous bundle were gone, Jessica turned to Daddy. "Is she going to cry like that all the time?" she asked.

Daddy laughed. "Only when she's hungry or needs her diaper changed—or just wants to be picked up."

"How often is that?"

"It depends," Daddy answered. Then he put his arm around her shoulders. "I'm afraid things are going to be a little different around here for a while, sweetie," he said. "Mommy's going to have to spend most of her time taking care of Sarah, and we're all going to have to adjust. Do you think you can do that?"

Jessica wondered just what kind of adjustments she'd have to make. "I guess so," she said reluctantly. "If you want me to."

Daddy squeezed her shoulders. "That's my girl."

But the adjustments they asked of her were too much. It wasn't that Sarah cried a lot or got all of Mommy's attention. No, what was more than she could bear was what happened to Daddy.

Whenever Mommy was resting—which seemed to be a lot—Daddy would take care of Sarah. He'd go into the nursery and do whatever had to be done, and then he would carry her over to the rocking chair and sit and rock her back to sleep.

Daddy didn't even seem to mind the filthy messes Sarah made in her diapers or the fact that she couldn't eat like a normal human being and was always dribbling or drooling all over herself.

At first, Jessica thought he did all this for Sarah only because Mommy was napping, but then Jessica began to realize that Daddy actually *enjoyed* taking care of Sarah.

Jessica couldn't believe it. But when she stood just

outside the nursery door and listened to Daddy talking to Sarah, her feeling of horror grew. Daddy was saying things to Sarah that he should only say to *her*!

"You're my little girl," he'd say in that silly cooing voice adults used when they talked to babies. "My precious little girl—and Daddy loves you. Yes, Daddy loves you very, very much."

And then Jessica peeked just around the edge of the door and saw him kissing Sarah's cheek and nuzzling her forehead. *Daddy, how could you do that to me?* she had wanted to scream. But she had kept her silence and gone on listening, growing increasingly afraid with every word of tenderness that Daddy uttered that he didn't love her anymore.

That was when she had made up her mind to get rid of Sarah. It seemed to be the only way she could get her Daddy back and not have to share him with anyone—most of all such a disgusting monster as Sarah.

It shouldn't be too hard, Jessica reasoned. All she had to do was hold a blanket over Sarah's face until the little worm stopped squirming.

But it turned out to be harder than Jessica thought. Mommy had somehow sensed what Jessica was planning to do.

Jessica always wondered how Mommy had figured it out. Had she seen Jessica watching and waiting for the perfect moment when Sarah would be alone in the nursery, when Mommy would be busy elsewhere?

That was probably it because one time when Jessica was in the nursery and had been just picking up the blanket Mommy burst in. "What are you doing?" she shouted. "Get away from her!"

"I-I was just putting her blanket back on," Jessica said, trying to cover up her guilty surprise. "It slipped off."

Mommy's eyes narrowed suspiciously. "It was fine

when I looked in on Sarah two minutes ago," she said. "What were you really doing?"

Jessica dropped the blanket and backed away from the crib. "Nothing," she said. "I wasn't doing anything."

Mommy didn't say a word but continued to glare at Jessica, and she could see that the seed of doubt was already planted in Mommy's mind.

Mommy never said anything more to Jessica about the incident. But from that day on she would fly into a rage if Jessica so much as went near Sarah—especially when no one else was around.

Jessica's biggest fear was that Mommy would say something to Daddy. But for some strange reason she never did. Instead, she began drinking.

Jessica had never seen Mommy drink before—except a little wine. But it amazed her to see the effect that drinking had on Mommy.

She started out gradually—mostly so that Daddy wouldn't catch on, Jessica guessed. But within a couple of weeks she was going through more than a bottle of Scotch a day—and not bothering to hide the empty bottles or to conceal her drinking from Daddy anymore.

The drinking turned Mommy nasty, and she said mean, terrible things to both Daddy and Jessica. It upset Daddy, and he began to get dark circles under his eyes and look worried all the time. It bothered Jessica to see him like that, and—since it was all Mommy's fault—she decided that Daddy would be better off without Mommy.

So Jessica made her plans and waited for the right moment. It happened one day when she came home from school and found Mommy slumped over the kitchen table, an empty Scotch bottle nearby. Jessica went into the dining room, got a fresh bottle out of the liquor cabinet, and brought it back into the kitchen to Mommy.

As Jessica placed the bottle on the table, Mommy lifted her head and looked at Jessica with bloodshot, watery eyes. "Oh, it's you," she said thickly.

"Yes, Mommy," Jessica replied. "Here's another bottle."

Mommy gazed at the new bottle and mumbled something that Jessica couldn't understand.

Jessica waited while Mommy broke the seal on the bottle and, using two hands, poured out a glass. When Mommy tilted her head back to drain the glass, Jessica slipped in front of the knife rack and pulled out the butcher's knife. Holding it behind her, Jessica began to edge away from the table.

Mommy banged her glass down. "What are you doing there?" she asked sharply.

Jessica froze. "Nothing," she said, her fingers tightening around the handle of the knife.

"Then leave me alone," Mommy said, dismissing Jessica with a shooing motion of her hand.

Her eyes downcast, Jessica sidled away from the table, the knife concealed in the folds of her school skirt. Once out of the kitchen, she walked rapidly to her own room and closed the door behind her.

Sitting on the edge of the bed, she ran her fingertips gingerly over the razor-sharp blade of the knife. She wondered why her heart was pounding so—almost as if she had been running around the block. But she wasn't scared—she knew exactly what she was going to do. Within a few minutes it would all be over.

Would Daddy believe the story she was going to tell him? Don't be silly, she told herself. Why shouldn't he? Daddy always believed everything she told him.

Then there was nothing else to worry about.

She got up off the bed, went to her door, and

peered out. No sign of Mommy. So she tiptoed out into the hall and across the dining room to a point where she could see into the kitchen. Mommy was still sitting at the table, absorbed in her drink.

Jessica retraced her steps, then went down the hall to the nursery. The door was wide open. Mommy always left it that way so she could hear Sarah's cries.

Sarah was on her belly in the crib, her face turned away from the door. But Jessica was pretty sure that Sarah was asleep—it was about all she did, anyway. That and eat and cry and make messes. What a useless thing she was—it was going to be such a relief not to have her around.

Careful not to make a sound that would rouse Sarah from her sleep and make her cry out and bring Mommy too soon, Jessica crossed the nursery to the crib. She stood there, dispassionately observing the gentle rise and fall of Sarah's back with each feathery breath and the fat curve of her pink cheek where her face pressed against the crib mattress.

Then, like an ancient priest wielding the sacrificial blade, she lifted the knife over her head and held it, poised for a single, breathless moment, and then thrust it with one purposeful blow deep into Sarah's back. She wrenched it out and plunged it again into the resilient flesh—then again and again.

The pink terrycloth sleeper was now soaked red with blood and slashed into strips. The tiny form in the crib had long since ceased to breathe, but still Jessica stabbed at it with the knife.

Once she missed, and the knife went into the furry brown teddy bear lying in the crib next to Sarah. The stuffed toy was already soaked in baby Sarah's blood, and as Jessica pulled the blade out, large chunks of stuffing came with it, making the bear look as if it had been disemboweled. Jessica suddenly felt very bad about stabbing the teddy bear—she hadn't meant to hurt it.

Then she heard the shuffling, uneven footsteps in the hall. Mommy. She was coming to check on Sarah—just as Jessica knew she would. Jessica turned toward the door, holding the knife behind her back.

Mommy came through the doorway and stopped when she saw Jessica. The light in the room was dim, and she couldn't see the blood spattered on Jessica or on the wall by the crib. She reached out an uncertain hand to hang onto the doorjamb for support. "Jess'ca, wha're you doing?" she asked, unable to control the slurring in her voice.

Jessica stood in front of the crib, blocking Mommy's view. "Come and see, Mommy," she said, looking slyly over her shoulder.

Watching carefully, Jessica waited as Mommy staggered toward the crib, and at the precise moment when the horror registering on Mommy's face showed that she had caught her first glimpse of the bloody lump that had been Sarah, Jessica turned, whirling so suddenly that Mommy had no chance of escape. The knife held high, its blade still wet with Sarah's blood, Jessica lunged straight at Mommy's chest.

Mommy struck out with her arms, desperately trying to beat Jessica away. But she was too confused from the alcohol, and Jessica managed to stave off her harmless blows and jam the knife into the left side of Mommy's chest. She could feel the blade encounter an initial resistance, and then it slipped smoothly through layer after layer of tissue, burying itself up to the hilt. A thin stream of blood spurted out, some of it splashing onto Jessica's clothes and her hands and face. The blood was hot; Jessica didn't like the feel of it on her face so she quickly wiped it away with a corner of her skirt.

Mommy was still bleeding a lot, only now the

blood was oozing out more than gushing. It was all over the place: the front of Mommy's dress was soaked red with it, lines of it were running down her arms and legs, and there was a big puddle of it on the pink carpeting at her feet.

She was gasping and stumbling, and then she went down on one knee and swayed there for a second before she fell on her back. Her eyes were bulgy and glassy now, and they stared up at Jessica.

"Mommy," Jessica said, shaking her head as if she were talking to a naughty child. "You should never have had Sarah."

Mommy began to wheeze now. "I know," she said. (Or maybe she said, "No, no." At that point Jessica couldn't be sure—Mommy's voice was so weak.) Then her hands slithered through the trickling blood on her chest and began grasping and pulling at the knife handle.

Jessica stepped back, suddenly afraid that Mommy would pull the knife out and get up.

But Mommy's hands began to flutter, like two doomed moths beating themselves senseless against a windowpane. Then she sighed, a strange, wistful sigh, and her hands stopped moving, and her eyes turned toward the ceiling.

Ever so slowly, Jessica inched in closer, alert in case Mommy was playing a trick on her and only pretending to be dead.

But Mommy remained motionless, like a windup toy that had suddenly wound down.

"Mommy?" Jessica said, still unable to comprehend that the game was over and that she had won.

Mommy didn't answer. And for the first time, Jessica understood what death meant.

It suddenly felt funny being alone in the room with those two lifeless bodies. It wasn't scary—it was more like they had some kind of sickness or germ that

Jessica might catch. So she bolted out of the nursery and down the hall to Mommy and Daddy's bedroom, where she went into the bathroom and locked herself in. Nothing or no one could get at her in there.

While she was in there she heard the phone ring several times. She supposed it was Daddy, but she wasn't going to unlock the door to find out.

She stayed in the bathroom until she heard Daddy's voice outside the door. Then she knew she'd be safe.

When she opened the door and Daddy asked her what was wrong, she didn't know exactly what to say. So she simply pointed toward the hall, hoping that he'd understand so she wouldn't have to go and look at Mommy and Sarah again.

After Daddy went down to the nursery and came back, he looked almost as pale as Mommy had looked, lying there on the floor. He didn't say anything to Jessica for a long time, but he sat with her on the edge of the bed, his arms holding her in a vise-like grip.

Then, slowly, he began to ask questions and Jessica told him, little by little, the story she had prepared: "Mommy was crazy, Daddy," she said between sobs. "She killed Sarah . . . I saw her . . . she was in the nursery when I came home, and at first I thought she was hitting Sarah—but then I saw the knife . . . and I said, 'Mommy, what are you doing to Sarah?' . . . She looked at me real funny . . . then she grabbed at me, and I realized that she'd killed Sarah and—and she wanted to kill me, too."

Then Jessica broke down in great, choking sobs, and Daddy pressed her head to his chest as he wept along with her.

When the wave of tears had passed and both of them had wiped their eyes, Daddy said softly, "How did you get away from Mommy, Jessica? Can you tell me that?"

Jessica took a deep breath. It was all going good so far, just the way she'd planned it—except that she hadn't thought it would be so messy. But now everything depended on how well she answered this question. "I didn't, Daddy," she said, afraid to look at him. "She—she attacked me and I had to fight with her—"

Daddy gasped and slowly shook his head. "Oh, God, no," he moaned.

Jessica shot him a quick glance. What was the matter—didn't he believe her?

"Oh, my poor baby." Daddy sighed, his arms tightening around her again. "You killed her, didn't you? You killed her in self-defense."

Jessica nodded solemnly, her eyes wide. "It was an accident, Daddy. I don't know how it happened."

"Of course, darling, of course," Daddy said. "And don't you worry about it because Daddy's going to take care of everything."

Jessica looked closely at him, wondering what he meant by that.

Then Daddy put his hands on Jessica's shoulders and turned her so that she was forced to look squarely at him. "Now listen to me, Jessica," he said, a distinct sense of urgency in his voice. "Mommy killed Sarah and then she killed herself. They were already dead when you came home from school. You walked in and found their bodies—*but they were already dead.* Do you understand me?"

Jessica stared at him. Why was he doing this? Didn't he believe her story?

Daddy shook her gently. "Jessica, I'm trying to protect you. Don't you see? If we tell the truth, some people may not understand—they'll always look at you a little differently, maybe even say things behind your back. I can't let that happen to you, sweetheart."

"You mean you want me to lie, Daddy?" Jessica asked ingenuously.

"In this case a lie is better than the truth," he said, his face a sober mask.

"All right, Daddy," Jessica agreed. "I'll do it if you want me to."

Things were working out even better than she had expected—Daddy's lie on top of her own made her seem completely innocent. She almost wished she'd thought of the second lie herself.

Then Daddy had made her take off her bloody clothes and wash her face, and he went into the nursery and did something to put Mommy's fingerprints on the knife, and then he called the police. They came, a whole bunch of them, going all over the apartment, taking pictures and poking around. They talked to Daddy for a long time, and then they asked Jessica a couple of questions about how she had found Mommy and Sarah. The man who spoke to her listened to her answers patiently, nodded several times, and wrote something in a notebook. And that was all.

After they were gone Daddy made Jessica go into her room and lie down, and then a doctor came and gave her something that made her sleep. When she woke up she wandered out into the living room, and Aunt Fran and Uncle Jerry were there, talking to Daddy. When Aunt Fran caught sight of her, she came rushing over to Jessica and gathered her up in her arms and fussed over her with slobbering sympathy. She explained that Jessica would be coming to stay with them for the next few days, relieving Daddy of the burden of having to take care of her.

Jessica was not about to go along with this arrangement. So she staged her first temper tantrum—and discovered what a potent weapon it was, one that she would use again and again, whenever things were not going her way.

"No!" Jessica shrieked, wriggling out of Aunt Fran's embrace and flinging herself toward her father, clasping him around the waist. "Please, Daddy, please! Don't send me away!"

Daddy looked down at her with guilty pain in his eyes. He hesitated only a moment before he said, "No, sweetheart, I won't send you away. You and I have to stay together—we're all we've got left in this world."

From then on it was just the way Jessica had planned it. She had her daddy all to herself—for three wonderful years. Until Karen came along to spoil everything.

It had been a shock to Jessica when she found out that Daddy was planning to marry again—she hadn't counted on that. She had been so happy and satisfied with their life together that it never occurred to her that Daddy might want to share it with someone else.

By the time she met Karen, Jessica knew it was too late. She couldn't stop Daddy from marrying her. So she decided to go along and pretend that she approved of the whole thing, all the while hoping that Daddy would come to his senses.

But after Karen had moved in with them, Jessica realized just how slight a threat she was going to be: anytime there was any kind of conflict between Karen and Jessica, Karen was almost always the one who came out on the short end.

Just like with Mommy, things were fine as long as it was only the three of them. Then Karen started talking about having a baby, and at first Jessica had thought it was just a silly bluff because Karen was obviously too old to have a baby.

But now it *was* true. So Jessica would be forced to make her plans once again.

It shouldn't be too difficult; Karen was so clumsy she seemed to have more than her share of accidents, anyway. Funny how she thought that Jessica had been trying to kill her when she only had herself to blame for all those dumb accidents that happened to her.

And it had been really weird that Karen had sensed the truth about Mommy and Sarah—just like Mommy had done earlier when she saw that Jessica wanted to get rid of Sarah. Had Jessica given herself away somehow to each of them?

Well, that didn't matter now since Karen was convinced she was wrong. She trusted Jessica. She wouldn't be on her guard anymore, and another accident should be easy to arrange. It'd probably be better to wait until they got back to New York and Daddy wasn't around.

However it happened, both Karen and her baby must die. Because there mustn't be another baby again—*ever*. One of those horrible little creatures would never have another chance to steal Daddy's love.

"Jessica, are you listening to me?" Karen suddenly said, breaking into her thoughts.

Jessica tore her eyes away from Karen's belly and looked straight into her eyes. "Sorry," she muttered. "Guess I was daydreaming."

"That's all right," Karen said, smiling benignly. "I understand. You were probably thinking about the baby, weren't you?"

Jessica nodded as she let a slow, shy smile work its way across her face. She had something to smile about now—because soon, very soon, she would have her daddy all to herself once again.

"Gruesomely effective.
A scary, engrossing book."
—Stephen King,
author of *Firestarter*

The Unforgiven
by Patricia J. MacDonald

Maggie tried to forget the body of the man she loved, the murder trial, and the agonizing punishment. Now she was free to start a new life on a quiet New England island—until the terror began again.

"A terrific psychological thriller." —Mary Higgins Clark, author of *The Cradle Will Fall*

"...one of those rare books that, once started, you can't put down." —John Saul, author of *When the Wind Blows*

A Dell Book $3.50 (19123-8)

At your local bookstore or use this handy coupon for ordering:

Dell | DELL BOOKS   THE UNFORGIVEN $3.50   (19123-8)
P.O. BOX 1000, PINE BROOK, N.J. 07058-1000

Please send me the above title. I am enclosing $ _____ (please add 75c per copy to cover postage and handling). Send check or money order—no cash or C.O.D.'s. Please allow up to 8 weeks for shipment.

Mr./Mrs./Miss _____

Address _____

City _____ State/Zip _____

First *Sybil*, then *The Exorcist*
Now...

The Owlsfane Horror
by Duffy Stein

Owlsfane—a quiet, quaint Vermont village where city pressures evaporate under crystalline skies. For Sandy Home, it was a place where she and David would share a week of adventure. Then she was thrust through a doorway in time, plunged into a dark, terrifying world that claimed her mind, body and soul.

A Dell Book   **$3.50**   **(16781-7)**

At your local bookstore or use this handy coupon for ordering:

Dell | DELL BOOKS   THE OWLSFANE HORROR $3.50   (16781-7)
P.O. BOX 1000, PINE BROOK, N.J. 07058-1000

Please send me the above title. I am enclosing $ _____ (please add 75c per copy to cover postage and handling). Send check or money order—no cash or C.O.D.'s. Please allow up to 8 weeks for shipment.

Mr./Mrs./Miss _____

Address _____

City _____ State/Zip _____